# BLUE MONKEYS

**L. Shapley Bassen**

Copyright © Shy City House 2025

*AFTER THE VOICES by W.S. Merwin*

*Youth is gone from the place where I was young*
*even the language that I heard here once*
*its cadences that went on echoing*
*a youth forgotten and the great singing*
*of the beginning have fallen silent*
*with the voices that were the spirit of them*
*and their absences were no more noticed*
*than were those of the unreturning birds*
*each spring until there were no words at all*
*for what was gone but it was always so*
*I have no way of telling what I miss*
*I am only the one who misses it*

### *Introduction - from Blue Monkeys by Paloma Shapiro & Pearl Feria*

*The history, ceremony, and mystery of toreadors and the bull ring are a long-dimmed memory. The first letter of the first alphabet, A, is an upside-down and abstracted image of a cow's head.*

*Four millennia ago, a bare-breasted young woman vaulted through the lethal horns of a pied bull, flying over its back into the waiting arms of a partner. A stockaded courtyard of standing congregants gasped and sang a prayer thirteen times, as each one of the sanctified gymnasts, like Pasikennae, survived the ritual. The bull-leapers were young, slim, and bare-chested, their hair long and curled, both boys and girls in loincloth, wearing decorative bracelets along their arms. In Cretan fashion, bare-breasted bolero shrugs for women were the norm, so there was nothing remarkable in bare-breasted worship of the bull. The bull-leapers were unarmed; they were not fighting the bull but celebrating it with gymnastic, athletic fervor.*

*Some bulls were black, some brown, some pied. The white ones were kept for the most sacred sacrifices, not for this lunar calendar rite. Bulls were HER consorts. Four millennia ago in the Mediterranean, SHE was the Cow of the Milky Way. HER horns crowned the roofs of HER palaces, and HER Temples were the archway between Life and Death. Safe passage through the Strait of Gibraltar [first named 'Great Horns'] shared the same word with the vaulting ceremony that was called 'Through HER Crown.' The word 'crown' <u>meant</u> bovine horns. Bull-leapers and sea-farers were HER favorites. They both jumped over the Moon (risked death = died) and SHE allowed them to return (live).*

*HER daughter Pasiphae was (in <u>much</u> later Greek) called Iphiánassa ("mighty queen") over an empire from Crete through the Great Horns, its outposts reaching along the Spanish/ Portuguese coasts north to the tin mines of Britain, farther north to the Scottish Orkneys and Faroe Islands, where the northern journey began to the boulders and mines of copper that SHE* *craved, located in the distant west of the proto-Ojibway on current day Lake Superior, French-*

*named Isle Royale.*

*HER ancient Cretan empire and era were later patriarchally renamed Minoan, for Minos,*

*consort of Pasiphae, a bull for The Cow, a drone for the Queen Bee. 'Minos' was not a king's*

*name; it meant Consort. Then, Crete was Keftiu to the Egyptians, in Hebrew Kaftor or Caphtor,*

*and its three-ringed Vatican island to its north was called (in its ancient language, Linear A)*

*Mnkallis. Long after its catastrophic eruption, it was named Thera, and much later for Saint*

*Irene, still in the current day, Santorini. Mnkallis's volcanic annihilation by HER, seen in Egypt*

*and as far away as China, was the first place where the end of the world began, its survivors the*

*first diaspora.*

2019

*Chapter 1 April, 2019 - Neighbors on the 9<sup>th</sup> Floor*

Postcoital, Alan turned to his husband and drawled, "So what's the story with our new old neighbors? They here when the building cornerstone was laid?"

In the moment, David appreciated (1) Alan's complimentary pronunciation of *laid*, (2) Alan's belief that David knew all the answers, and most of all, (3) Alan's beauty.

David said, "Pal and Pearl aren't that old. This building is 1927 faux Beaux Arts," he spoke quietly as if they were still in their LA home where Arno and Dylan had slept in an adjoining bedroom. Here, the twins' bedroom was on the other side of the co-op, next to the nanny's. "*Fo-Bows-R?*" Alan imitated. "Pal? Pidge and Pearl. She's called Pidge."

"Professor Shapiro. Ah. *Paloma* means *pigeon.* You know more about our neighbors than I do."

"No one knows more about anything than you do." Sleepily, Alan added, "But I'm taller."

"And younger. Etcetera."

"Pearl Feria is a Shoshone princess from Wyoming. No one in New York City was born here."

"Well, I was. Pidge and Pearl are both Baby Boomers like my 'rents. Be impressed: P and P deciphered Linear A."

"Old know-it-all," Alan yawned.

He stretched, arched, and yoga-breathed under the sheet and comforter. It was dark, but a nightlight dimly illuminated plaster copies on the wall of three Minoan scenes: a nude youth holding catches of fish in each upraised hand, the famous one of the bull-jumpers, and the Picasso-like profiles of black-eyed palace ladies.

Just two weeks earlier on April Fool's Day, Alan Tapley and David Rochester had moved from LA into this NYC apartment. Since then, a *New York Times* photo-headline announced: *Darkness Visible, Finally: Astronomers Capture First Ever Image of a Black Hole.*

Eyes shut, falling asleep, Alan drawled, "Wow, Linear-fuckin'A."

David started to drift off as well, imagining a pair of their self-portraits. For over the living room fireplace to replace the blue monkeys fresco? Alan's portrait should be Warhol-size, all that perfect face. His own? collage, better to mirror the parts whose sum would never add up.

Then, as usual, David couldn't sleep.

### *October 1, 2019*

The seventeen-story faux Beaux Arts building faced north and south near the corner of Riverside Drive in New York City's West Eighties. It had opened its brass and beveled glass doors the same year Lindbergh flew the Atlantic and New York's Holland Tunnel became the world's first vehicular tunnel. On October first, at early breakfast in the third apartment on the south side of the ninth floor, Dr. James Beekmans read aloud from *Entertainment Today*'s description of their neighbor, an actor known for accents and impressions, Alan Tapley, "in *HITTITE QUEEN,* one of the three brightest stars in a constellation going SUPERNOVA." "How many things are wrong with that sentence?" James asked his wife as he read the tablet on its counter-stand while stirring honey into yogurt for their three-year-old daughter.

Micheline had nearly dressed herself but brought four unmatched socks to the table. She was trying two on as gloves and singing, "*Ya-ya-ee, ya-ya-ee, ya-ya-ee, ya-ya-ee, Blame it on my juice, blame it, blame it on my juice.*"

"Why are you even looking at that?" Susanna scolded James in the same breath she asked Micheline, "Where did you hear Lizzo?"

The child ignored the question but stopped singing.

"The twins have two fathers. Mr. Tapley is *Da,*" Micheline said. "Mr. Rochester is *Daddy.*"

"Well, you've got a *Mommy,*" Susanna said.

"I can be a father when I grow up."

*"Che sera, sera,"* James said, "but I advise eating yogurt without gloves on. Just a suggestion." Dr. Susanna Duckett rose from the table, already focused on a stressful morning ahead at the hospital. She stopped herself.

"A supernova is by definition short-lived. Star's brightest before it fades. Hardly a compliment. *Constellations* don't go nova or super. Stars do, when they collide and/or die." Micheline tucked into the yogurt but looked up at Susanna. "Mommy does *brain* surgery with gloves on."

The parents exchanged a look. The little girl's hand lifted her spoon like a magic wand.


Filmed in Manhattan, the first season of *"HITTITE QUEEN* is a *HIT,"* had caused Alan's, therefore David's, return to the East Coast. The series was a hybrid story of a thirteenth century B.C.E. Hittite love triangle between monarchs and their chief advisor. Scenes were intercut between costumed Turkish history and the same actors in their modern-day New York lives. Pundit-critics proclaimed, *"HITTITE QUEEN* comes from a pre-gender-hierarchized world in which lust was both fluid and normal – 'comin' 'round again with a'plenty of *bang.*"

Alan had originally been cast as the king, but as the Prime Minister he could be lover to both monarchs, with Hittite Queen Puduhepa as the dominant figure. Even though it was TV, the role lured the most A+ list actress in Hollywood. True to her status and the queen's character, she demanded Alan play her Prime Minister.

This October morning, though, Alan was neither at the TV studio across the East River or location shooting in Manhattan. Pidge came upon him in the apartment lobby after a fifteen block walk back from shopping at Fairview Market. A new tenant was moving in.

Professor Paloma Shapiro wheeled her grocery-filled cart and made sympathetic eye contact with the Latino doorman in his 'uniform,' a white shirt and black tie/slacks.

"*Abogada*," he mouthed, nodding toward a tiny middle-aged woman directing huge moving men. "Elena Luster, *el Don*."

"*Esquire*," Pidge translated. At least 'lawyer' had a feminine formation.

"No, no, the <u>fourth</u> floor!" the new resident yelled.

Prof. Shapiro navigated boxes, furniture, and movers as her eyes adjusted from the bright street into the low-ceiling dimness of the marble and plaster lobby. Instead of gilt-framed dark oil paintings, a full-length mural filled the wall facing the entrance doors. It had been painted in the 1930's by WPA artists. To her left, the professor saw Alan in the leaded-glass bay window's upholstered seat. She had to pass him en route to the elevators. Even with the hubbub in the lobby, Alan's exhaled sigh was hard to ignore. And best to avoid the elevators for a while.

Be honest, Pidge, she scolded herself. Young man was a magnet. Those pale blue eyes under a wave of dark hair on his forehead. She gave herself a smile. She liked to call herself by the nickname Alan thought he had given her. She still had sufficient iron filings in her blood to align in the actor's direction.

On most floors, there were four apartments on either side, south and north facing, but Alan's and David's had been created from a combination of two in the south wing. The three couples on their half of the ninth floor had seen each other in aloof urban passing since April, but friendships had begun during and after a September blackout that sent them all into the hallway with flashlights. The outage had lasted for candlelit hours together in the large Tapley-Rochester co-op. Under a nanny's care, the children had bedded together (the twins had bunkbeds with a trundle), and the younger adults began to share biographies like summer campers around a firepit. The old women hoped just to listen. Age allowed curiosity to supersede assertion. But the south side of the ninth floor was inquisitive about Linear A: a doctor and scientist, a journalist and a master of mimicry, they were professional questioners.

Pidge and Pearl had been interviewed before.

Pearl said, "For years, there was too little available to translate, and little mention of the magnificent empire, contemporary with Egypt nearby and far away, in China, where they chronicled the Bronze Age Mediterranean volcanic eruption. Etched stones and cuneiformed clay tablets – found at a contemporaneous Orkney burial site -- became our Rosetta Stone. A place called The Knowes of Trotty. Their author, Pasikennae, rarely named herself. We know she was female from the tablets' language -- she refers to *her* baby buried at Lake Superior."

"From Crete to Lake *Superior?*" David doubted.

"The Great Lake was *Kitchi-Gami*. The island in it is called Isle Royale now," Pidge took over.

An October breeze through a dark window had flickered candles around the living room. "Pasikennae was a sea captain, ordered by HER to bring 'heavy cargo' back to Crete. Then she sailed home to 'Mnkallis' – now Santorini – the island destroyed by the cataclysm. When she had arrived at the Minoan outpost at Gibraltar, re-entering the Mediterranean, a sister there warned her not to go any farther, but Pasikennae was still compelled by divine order. It must have been an even worse shock than her baby's death, which she understood as punishment for not returning sooner, to see Crete's blasted harbor, and worse, the annihilation of her natal island. Mnkallis had been the center of – it was like Crete's Vatican City, an island of three concentric circles. Pasikennae believed Mnkallis had been divinity-manifested, a trinity of Maiden-Mother-Crone. SHE left only a judgment of ash."

From the actor, listening for motivation, "Was that the shock that sent her to the Orkneys?"

Pearl answered, "It was hard enough to translate. We don't like to speculate. The Orkneys were the embarkation point for the equally astonishing distance to Lake Superior. Pasikennae's Mediterranean life was over."

Dr. Susanna Duckett's Arkansas accent still surprised the neighbors. "And she wasn't even allowed to die. All her people must have felt such guilt. Why were they punished so brutally? Where could – Pasikennae? -- belong?"

"Many reasons not to go back to Lake Superior," her husband James said.

"You can only imagine," Pidge said. "We don't know."

David had been thinking. "They saw Gibraltar as another incarnation of the Horns of Goddess, like the bull horns they jumped through. It was a world of signs and omens. What a story. I've got a great agent for you."

After that night, Alan/David, Pidge/Pearl, and James/Susanna said more than hello. Their three year-olds attended different daycares but played together, often with the septuagenarians' aged dog. Sixteen years earlier, the professors had rescued Ginger as a puppy mix like Lady and the Tramp's, if Lady had been a King Charles, not a blond cocker spaniel. Alan trusted Pidge. In the lobby, when Alan saw her coming towards him, his eyes filled. She sat down beside him.

Alan eyed her groceries in the shopping cart. "Will they melt?"

She wiped away his tears with a tissue. "Not as fast as you. No, we take a taxi when there's frozen stuff. What happened, dear?"

This was the way she spoke to graduate students. 'Dear' defined roles.

"David is furious that I bought something with my own money. But he bought this co-op!"

"What did you buy?"

"I thought I was doing the same thing he did. Property in Orient, Long Island."

"Alan, I have no idea where that is. My boundaries are The Cloisters to the north and The Battery to the south. East is the Mayor's Mansion. And we're on the Wild Upper West Side."

He smiled briefly. Pidge thought *angels wept*.

Alan explained, "Long Island looks like a hundred-twenty-mile-long fish east of Manhattan. A fish with a two-forked fin at the end," he gestured with his left fist and two fingers. "Orient Point is the end of the north fork. The Hamptons are in the southern one. Montauk Point is the south. It's like this building, south and north, only bigger. With Gardiner's Bay instead of the elevator bay in between. According to David, Orient's on the wrong fork, and *he's* the money man. Because he sits on his inherited hedge fund. He says I don't know what I'm doing with money. I bought it with *my* money. That's another thing. He says it's *our* money. But *he's* the investor."

"Did you mean to surprise him, like a gift to share?"

Alan shook his head. "I knew he didn't want it. I'm away on locations too much as it is. But I didn't want another argument."

"So?"

Alan also paused and looked at Pidge, appreciating her timing. It gave him the moment to retrieve at least a decade of maturity.

"I want a place away on the water. To go to in the summer. And hiatus. Get out of the City. I could paint. You should see the property. An old barn to convert into a studio. Honeysuckle. Trees.
The ocean. Okay. I did. Want something of my own."

"Does he want something of his own?"

"He wants me. Did you and Pearl fight when you were –"

"That's a long voyage into the past, dear. This food may not melt, but it could spoil. The short version is that Pearl and I were divorced with toddlers and in competition doing similar research. Archaic translation. Yes, people compete over that. We loved the Minoans – well, *Pasiphaens*. We were decoding language, finding remnants of objects and words throughout the Mediterranean up to the Orkneys. To Lake Superior! We were crazy in love with the work -- it had nothing to do with an *us*. We got married when it got legal. Pearl and I were never sexy."

"So?"

Pidge laughed at his imitation. "I was born into my apartment. Rent control, forgive the expression, *trumps* sex in New York."

"David is also a New York native. I escaped from a Lone Star state of mind. It was like stripping off a prison uniform, going naked."

"You wear costumes brilliantly, m'dear," Pidge said. She patted his hand. "Easier to decipher a language than a self. Need more than a Rosetta Stone and a Phaistos Disk, don't you think?"

The doorman approached them. He gestured that the lobby was momentarily quiet.

"Professor Shapiro," he said, "you want to get upstairs while the going's good?"

"May I help, Pidge?"

She demurred Alan's halfhearted offer. In the elevator padded for the lawyer's movers, her thoughts drifted away from the actor to Fernando, the doorman nick-named *Azul*, whose dusty blue skin was yet another familiar mystery.

Six years earlier, when the GOP had shut down the United States government on October first, Pidge's college roommate Tereze Sedgwick was one of the DOJ lawyers furloughed in Manhattan. Half a century plus, as freshman roommates, it had been tiny Tereze – five feet tall -- who first translated *Paloma* to *pigeon* to *Pidge*. Laden with bags of delicatessen from Zabars, Tereze had suddenly appeared out of years of estrangement at the ninth-floor apartment door Pidge now unlocked. Though different in so many ways from Pearl, whose path had been from U. Montana (paleontology> Berkeley – archeology> Columbia - ancient language), both friends had been foils for Pidge's wary inhibitions.

Pearl wasn't home, but their aged spaniel was, still on the floor by the couch, though now the sun had moved to bathe sixteen-year-old Ginger in *OCTOBER LIGHT*, John Gardner's title.

Addled by her chat with Alan Tapley, Pidge's mind heard an echo in *OCTOBER THE FIRST IS TOO LATE,* a sci-fi novel by Fred Hoyle & Son. In it, separate eras existed simultaneously, spread out across the entire Earth. Pidge imagined sailing off to Pasikennae's Mnkallis when it still remained the three-ringed center of Cretan religion. If only!

But instead, she maneuvered the grocery-filled cart to the kitchen. She didn't mind unloading it herself, thinking about the book she and Pearl were trying to put together. According to the literary agent they now shared with David, *Blue Monkeys* needed a "frame." Tereze had died of cancer a year before, in December. Diagnosed and dead in four months' time. She had left Pidge one of her Hermes silk scarves.

By the end of this October, Elena Luster was also dead, murdered in her new fourth floor apartment.

***Chapter 2 November Memories***

Pidge and Pearl had collaborated over decades, but never on anything nonacademic as David's literary agent urged. Three years earlier, before the election, at the start of a sabbatical semester that tripled, they had accepted an urgent invitation to the Orkney Islands north of Scotland to evaluate archeological discoveries presented with tighter security than currently surrounded the murder investigation in their Manhattan building. When the two linguistics experts had seen what was subsequently called the *Pasikennae Find*, they had been uncharacteristically beyond words.

Minoan Linear A on one side; Egyptian hieroglyphs on the other – a way to decipher Linear A at last!

On the Orkney island, birds flew overhead in the ocean-salty sky, curlews and oystercatchers, they were told. The professors looked out over low, heathered hills at grassy mounds lined into barrows. The *Knowes of Trotty* meant 'the mounds behind the marshes where the trowies (*trolls*) live.' They'd been invited by the Orkney Research Centre for Archaeology. A gloved specialist from Edinburgh had stood beside them. He turned over an etched stone for

Pearl's examination. She breathed a name.

*"Pasikennae."*

"A signature," Pidge echoed, "two centuries after Egypt's *Sinuhe*!'

"1800 B.C.E.," the Scot agreed. "This is circa 1600."

The trove of nearly 4000-year-old 'chapter stones' had contained writing etched or carved in fired clay, stone, and most rare, some cached inside copper cases. One of the two most remarkable appeared to be the very earliest, a beach stone later believed to have been

Pasikennae's -- as a child. The others included lists of cargo, passengers, sailors, events and stories, and some few maps implying that Pasikennae used a northern route from the Mediterranean to Lake Superior, not an also-disputed southern passage via the Caribbean/Mississippi.

Pearl had looked at Pidge and the Scot and invoked the Rosetta Stone's Champollion's 1822 triumphant shout, "'*Je tiens l'affaire!*'"


The co-op committee created a memorial for Elena Luster in the rooftop common space covered for the autumn/winter with a high-ceilinged, bubble-insulated, heated tent. Clocks had returned to Standard Time on November third. Night came too soon. The Committee had argued against the bowls of leftover Hallowe'en candy, but they'd lost that vote. An easel held an enlarged photo-poster (from a website) of the petite lawyer. The roof was scented by orange and yellow chrysanthemums and spiced-pumpkin candles as well.

Pidge and Pearl clustered with their ninth-floor neighbors and when asked, shared requested details about deciphering Linear A. David pursued Pidge, apologizing again for his agent's insistence about "getting" the professors to write a "reverse Rumpelstiltskin" popularization of "the first end of the world. Make hay out of golden scholarship!"

Pidge ignored his apology and avoided mentioning Alan's obvious absence. She was relieved when David went in search of more wine. This was no time to be judgmental. She and Pearl remained uneasy about the book contract. Instead, Pidge picked up a chocolate Reese's peanut butter cup and unwrapped it, looking out for Pearl's watchful eye. An elevating sugar A1c number was a genetic hazard for Pidge. She put the chocolate in her mouth before turning to look up and listen to James Beekmans. He had borrowed Pearl's first edition of the Hoyle novel Pidge had recently mentioned.

In a hushed voice, the tall geneticist talked about the sci-fi story with Pearl. He sounded like the former President, Black, regal, and brilliant.

"Great how Hoyle shows the past, present, and future happening simultaneously all over the globe. They're iterations. Just like this building, the City, the whole country. It's called *fractal amplification*. Like paisley. The number of repeating patterns at different orders of magnitude can make you dizzy when you add fungi and bacteria."

Dr. Duckett, his wife, added, "I often get the feeling we're constantly bombarded with coded messages that haven't been deciphered --," she paused, admiring Pidge and Pearl, "-- yet."

"*O, Susanna,*" Pidge sang off key, "what a lovely compliment."

Pearl smiled but was noticing, not the candy, Pidge was relieved to see, but across the enclosed roof, the NYPD detective who had been leading the investigation in the building. He was standing near a young woman, another research scientist who lived on the sixth floor. Pearl's dark eyes also narrowed at a couple from the fourth floor, next door neighbors of the murdered lawyer.

"The Doctors Persaud-Kimani have a four-month-old," Pearl said. "Who is with the baby, if not over there – what's her name who does research with James?"

"— Marwa Al-Halimi," Susanna supplied. "Dayita Persaud's mother stays with the baby. Not to worry, Pearl. Marwa is James's undergrad ex, but they don't work together at Rockefeller. James is genome. Marwa is brain. She's got synesthesia herself. Sees things in Crayola crayon colors. Marwa fills in for Dayita's mother in a pinch just like she sometimes saves us, staying with Micheline. We don't like to ask the twins' nanny. Marwa won't take money, either. She says it's research."

"So," Pearl as usual sounded like an oracle, "she's blood under the bridge."

"Old (Wo)man River," Pidge chided, "is supposed to say nothing but just keep rolling along."

"Well, you do have to wonder how ethical, I mean," some Arkansas came out in Susanna's edgy voice, "the detective…and Marwa. What's up with that, I wonder."

"Why?" James said. "Just means she's not a suspect. Am I? He just asked me about Azul. I told him *Methemoglobinemia*. Rare in a Costa Rican, associated with Kentucky, of all places. Treatment is, counter-intuitively, methylene blue dye, changes the blue skin coloration pink in minutes. As long as Azul remembers to take his meds, no other symptoms. Cold or anger can trigger it."

David returned with a small tray of wine glasses.

"What might get this memorial rolling along?" he said. "Is anyone going to speak? Give a eulogy?"

Relieved, James offered, "Likely that's just what the detective is waiting for."     Pidge and Pearl had guessed that Detective Donnelly's too many irrelevant questions translated into romantic curiosity about Dr. Al-Halimi. Pidge gave Pearl a look, and this time the oracle remained silent.

Finally, the co-op president moved to the longest table with the largest floral arrangement and tapped her wine glass for everyone's attention.

"A month isn't much time for seventeen stories of busy New Yorkers to make memories with our neighbor…Elena Luster... Seventeen stories times seven or eight apartments per story," the accountant wandered about in numbers. Then she introduced a stranger who expressed banalities.

An unfamiliar woman from another floor confided to Susanna, "That's the *masseur*. Elena told me she'd never have a *masseuse* in to celebrate winning a case. She couldn't trust herself with a woman touching her, she said. Y'know, Elena wore a wedding ring, but her wife had left her."

A man nearby scolded the gossip with his own. "The move was work-related. Elena Luster received threats. Refused Witness Protection. She was a DOJ attorney working for ICE."

"ICE isn't DOJ," Pearl pronounced.

"What is it?"

"A component of the Department of Homeland Security."

"That's not DOJ?" the man countered, but Pearl never lost contests like this one. This time, she just shrugged.

A few other neighbors spoke briefly. Detective John Donnelly learned little he didn't already know about the murder victim. "She was a smile, a hello at the garbage chute." In the elevator or lobby, though, she had talked to the actor. The "irresistible" Alan Tapley was absent now. Nothing new about Luster's other phone. The one they had was hardly older than her move. Her building memorial was a sad affair. He was hoping to begin a happy one.

### *Chapter 3 - from Blue Monkeys by Shapiro & Feria...*

*Pasikennae knew a proto-Greek myth about the punishment of Prometheus for his theft of divine fire to benefit humanity. She lived almost four thousand years ago in the Mediterranean, by which time people could forge copper and alloy it with tin to create bronze. Pasikennae lived on a small island of three concentric circles that lay sixty-nine miles north of Crete. HER rings identified it as the chief deity's home, a Cycladic Vatican for the trinity of Maiden, Mother, and Crone. SHE was the Creator and Destroyer of all things.*

*"Cyprus" meant 'copper' and was the region's greatest source of the shining element. Tin was mined in Cornwall and Brittany and to a far less extent in Turkey, where small children slaved in narrow tunnels. Until the volcanic disaster that ended it, the Cretan Empire was a center of Bronze Age trade, notably in metals like copper, tin, and silver from as far away as Norway, where Linear A inscriptions were found at Kongsberg. As much a mystery as its language, Linear A, was the life of one of its speakers, bull-vaulter and sea captain, Pasikennae.*

*Before her long life ended in a remote outpost of a shattered empire, Pasikennae created two-sided relics obviously treasured by the people who buried her. One side of carved stones and etched clay told stories in Linear A and the other in Egyptian hieroglyphs. This find moved translation of the extinct language well beyond the powers of the Phaistos Disk, a small clay circle with symbols stamped on both sides in a spiral formation, discovered in 1908 in a second millennium B.C.E. palace at Phaistos, Crete.*

*All but one of Pasikennae's relics began with the same inscription, an invocation of the 'Holy Holy Holy Horned Crown, Snake-armed Divinity.' On one relic, set tightly inside a lidded copper case, archeologists found a shaped four by three-inch black stone from an Orkney beach, identified as a prayer repeated thirteen times during a calendar rite. A female bull-vaulter was enameled on the lid whose vanished colors were detectable with photography, chemistry, and ultraviolet light. Repetition was indicated by four icons denoting a drum, cymbal, flute, and harp plus the sign for the number thirteen.*

*The original prayer, Feria & Shapiro speculated, had been sung to an oceanic, heartbeat sine wave rhythm, meaningful to a culture defined by the sea. Vastly amplifying the mystery of the Pasikennae Find, the copper of the minaudiere containers (some with veins of silver as part of a design) came not from Cyprus but from North America, from the northern shore of Lake Superior on Michigan's Isle Royale.*

*Much later Indigenous stories describe huge boulders of copper shining in the sun. Like Homer's four-hundred-year-old memory of the Trojan War, six centuries <u>after</u> the Cretan Empire's end, fragments of Ojibway stories suggested a distorted memory of Pasikennae: 'Long, long ago, when Ancient Turtle was young, careless cranes flew over the island and spilled from their beaks all but one memory stolen from a faraway Manetoowa. Her memories fell as huge copper boulders which were only the size of beads to the Manetoowa. As Turtle grew older, he walked more slowly, pressing many of Her beads deep into the ground. But he left some as a necklace around the shore of the Great Sea.*

*Long ago, a good Chief taught the people to dig out the copper, and they traded near and far. One day, the faraway Manetoowa demanded her stolen memories be returned. She sent Rippling Hair in an enormous canoe with thick skin wings, long wooden hands, and a giant belly. No one had ever seen anything like it or knew where it came from. No one had ever seen a tiny blue-*

*faced, furry man who danced in the canoe for Rippling Hair and made everyone happy.        Black crows welcomed the strange canoe, but the cranes flew away in fear. Rippling Hair disobeyed. She did not pack up sacred memories. She loved the young Chief, and their daughter Many Smiles –* Sueaysua *-- was born. The Sun gleamed on the Great Sea's copper necklace.*

*Then the cranes returned and admitted their theft. Little Blue Man died. Sueaysua died. Rippling Hair knew Manetoowa punished her. The Chief filled the belly of the winged canoe with Her memories. Rippling Hair had to leave. Crows cawed a sad song they sing to this day.'*

*Another shred of memory appeared in a nursery rhyme (IKWE means woman in Ojibway):*

*'Ikwekken, ikwekken, Fly away home! Your
canoe has blue wings And your baby is
gone. Ikwekken, ikwekken, Fly away home!
Take away copper!
You must leave us some!'*

*Chapter 4 Before the party, December*

*'Hey diddle diddle,*
*The Cat and the fiddle,*
*The Cow jumped over the moon,*
*The little Dog laughed to see such sport,*
*And the Dish ran away with the Spoon'*

Before Christmastime, impeachment was as much in the cold air as the sound of carols and steam of roasting chestnuts from Manhattan food carts. In China, coronavirus had begun to swing its scythe. The first known patient started experiencing symptoms on December first. He had not been to the Hunan Seafood Wholesale Market of Wuhan. No epidemiological link could be found between his and later cases.

Micheline, the three-year-old daughter of Susanna Duckett and James Beekmans was again 'reading' a book of nursery rhymes she had chosen at the ground floor children's room at the branch of the New York Public Library a twenty-minute walk from their building. Micheline paused for her mother to make the same comments she made every night as they 'studied' the book.

Susanna complied, "You know that the Cat and the fiddle are –"

"Constellations," the child recited.

"Yes, the constellation of –"

"Felis is the cat –"

"Latin for *cat*, or it also could be –"

"Leo the lion!"

"*The Cow jumped over the Moon* is Taurus that moved over the moon."    Micheline took over, "*The little Dog laughed to see such sport* --" and paused. "The constellation of *Canis Minor* is the dog –"

"Smaller dog," the child corrected. "*And the Dish ran away with the Spoon!*"

Bringing it home, Susanna concluded, "*Ursa Major,* the Big Dipper, and *Ursa Minor*—"

"*Little* Dipper are the dish and the spoon! Now do Paul Bunyan."

Later, as they cleaned up dinner dishes, Susanna remarked to James, "You know, you try not to gender-stereotype, and then the twins get our little girl swinging two-headed axes and trampolining in their kitchen."

"I bet it was her idea," James assessed their cramped space. "That kitchen *is* big enough for a trampoline."

"Daycare reports that she's also fixated on the letter 'x'."

"Why?" James asked.

"And I quote our daughter, 'Paul Bunyan carries an axe with two-they-say 'heads' and he has a blue *ox*. Arno and Dylan have a picture of the Minoan axe just like Paul Bunyan in the room with the blue *monkeys*.'

"She said *Minoan*?"

"They make axes out of construction paper with the nanny."

Then Susanna imitated Micheline putting her hands to the sides of her head like horns. "She tumblesaults on the bed, proclaiming she's 'just jumping over the moon!'"


Before Christmas, the holiday party initially planned by Susanna and James had transformed from an intimate dinner for six with Pidge, Pearl, Alan, and David into an event to be hosted at the Tapley-Rochester more spacious co-op. David had doubled the number because their dining room table easily sat a dozen. Sixth-floor Marwa Al-Halimi and "her" detective were to be guests along with fourth-floor physicians Dayita Persaud and Esau Kimani. A formal invitation also went out to David's literary agent and his young second wife, Vera Mifeng.

Though David had asked for his suggestions, Alan had begged off with too much going on shooting *HITTITE QUEEN*.

"And building your Island house," David said.

"Just call the planner along with the Juilliard quartet. You don't need me."

"But I want –"

"Early makeup!" Alan called over his shoulder as he shut the door.


The day of the dinner party, James had already driven Micheline up to Belmont, Little Italy in the Bronx, to stay overnight with his parents. He and Susanna would follow the next day for the long Christmas weekend. He watched Susanna as she got dressed. Admiring his wife, he thought of his original impression of her in '10 when they were both first years in Gross at Columbia. Susanna had long fingers and more knowledgeable hands than the rest of them. After graduating from U.Arkansas's Honors Program, for five years she'd saved most of her income living in her mother's trailer and working in a Medical Examiner's office. Nine years later, at thirty-six, she still looked – great legs.

Susanna turned to him and twirled in a black slip and black velvet skirt. "Deep thoughts?" she asked.

"It's quiet without Micheline here," he said.

Street noises easily reached the ninth floor. Sirens. A jet overhead.

"Well, as quiet as it ever gets in the City."

There was a smile in Susanna's voice. James imagined more of his body rising from the bed and embracing her, but he was too tired from an overnight in the lab plus the drive to and from the Bronx.

He said, "I was just thinking of that line from *RIDDLEY WALKER*, 'What we been, what we come to,' but that was to a future dystopia where Riddley finds a gigantic generator from the past without understanding what it was except a commentary on the ruin of the future. And what you and I been, what we come to … not so bad, huh, Doctor?"

"I've got another year, but… we're okay." Susanna sat on the small chair facing the bed. The smile had moved to her face. Neurosurgery residency took seven years. She had the night off. "Just have to put on makeup and then -- The Splurge!"

A copper-spangled sheer black blouse was on a hanger over the closet door.

In the bathroom, in the mirror, Susanna thought "what we been" and hardly paid attention as mascara and the rest masked her face. She thought of her single mother whose minister father had thrown her out when she got pregnant at sixteen. Susanna had never known him or her grandmother. A Latin teacher at the high school had given them a home in her apartment. Susanna learned to call her *Avia*. She had given toddler Susanna Latin primers along with *GOODNIGHT, MOON*. When she died, Avia left Susanna's mother enough money for the trailer.

Born Again Mom, who worked for the Catholic Diocese of Little Rock (Prison Ministry Office), hadn't been able to swing college for Susanna. Over the years, their conversations had revealed versions of a life story. Susanna had worried that she was the child of rape because Mom would never tell her about her absentee father.

Finally, Susanna had asked, "Was he in some war and never came home, or his parents didn't want their upper-class son to marry you?

"He was smart, like my mom's father. Like you. Your father could read Latin and Greek. He was a married man," Mom said.

Seeking something other than her harsh father's church, Susanna's mother had found not only

Catholicism, but also a not-so-virgin birth. Susanna's father had been a priest.

"He said he was married to God."

Teenage Susanna sniped, "In Latin or Greek? I thought that was nuns. So, his was a gay marriage?"

Then she had won the writing contest that helped her get a full scholarship to UArk. Mom had named her *Susanna* for the rape in the Apocrypha whose meaning Susanna changed in her poem. She'd been inspired by Jack Miles's better explanation of Job's understanding of the divine Bully. Her mother rebuked her. Susanna's marriage to James was another *anathema,* Mom's favorite big word. She'd turned out as fundamentalist as her own Dad. Perhaps Susanna *was* like her maternal grandpa and priest father, too. James studied genetics, not her. Lord help her not to be like her Mom!

Makeup and hair complete, Susanna returned to the bedroom. James was sound asleep. As he had watched her dress, she enjoyed him now. There he was, her guide Through the Looking Glass, his negative to her positive, his Black to her white. How wary but intense he had been, but how certain about *her.*

He'd said, "I admire brilliant, alienated women."

Susanna sighed. James stirred.

Pidge and Pearl had admired Susanna's winning poem. She wasn't sure how they had wormed it out of her. Sometimes, she thought the two old women were witches. They reminded Susanna of her *avia.* They'd had the poem artfully calligraphed and framed as a gift for her December 8th birthday. It was new on the wall beside the closet and her blouse. She read it again.

*SALIX BABYLONICA*

**This is how you both have been dealing with the daughters of Israel, and they were intimate with you through fear; but a daughter of Judah would not endure your wickedness.**
**APOCRYPHA, Book of Susanna, 57**

*1*
*Daniel, I call to God through you.*
*I remove my veil before you*
*and reveal what two elders saw*
*in my husband Joakim's house*
*here in Babylon where God*
*has allowed us all to be taken.*
*My beauty, they say, justified*
*their intended rape. I resisted*
*them, trusting to God and you.*
*Now I am condemned to die*
*for adultery they say I committed*
*with a young man too strong for them,*
*who opened the doors of my garden*
*and dashed away. They say they seized*
*me then and demanded who the young*
*man was, but I would not tell.*
*Daniel, I call to God through you.*
*I remove my veil before you*
*now I am condemned to die.*


*2*
*Then God aroused the holy spirit of a young lad*
*named Daniel, and he cried among the captive Jews*
*of Babylon with a loud voice, speaking for God,*
*"I am innocent of the blood of this woman."*
*All the people turned to Daniel and said, "What*
*is this you have said?" Taking his stand*
*in the midst of them, he said, "Are you such*
*fools, you sons of Israel? Have you condemned*
*a daughter of Israel without examination*
*and learning the facts? Return to*
*the place of judgment. For these men*
*have borne false witness against her."*
*And so they returned to the scene of the crime,*
*to the pool in the garden of Joakim, honored*
*Jew of Babylon, where Daniel separated*
*the suspects and questioned them cleverly.*
*"Under which tree in this garden did you see*
*beautiful Susanna lying with a young man?"*
*"Under that mastic tree," said the first, pointing.*
*"Under that evergreen oak," said the other, the same.*
*So the first was cut in two, as his tree was named; and*
*the second was sawed in half, as his tree was named,*

*for their false witness against The Name and Susanna.*

*3*
*Hosannah to justice and God who are One!*
*served by Susanna and Daniel who knew*
*those liars for what they were! As penance,*
*Daniel served the Lord all his days,*
*crying out in the streets*
*of the captive Jews of Babylon*
*for the justice of their God –*
*and I, Susanna, never again loved Daniel*
*beneath the weeping tree named for Babylon.*

The Tapley-Rochester co-op and dining room table were decorated for the holiday season. The overall effect was evergreen scent and twinkling. Dr. Dayita Persaud had never seen anything like it. She and Esau rented. She'd had no idea there were co-ops this big in their building. Baby Sandra was asleep five floors down in her tiny space off the kitchen. Dayita's mother, relieved at last to have a grandchild, was as usual watching Sandra and would sleep over on their living room couch that opened to a queen-size bed.

The Tapley-Rochester living room faced a wall of high windows now black and reflecting the glittering salon that overlooked Riverside Park and the Hudson beyond. The furniture was designer, the thick area rug pattern-carved in wide sweeps of grey, cream, and brown. The windows were bare, their blinds invisible inside layered glass. An anomalous, ornate marble fireplace centered one wall. Displayed on its carved mantel were fragrant evergreen garlands decorated with Christmas balls in silver, bronze, and copper. Strands of tinsel lights repeated around the room and circled a tall, live Christmas tree in a corner window behind a baby grand piano.

Pidge and Pearl had wondered how much David and Alan tipped the superintendent and nine other doormen and porters, their own greatest Christmas expense. Above the fireplace Pidge missed the large painting of an ancient fresco, fragmented images of blue monkeys on a peeling red, orange, and cream background. It had been replaced by another Minoan copy of long-haired wrestlers grappling. Within the fireplace were an assortment of flameless LED candles of different shimmying heights. Faceless Cycladic statues of various sizes were haloed in lights on glass end and coffee tables. On the piano was a polished heirloom menorah. Winter had begun that Saturday in the northern hemisphere; New York City knew the next sunset began the eight nights of Chanukah.

To Dayita's left, the way to the living room led back to a wood-paneled foyer and master suite hall. To her right was a formal dining room, the kitchen, a den and the twins' and nanny's bedrooms. Alan Tapley had taken her on a tour. Dayita was surprised she'd been able to pay attention to anything beyond the celebrity's flawless features. Otherworldly pale eyes. Really, a plastic surgeon would've invoked Galatea. But Dayita had gaped at a strange toilet in the master bathroom.

Alan laughed and explained how easily it worked, bidet included.

"I had the same reaction when David and the decorator chose it. Sales pitch, 'A high-tech toilet whose lid rises and its seat heats as you approach. As the lid opens, music plays from a sound card, and the deodorizer is turned on. When you leave, the toilet flushes on its own.'"

Dayita blurted, "I wouldn't want to know what that costs!"

Charming away her embarrassment, Alan said, "Neither did I!"

By the time Dayita and Esau had come up from the fourth floor, all but one other of the "six unlikely couples" were present, shiny in velvet and jewelry. Catering servers offered trays of drinks and hors d'oeuvres.

Marwa Al-Halimi was accompanied by a building outsider, the detective, John Donnelly. They were sipping wine and scotch, respectively, in conversation with Dr. Esau Kimani. After Marwa, of course, Esau and his wife Dr. Dayita Persaud were the people John knew best at this party. Marwa's co-op was two floors directly above the crime scene apartment; the doctors' was next door to it. The investigation had reached a bad pun: dead-end. A new tenant had moved in.

John knew that unlike the former President, Dr. Kimani did have a birth certificate from

Kenya; he was forty-six, an American citizen for twenty years. His in-laws were entrepreneurial Indian immigrants now retired in north Manhattan's Inwood neighborhood. At the party, John was to call the doctor's doctor-wife Dayita – she was forty-three, born in the City's northern suburban county, Westchester, in Hastings-on-Hudson. The detective was curious about whatever the couple might say about their new neighbor.

Marwa was asking Dayita, "Do you ever go upstate in the winter?" She paused to explain to John that the neighbors had generously let her escape to their Cold Spring house when they didn't rent it or go themselves.

"Cold Spring is near Poughkeepsie," Marwa's dark tan reddened.

John understood she was embarrassed he might think she was requesting a romantic getaway for the holidays. He took a long swallow of a fine single malt. Cohabitating did look hopeful. Marwa had agreed to a Christmas tree. They had confided edited autobiographies. Last night's sleepover was a first. John held up his crystal glass for distraction.

"Waterford," Dayita supplied. "What an apt pattern for tonight. That's 2011's *Snowflake Wishes For Joy Lismore.*"

Esau signaled for a refill for their glasses, gently tapping his to John's, adding, "Dayita knows things."

Sipping strongly-rummed eggnog, Dayita said, "New York City had the best homicide clearance rate in the country this year, eighty-six percent, when fifty-four percent of the City's murders involved a firearm."

Esau beamed at his wife. He asked, "Do you know if genetic genealogy might be apt for the Luster case?"

Dayita looked at Marwa, then the detective.

Marwa said, "Identifying crime DNA via relatives in databases? I'm not genes per se."

John offered, "The Golden State killer, two years ago? NYPD possesses eighty-two thousand-plus genetic profiles."

Dayita laughed. "John, do you ever answer questions? You must be dying to ask us about our new tenant next door."

John felt the scotch warming him towards Marwa's neighbors. "You know the E. E. Cummings poem? 'Dying's fine, but death, oh, baby.'"

"English major at Cornell. He can't help it," Marwa explained.

"It must be genetic, Detective," Esau said, accepting a miniature potato pancake hors d'oeuvre offered by a server. He dipped it in applesauce.

Dayita dipped hers in sour cream. Like her husband, she avoided several other gourmet topping choices.

"We love the latkes," she said, "but we're 'don't ask, don't tell' about food. I did ask Azul the move-in's name. Cage, I think."

Esau shrugged. "So far, he's all rumor. All we know is, he's not a renter like us, but a buyer. Not even that for sure."

John saluted with his scotch glass, sipped, and said nothing.

The doorbell rang, and David crossed the room from the Juilliard string trio and piano where he had been entertaining Pidge and Pearl. He led Drew Burgos and his young wife, Vera Mifeng, into the living room. Vera wore a fur coat.

"It's *faux*! It's *faux*!" she announced. "We are not *sauvages*!"

Drew apologized for being late. "But we're the ones who didn't get here by elevator. We actually had to cross town. It's not snowing yet, thank god."

The windows were dark, reflecting like mirrors. Conversations moved in shallow dinner party

eddies of biography and commentary, with the occasional intimate asides occasioned by alcohol

and proximity whose loss to a plague no one could yet imagine. In passing, Alan accepted

champagne from a young waiter and answered his question, "Yes, the Joan of Arc statue is just a

ten-minute walk from here."

Then the musicians segued from Chopin to Christmas carols, cueing sing-along laughter, which

distracted Pidge and Drew who had seen David, across the room, notice the flirtation they had

overheard.

Drew continued chatting with Pidge about the four young musicians, "David's on the Board at

Juilliard. Do you have a cat?" he asked.

"No," Pidge said. "Just an old dog, no new tricks among the three of us."

Drew nodded toward Alan. "He's catnip."

Also near the music and trying to hear above it, Pearl was listening to Drew's hyper wife. She

encouraged Vera to eat hors d'oeuvres, wondering if the Asian sylph ("I'm twenty-five! My

literary agent husband sent me a manuscript as an excuse to meet!' I'm a new editor at an old

publishing house!") had an eating disorder. Would they ever sit down to dinner?

Gesturing with her champagne flute, Vera said, "I love New York! Your *Pidge* – I *love* that! –

is Puerto Rican, father Jewish so she's technically not, Drew says – but what a great Jewfro on

that genius head!" Then sadly, she pouted, "*Our* hair is bone straight," then brightened. "Two

Africans, one Indian, one Indigenous, one Chinese, two and a half Jewish – we outnumber

Handsome Texas Hold 'Em -- did you even know eyes could get that white? and the detective?

Donnelly? Irish?" Vera pointed across the room at James Beekmans. "He's Blacker than Kenya-

Kimani. In this room of giant men, how tall *is* he?"

Pearl was inured to the adolescent need to shock. Perhaps the girl was on drugs. Or had missed a dose. Hoping to calm her, Pearl talked above the music.

"James Beekmans is six foot six, I believe. When he was little, he lived near the Bronx Zoo. He thought it belonged to his grandfather because he took him there daily. You know South Street Seaport, Beekman Street?" Pearl asked as Vera's eyes wobbled around the room "James told us he's those Beekmans. His family dropped the master's apostrophe three hundred years ago. They moved north into the Manhattan woods and swamp before Olmsted started terraforming Central Park but got chased out when that real estate became worth something. Once they were in the Bronx, they owned land they weren't being run off anymore. His great-grandfather took photos of the Italians when they first arrived, and he delivered mail to the ones who could read."

Vera blinked (awake?) and heard the nearby Christmas carol's lyric. She sang instead, "We're the only *Asians* here!"

"*We* left Asia at least twelve thousand years ago. I identify as old," Pearl said.

Vera ignored the professor's tone. "How BIPOC. What tribe? Where?"

"Shoshone, Wyoming," Pearl began. "My older brother and nephew inherited a store in Gardiner, Montana. That's the original, northern entrance to Yellowstone Park. Whole family works there, one way or another. Below Yellowstone is the world's most massive active volcano. The last time it erupted was 640,000 years ago. It's a *caldera*. Paloma and I've been several times. We stay in Jackson Hole. I grew up discovering fossils. I hope to become one."

Vera burped. She repeated, "I love New York," and concluded, "Orchids and weeds thrive, but no shrinking violets."

Stringed arpeggios and a flourish on the piano announced dinner. The couples filed out of the living room through the open hallway to the other side of the wall into the dining room. Its two sides were painted a shining copper, and the same holiday décor was aglow, this time with lighted wax candles on a damasked table whose ornate, heirloom settings contrasted with modern chairs and side furniture. The carved area rug was similar to the one in the living room but with metallic glints, and the surrounding dark wooden floor gleamed.

Alan and David sat at either end of the long table. As they located their names on place cards and took their seats, the guests saw they were also separated from their partners.

"How *colonial*," Vera looked up to her right at James Beekmans, who even seated, towered above her. Pearl was on her left, pleasing neither. Susanna was at the other end of the room, next to Alan, who along with the rest of the table, couldn't fail to hear Vera's comment.

"David left seating to the planner," Alan said. "We were going for something between random and toss-up. I'm left-handed, so it's good I'm at an end."

Marwa turned to Drew Burgos. "I'll be careful. I'm also a lefty."

Dayita observed, "The night turns these windows into mirrors, so you don't need them."

At the end of the table with his back to the reflection, Alan said gently, "I avoid mirrors."

Sitting across from her, James saw Marwa startle, and to his right, beside Dayita, John Donnelly had been closely watching Tapley as well.

But the star attraction in the dining room was the theatrical effect of the two saturated-color canvases newly hung on the facing walls.

Pidge thought, *So that's why Alan wants a place to paint. He's good.* She turned to her left and asked David, "Where did the blue monkeys go?"

"The twins wanted them in their room. They've given them their names, are drawing pictures of them, and making up stories -- it looks like the boys think they *are* the monkeys. They keep finger-painting each other blue."

As the dinner was served and eaten, Alan answered questions about his oversize paintings.

Vera said, "The color is so *fauve*... odd abstractions –"

From the other side of the table, Drew corrected her gently, "Not abstractions, really. Texture studies?"

Alan said, "Actually, I was interested at what point and how something gigantic and something microscopic can become color and shape to the eye and mind."

Marwa and James exchanged a look over the candles and holiday centerpiece.

Seated facing each other in the middle of the table. Marwa asked him, "Like your dataset, the forty-eight terabytes?

James nodded. "And your compass cells? Coincidence? Zeitgeist?"

"The two paintings are a diptych?" Vera attempted, but it came out, "Dipstick."    No one laughed. Instead, Drew looked to David and said, "Our wordsmith *par excellence* must've named the pair?"

David lifted his wine glass and said, "*Orders of Miniature and Magnitude.*"    Drew looked to the other end of the long table and asked Alan, "Did you approve?"

"Above *par,*" Alan drawled to relieved laughter.

Four servers distracted the guests with platters and pouring while Vera's husband Drew sent her a supportive smile. He had the Nile-haired Egyptian on one side and his new client on the other.

"Professor *Shapiro,*" he turned to her, "I'm always glad to see I'm just a smidge, just a *Pidge* away at the hallway end of the table. Don't *we* always look for an escape route?"

Pidge stopped with her wine glass near her lips. She had to lower it to accept a toasting tap from Drew who was humming music she couldn't hear.

After the party, she and Pearl discussed the pronoun *we.*

"Was Drew being imperial, like Queen Victoria?" Pidge said. "Escape from what? The party?"

"He meant you're Jewish," Pearl said. He was singing *Tradition* from FIDDLER ON THE ROOF."

"You could hear that from the other end of the table and I was right next to him? My ears! There is no justice." Pidge touched her corona of white hair. "I'm going to seed like a dandelion and you don't even need hair dye."

"Yes," Pearl echoed, "the European conquest of North America was all about hearing and hair," Pearl said, and then even more tartly, "Vera reported that Drew actually denies your paternal Judaism because your mother wasn't. She mentioned your *Jewfro* hairdo."

Pidge lifted her chin and tossed unmoving curls. "You didn't correct her? My father's hair was wavy, yes, but this bouffant crown is as much Mom's do-ing as," she put a palm against her cheek, "whatever shade my Black is Beautiful skin is –" she stopped. "I'm too tired for this. All I am is a lapsed atheist and ready for bed. Does Ginger need a walk?"

"I put out newspaper. She's older in dog years than we are and doesn't want to go out in the cold any more than we do."

"*We*," Pidge sighed. "Poor Vera was the kid at the grownup's table."

"Her grandparents still live in Hong Kong," Pearl said, "and her parents are longtime residents in Queens where she was born. She is Chinese-American, *not* Korean, and she was an English major at NYU."

"She's no shrinking violet," Pidge said. "What's so funny?"

*Chapter 6 The Party's Over - December*

He and Susanna were already in bed. As far as James was concerned, keeping Micheline for this overnight was his parents' real Christmas present. His arousal belied all the alcohol he'd drunk. Quite a list. *Grey Goose*, vintage wines, champagne with dessert, and after, David had insisted James "*savor* a glass of a truly memorable port." Ambrosia. Must've cost a small fortune. Sitting across from Marwa at the "table of unlikely couples" as David had also accurately described, James had appreciated the past was in the past. No regrets. He breathed deeply to *savor* Susanna's perfume.

Predictably, she was still wound up. Her back to him, James spooned, his left arm over Susanna's waist. The bedroom was darkened by blackout drapes. Riverside Drive was quiet in the falling snow.

"Who but Pidge and Pearl would turn dessert into a dissertation about *impeachment*? Susanna said.

James struggled to remember. Something about the peach pie? The ice cream? He was familiar with his wife's idea of foreplay. Ah, yes.

He whispered, "Pidge's ex-husband's grandmother called it *Fresh Peach*, and now Breyer's just labels it *Peach*."

Susanna moved into his embrace. Progress, but still spoons. No *forking* yet. He must still be high.

"The *etymology* of the word," Susanna whispered back. "Medieval law, no less. Mix-up of Latin *impedicare* with *impetere* and a Middle English verb *apechen*."

"Your Grandma Avia would've loved Pidge and Pearl. I love you."

"James, I am talking about im*peach*ment."

"You are unimpeachable," James said, as Susanna turned his way, "though you are a peach."

On the fourth floor, Dayita and Esau had managed to avoid waking Dayita's mother via the apartment's rare second entrance into the kitchen, one of the many oddities of the historical building. The kitchen shared a wall with the scene of the Luster murder. They could just hear the new tenant inside, possibly moving pots around. At this hour? Given the thickness of the walls, he must be making some racket in there.

They were both wide awake, anyway. Descending in the elevator, they'd checked their phone's baby monitor and heard only white noise waves. Sandra was sleeping soundly. Her thumb was secure in her mouth. They were eager to see her again. On the other side of an original pantry door, there she was.

Neither spoke. They watched their daughter breathe.

Esau considered the tiny nursery. In 1927, a bachelor's City pied-a-terre? Perhaps not a pantry but a valet's cubby? He and Dayita could never afford a place like the combined co-op up on the ninth floor. Esau's thoughts scattered: epidemic in China -- if pandemic, he was head of ED at Columbia Presby -- entry via the West Coast -- but if in Europe, then already here. Must send the baby to live with Dayita's parents in northern Manhattan? or the trio to the Cold Spring house north of the suburbs?

Dayita's thoughts ricocheted like Esau's. She was also an Emergency Department doctor in the same hospital, how they had met. At forty-three and forty-six, so late to marry and so lucky to have a healthy baby? Risk Sandra's and her parents' lives? If only there had been time to find a house in Inwood, or move generations together in Cold Spring or back to Hastings-on-Hudson where she'd grown up. Esau liked her Hindu parents. His family were Christians in Kenya. No cases reported in Africa. Only a matter of time.

Dayita took Esau's hand. They had to cross the living room to get to their bedroom. *Mam* was asleep and didn't stir. She hadn't turned off the colored lights garlanding the table Christmas tree. Red, yellow, blue, and green reflected on the thick glaze of an ornamented elephant Ganesh beside it. The shades were pulled down, but the wind was sweeping snow in gusts against the windows.

In their bedroom, the couple was suddenly exhausted. Silence continued until they could trust sleep to rescue them. Jarred momentarily awake by something in the bathroom, no, in the next-door apartment, the bedroom monitor broadcast the baby's cries and Dayita's mother's near-instant lullaby. Then white noise whooshed again.

But Dayita said, "Donnelly? John? The detective?"

And Esau answered, "Yes, he'll want to know."


Two floors directly above, the noise was inaudible in Marwa's apartment. She expected John to stay for the rest of the weekend. He intended to escort his mother to Christmas Midnight Mass on Tuesday. But Marwa saw eye to eye with John's father about "parting ways with metaphysics." Mr. Donnelly had been an AP physics teacher like her high school ace at Stuy. John's parents lived in a little brick Tudor house in Long Island's Nassau County just over the Brooklyn border.

John thought of Mass in East Rockaway with his mother as penance for the Christmas absence of her only grandchild. Though he shared custody of nine-year old daughter Beckett with Kirby, he imagined a double entendre bumper sticker, *$ trumps the law*. So the little girl was spending two private school holiday weeks in St. Bart's, a longtime redoubt of Kirby's old money family, and John Donnelly would be a poor stand-in for *Becky*. Her red-headed ("that was") Irish perpetually up, his mother refused to call her granddaughter "that *Murder in the Cathedral* name!" Though retired, ever the English teacher. Beckett had pronounced her *Gramma* without hearing the dropped *r* that became a family joke.

Standing, John was looking in the dresser mirror. From bed, Marwa's reflection watched him. He smiled at her.

Marwa said, "Did you notice upstairs they have no mirrors except in the bathrooms?"

"Tapley startled you when he said he avoids them."

Marwa considered the moment. John had detailed his failed marriage. She had told him about James Beekmans ("I ruined that") and the awful summer *hajj* in Mecca before her college senior year. But not about four years earlier.

John pulled his undershirt over his head.

His torso caused a synesthesia cascade in Marwa's eyes. Kaleidoscope Crayola colors. Heat. John enjoyed his effect. He gave Marwa time. Technique. Usually, people talked.

Finally, she spoke slowly.

"My family had moved into downtown Manhattan, to be near magnet schools. My senior year began with 9/11. I watched in math class when the Towers fell five blocks away. I rushed to my little brother's elementary nearby, and we were tug-boated by firefighters across the Hudson. In New Jersey, someone saw I was bleeding from my head. My colors were gone. In our Battery Park apartment building lived an international model. Pree had black skin, natural blond curls, and green eyes. He was on the jet from Boston that hit the North Tower. He was twenty-two. I was seventeen. In his will, Pree left me a giant diamond; my father invested it for me. His professional name was Denim Prix. They called him *Grand Prix*. 'Pre-what?' my friend Judy said. Pree didn't have mirrors even in his bathrooms. 'Reflection isn't reflection,' he said." It was snowing outside. Bare-chested, John felt the cold. Marwa got out of bed and stood behind him, both facing the mirror. She pressed her cheek against his shoulder blade. He didn't move.

Then she did, going to her desk under the window. She took an old manila envelope from a bottom drawer, removed tape over its metal butterfly closure, and opened it.      "It's Pree's letter to me in his will," Marwa said, handing it to him. "Also what the psychiatrist asked me to write down in 2004. That's everything."

"Not really," John said. 'Not anymore."

He waited several days. Then late on Christmas Day at his parents' house in East Rockaway,

John read the typed letter.

*August 31, 2001*

*Dear Marwa,*

*If you are reading this, something bad has happened to me, so don't be upset. Also, don't expect too much from this letter because I'm not one of your Stuy genius friends. I don't want you to get the wrong idea about the diamond. It's not like the movie Titanic or an engagement ring. If your reading this I'm right I can't see myself getting engaged. But I wanted you to have a diamond big enough to do that experiment you described and I know you will think of some way to use the diamond better than I could what it cost. Also, never think it is payment for anything except maybe in a good way of your affect on me.*

*I have the affect of being a drug on people they get physical around me. So I put a wall up around like I walk around wearing a mask. But behind the mask I didn't want anyone for a very long time until you. Not like you wanted me but that was okay. You knew so much and had so many questions about everything that was like a drug to me, like someone <u>could</u> know things. I didn't think anything could make sense but with you I saw maybe. Maybe not for me but at all but I want to understand more so I am going to California to try.*

*A model should be an example of something not a puppet. I have always been treated like a dummy (mannikin) not a person like I had no feelings or ambitions maybe I don't. But I never got a chance to learn how to do anything besides walk, pose, take direction. You once said how Muslims all have to face Meca 5 times a day in the same direction my whole life I have been facing cameras.*

*<u>The most dominating camera is someone else's eye/idea of what you have to do and be</u>, you said. A real model is like Jesus or Alexander or you for me. When you disobeyed your father to come to my birthday party I'd never done anything like that. When you came to my apartment for sex I knew your first time was a big deal for you which I did not think it could be to me anymore but it was because of you.*

*I don't know if I can go from being a model to a real <u>actor</u> that acts not pretends. I don't know what I can learn to do I never really went to school. I don't trust gurus. I don't know if I could sit in a library. Who knows how soon you'll be reading this. Not soon I hope. You make me want to know things I didn't know*

*Be yourself that's the hardest thing but I think you can do it don't blush too hard,*

*love,*

*Robert (my real name) Doucette*

John put the letter down and then read the pages she had written for the psychiatrist. They

appeared scanned and copied from diary-sized paper. No explanatory headings from 2004.

Marwa's handwriting. It must've taken her a long time.

"He misspelled *effect*, *you're*, *mannequin*."

Dr. Rawi looked at me. "And Mecca. What experiment?"

"So I killed him. He was on the plane to LA because I was such a terrific model. Now maybe I'll be the death of James Beekmans."

I counted the beats of the psychiatrist's silence.

"James Beekmans?" Dr. Rawi prompted.

"Shouldn't I tell my boyfriend about Pree? Can you give me a prescription for the pill? Is that how it is, every truth with one person gets to be a lie to the next? How can you be true to anything, to anyone? To Allah? To self? Does either exist? I'm afraid even to look at the diamond," Marwa said. "The experiment was, if you put it on your tongue, it's supposed to cool it. Like ice."

"Ice costs a lot less, and it melts," Dr. Rawi said. "It reminds me of the coal an angel placed on Isaiah's tongue.
What do you dream about Alexandria?"

"I find Alexander's *tomb*. Like Juliet when she wakes up and sees Tybalt. And Romeo. But it's the *plane*. I'm in it on fire in the *North Tower*. I've found Alexander, but *now I can't get out. I can't bear it!* But Pree *had to*. Why would an angel *do* that to Isaiah? Bushes burning, and sending people into a lion's den and furnaces, and burning a tongue?" I sounded like a taut string. "And who's responsible? Who's accountable? *Shame* on them! '*Shame!*' that woman said, and she was *right* –"

"What woman?" Dr. Rawi asked.

"When Condoleezza Rice just testified about the August 6th warning – the woman's mother had died in the North Tower, too. She went to the hearings -- they *had* 'way too much information not to do something, so by going to the hearing, she was saying to her mother, 'All right, I'm swinging back for you now,' and, '*It changes the rest of my life to know they had this level of information!* And she couldn't help it, she yelled out, '*SHAME!*'"

I jumped up, screaming, "*SHAME*," and rushed around the room, touching the desk, the chaise, grabbing a toy from the top of the bookcase, then turning, saying quietly, "My little brother is going to kill himself bouncing off walls – imitating those stupid teenagers, they run up walls and backflip from ledges, *tracers*, Joey says. My mother lives in terror," I stopped, then began tossing the small stuffed animal from one hand to the other.

"*Parkourists*," Dr. Rawi said. "I have seen them catapulting in Central Park."

"They climb up alcoves in Battery Park City."

"Very gymnastic."

"They - think - they - can - defy - gravity," I said. I fell back into my chair. I covered my face with my hands. "I can't – breathe," I said, but I was breathing, very hard, "*I'm on fire* –"

When I came to, I was lying on the chaise against the wall. A cold compress on my forehead. Dr. Rawi sat nearby.

I could only whisper. "Will my synesthesia come back? Will I get well? Will I get over it?"

"Like a mountain?"

So it was not a mountain, he meant. Me, the doctor, and Time, we were moving together in fractal ways and waves beyond current understanding.

"Was it all ever Whole and One?" I asked.

"Golf? Or before the Big Bang?" Dr. Rawi said. He gave me a referral to a gyno for the birth control prescription. They call this *abreaction*.

Midnight Mass with his mother wasn't as bad as he'd expected. John had more than lapsed; he'd forgotten how powerful the mixed scent of incense and evergreens could be. The church was darker than he remembered, lighted for the ceremony by flickering candles. He felt it like a drug hitting his senses – sight, sound, smell – hard to deny the Jesuit maxim, *"Give me the child for the first seven years and I'll show you the man."*

His mother wore a sprig of holly with a red bow she'd brought to pin on the doily over her grey hair. The choir chanted: *In splendoribus sanctorum, ex utero, ante luciferum, genui te.* When he joined her in line to take communion, her delight translated, "Before I created Light, I created You."

He'd intended to drive his mother home and go back to his nearby Oceanside condo, but when she asked him to be there in the morning to open presents, the powerful mood kept John in East Rockaway.

In the car, she said, "I'm not supposed to tell you what Becky left for you under the tree. I'm sworn to secrecy."

"She gave it to you? What's under my tree, then?"

"Oh, part of the mystery. You should be glad your daughter is more interested in being a detective than a debutante."

Christmas morning, he unwrapped a nine-year old's handmade book, red poster paper cut and folded into a pamphlet with green copier paper. It was a story with illustrations both hand-drawn and collaged from magazines. John breathed in a whiff of Elmer's Glue and pictured his daughter's hard-working little hands.

John turned it to the back cover where she'd pasted her small school photo, long red hair ablaze above her uniform. Then he read the childish calligraphy on the front cover, "*Dr. Solver & the Small Fry by Beckett Anne Donnelly.*"

"Dr. *Anne* Solver," John's father added. "For *Gramma*, Becky said."

"So you were in on this, too," John said.

"Guilty, Detective."

His mother couldn't contain herself. "Dr. Solver is the City coroner. The small fry help the police solve crimes. Dr. S can see the miniature kids, but the other police can't see them. They don't even know they're there. Becky wrote four whole chapters! Four whole crimes! Two in this book, two waiting under your tabletop tree."

2020

*Chapter 8  Early January*

In the Southern hemisphere, it was summer. Australia was suffering the worst heat wave in its history. It was winter in New York. On the ninth floor, Pidge and Pearl were struggling to find words for Pasikennae's story. It wasn't harder than deciphering Linear A. But things didn't fit together like a jigsaw puzzle. There were no straight edges to line up or organize by color or shape, nor any crossword clues when it came to a human life…

"…and one who lived and died almost four thousand years ago," Pearl tried to explain to literary agent Drew Burgos on speakerphone.

"Just remember *our* deadlines," Drew said.

"*Just*," Pearl repeated, rolling her eyes at Pidge, who stood nearby listening, looking out a morning window.

Below was an ice-glazed sycamore whose springtime green felt as far away as Pasikennae did. The tree's peeling bark left scars. *Our deadlines.* Pidge didn't need any help feeling old. She heard her father's advice: *bad mood? get a better one.* The sycamore was an ancient species that shed its bark as a snake did skin. The name came from Latin *sycomorus*, Greek *sykomoros,* a native Mediterranean fig tree.

According to a legend younger than Pasikennae, Hippocrates taught his medical students under the leafy canopy of a sycamore tree on Cos, an island northeast of her tri-circular Mnkallis. In present day New York, a sycamore was *Platanus occidentalis.* A book Pidge liked as a child, A TREE GROWS IN BROOKLYN, starred that plane tree. Did little girls even read it anymore? The Biblical sycamore was *Ficus sycamorus.* Egyptians used it to make mummy cases. It produced kinda lousy figs. Pasikennae might have known that.

Pearl put down the phone. She *hmphed.*

"Well, where are we with *Holy Holy Holy*?" Pidge asked.

Pearl sat down at the round oak dining room table where beside layers of folders, their laptops yawned open. The hutch behind her, emptied of Pidge's inherited china (sent to her daughter near Seattle for Nina's fortieth birthday that year), was now was crowded with books. Pronounced *Neen-yah*. Pidge returned to her chair and stared at the same images on her screen. The scholars were struggling with the lunar calendar ritual prayer recited at the bull-leaping ceremony.

Pearl examined the familiar dual-pages showing an ancient carved flatstone and its scholarly translation.

"Pasikennae jumped through the horns of a bull to the repetition of those words. How?" She shut her eyes and shook her head, muttering, "She captained a fifty-oared ship to Lake Superior, lived among the proto-Ojibway, then sailed back across the Atlantic to find her world *gone*? Then up north to the Orkneys for the rest of a long life? Why, why, why? How, how how?"

"Well, here *we* are," Pidge said.

Pearl snapped, "You're right where you were born. In your mother's rent-controlled apartment."

Pidge shrugged. No need between the friends to retrace missteps. Old tragedies were ever present, best forgotten: Pearl's teenage marriage, stillborn son, escape from Yellowstone; later, a second marriage, another son, Esa (*Wolf*), currently dedicating his life to Pearl's redemption by working for the Eastern Shoshone Tribe Attorney General in Fort Washakie, Wyoming. Both women had divorced Columbia University husbands, Esa's father (Anthropology) and Nina's (Mathematics), Pearl's less cordially than Pidge's. Pearl grated. Pidge soothed.

Pearl softened, "Well, you heard him. We have to '*span the centuries, build bridges.*'"

"Engineering," Pidge said. "Something else about which I know nothing."

"Drew Burgos thinks that Life is a four-star restaurant where you *just* place an order, and a server brings it."

But Pidge was engrossed by her screen, whispering to the long-dead woman. "What a hard life, Pasikennae. Apt to carve into stone."

Pearl focused on the image of the artifact and their translation of a crude expression in the prayer. She knew which glyph Pidge was suffering over.

"Well, we can't say *Vagina Tunnel* or *Cunt Thruway*, now can we?"

This time, it was Pidge who *hmphed*. "The rebus is obvious. HER squatting anatomy. But millennia replaced its sacred meaning with dirty words. If we translate it as worshippers saw it – the holy center of their Cosmos – then –"

"Prayer equals porn," Pearl said.

"Well, we've got to do something."

"I'll make coffee."

A morning of espresso with lemon twists and pacing around the apartment followed, during which Pidge and Pearl tried to find words for ancient feelings of awe, fear, lust, and adoration. After an epiphany that took at least a half hour of contemplating prepositions, they decided the only path for them *to* was *through* their own experiences.

Pidge summed up, "*Holy, Holy, Holy*! When have we ever felt anything like Pasikennae 3600 years ago?"

"All right," Pearl began. "I'll try. In Yellowstone, once I saw a lone buffalo. *Bozheena.* A great bull surrounded by the steam of a geyser. Steam that would poach a person. All that power, danger – I couldn't – didn't want to move. Maybe to kneel, accept Whatever. It eclipsed – everything. But," she shook her head. "in the same moment, I felt the other enormity: the herds that had been wider -- than great lakes. When they stampeded, the roar and shaking – like a tornado? an earthquake? The buffalo never even looked at me. Just grunted and walked away. Had made Its point. I don't like remembering, but I can't forget. It *roots* me. Can you even feel that in a city?"

Without mentioning she noticed Pearl's uncynical expression of 'just', Pidge spoke slowly. "I don't think it matters *where* one is impressed. Imprinted. Place writes on us, carves *in* us its own dialect. The underlying emotion must already be inside us. In the amygdala? Here?" Pidge tapped her head above her ear. "Maybe James or Marwa knows. So …for me, Riverside Park … I was a baby in a carriage there. Once a woman spat words at me, *shayna maidel,* and my mother said, *nina bonita.* Which, I suppose, is where Nina's name came from! Now when I walk in the park, I feel like I'm one tiny cell … a muscle cell inside a Giant's body where it's loud and pounding like … giant pistons in an ocean liner's engine room. I'm a cell inside an Arm near the pulse of an Artery. Not a buffalo, all right, but the Hudson River."

"*Mahicanituck,*" Pearl said.

Pidge nodded at the river's original Lenape name. "And on the solstices, when the sun lines up – they even call it *Manhattanhenge*. I didn't have the energy to go down to 57th last Saturday morning of the party, but I thought of it when I woke that day. If I'd ever been Wiccan, I'd be a lapsed one."

"Wasn't it cloudy last weekend?" Pearl said.

"Yes. And I was warm under the covers with old Ginger snuffling in her dog-bed nearby. Her poor old lungs."

"Well, we've tapped our amygdalas. You think curse words might be a path to true ones?" Pearl asked.

"Maybe. Emily Dickinson said, "*I like the look of agony/men do not sham a throe.*""

Pearl frowned. "Worst I've ever heard you say is *Jesus fucking Christ.* Your Jewish father? Latina mother?"

"My father's worst that I heard was *goddammit.* Never my mother. She'd cut the umbilicus from Puerto Rico, but if she was startled, really spooked, it came out, *"Que susto!* Real grief she'd hide from me – but when she mourned, she cried, *'Ay dios mio!'*"

Pearl could hear the memory catch in Pidge's voice.

"Well, bullshit, *Holy, Holy, Holy COW,"* Pearl said.

Pidge smiled. "Can you curse in Eastern Shoshone?"

"We avoid it. I don't see it getting us anywhere. *Holy* ... okay. New start. For HER divine ... *genitalia* – 'snug harbor' welcomes entry and egress, alliterates the 'h'. Meaningful to a vast maritime empire. Would a pun help with how it's got the sense of things *within* things? *Containing* things? Like the matryoshka doll? Like Mnkallis's concentric circles?"

Pidge took a swallow of espresso and dramatically chewed the lemon twist, grimacing, "Vitamin C! No to *snug*. Dirty diction. The angst of taboo!" She looked at her hands. "I'm shaking. I'll need a bath to calm down." She forced her attention back to the laptop screen. "Snakes coiled around HER arms," Pidge described. "They armed HER. They were HER weapons, servants. Inseparably part of HER, consort as part of HER body, hermaphrodite. SHE really *was* All That."

They worked, possessed, until Pearl heard Ginger whimper in her sleep on her floor cushion across the room.

"Well, we all missed lunch. Time to stop."

"My heart is pounding in my ears." Pidge looked at the screen. "But – I think we've got something."

She tapped Save and closed her laptop.

Pearl read the prayer aloud.

*Holy Holy Holy*
*Horned Crown*
*Snake-armed*
*Holiest Mistress*
*Please open Your Harbor*
*Please allow passage*
*May our pleas please You.*

"I feel like we leaped through HER horns ourselves," Pidge said. "I ache all over," she touched her forehead.

"You take that bath. I need to get outdoors. I'll borrow the stroller again from down the hall for Ginger. I think James is still home. That was some cold they had. The flu?"

Pidge stood. "Less espresso in the future! Only Micheline had fever. That's why James had to stay home with her again. Daycare *rules*."

The double meaning (noun *and* verb) made Pearl smile to herself as she phoned their neighbor. Soon after, James Beekmans answered his door. Micheline, smelling of Vicks VapoRub and wearing footed pajamas, stood beside him.

"I'd invite you in," he said, "but we've got all kinds of *norcas* around here."

"That's my word, Prof Pearl," Micheline announced. "I made it up. It's a –" she looked up at her father.

"Neologism," he supplied.

"It's *new mucus*," Micheline beamed. "And it's *orky*."

He rolled out the three-year old stroller. "We really should just pass this along to you for Ginger, but Someone isn't ready to relinquish."

As Pearl swiveled it, James sent Micheline on an errand.

"About your walk in the cold," he began, then stopped. "I know you and Pidge are on flexible schedules at the University, but." He stopped again.

"What?"

"Well. Things are happening. Sue's at the hospital, and me at the lab, and I've got my parents near the Bronx Zoo – it's not clear what's going to happen. Departments, labs are shifting priorities. Epidemic. Pandemic. It's crafted by a molecule that's been omnipresent on Earth for four billion years. We don't know about daycare for Micheline. You and Pidge – no talk yet at Columbia?"

Her palms gripped the stroller's handle. "James?"

"No one wants to be alarmist, but. If it's here, it's *here*. And if it's here, it's – bad. Plans need to be made."

Pearl closed then opened her eyes. "I hear the passive voice. My blood is now espresso. I will panic – and plan – later."

The tall Black man nodded.

Back in the apartment, Pearl could hear singing in the tub. Pidge always left the bathroom door ajar. The song lifted the weight on Pearl's heart, but the palpitations continued to throb. She found her coat, hat, and boots in the closet along with the blanket they put over Ginger in the stroller.

Pearl knelt to wake Ginger, but her hands flew to her own chest.

"*Gai, gai, gai,*" she breathed the denials in and out slowly. She mirrored the animal's stillness. In Shoshone, she whispered an endearment, "*Nootsi,*" and began a prayer, "*Dammee Ape,*" for safe journey. Then Pearl walked slowly to the bathroom.

Pidge saw Pearl's face. Instantly out of the tub, wrapped in a towel bathrobe, Pidge rushed into the living room. She knelt, keening over the small blanketed body. Pearl bent beside her.

Through closed eyes, Pidge saw their pieta and crooned, "*Ay dios mio! Ay, ay, ay!*"

***Chapter 9  Late January***

***from Blue Monkeys by Shapiro & Feria... Pasikennae at Pylos***

*Though no more so than bull-leaping, in the winter it was especially dangerous for Pasikennae to sail from Crete to Pylos. (To picture where Pylos was, hold your left hand down, palm facing you. The Peloponnese Peninsula looks like a four-fingered hand without a thumb. Mid-pinkys's left side, the western coast, that's where Pylos -- modern Pilos -- was, its fine harbor protected by an island breakwater.)*

*It could be a very nasty sail in winter winds. That part of the Mediterranean was famous for horrific, sudden storms out of Europe that crossed over to North Africa.*

*"The sky turned brown, and a huge wind and sand hit ships and sailors," Pasikennae wrote. On a tablet, she had pressed the word/sign for a "sister" who ruled the Minoan port on what in time became known as the Greek peninsula. Centuries after Pasikennae, a king of Pylos named Nestor ruled there. In THE ILIAD, King Nestor of Pylos was a wise elder. In later accounts, Nestor was named as the grandfather of Homer.*

*In the 21$^{st}$ century, archeologists unearthed the significant role Nestor's proto-city-state played in the Cretan empire. As Pylos was a natural harbor on the southwest coast of the Peloponnese peninsula, it was a first stop on the shore-hugging, compass-lacking, sea-faring west of Crete's domination of Mediterranean trade.*

*On a series of tablets, Pasikennae wrote of her fleet's approximately 200-mile journey to Pylos from Crete: "Five ships, thirty oars each carrying giant jars (amphorae) of oil, olives, grain, and textiles." Metals listed included "Norwegian silver." This astonishing detail was supported by evidence discovered by archeologists at a site in Kongsberg (which meant 'King's mines').*

*"Artisans with artworks from Crete were on board, also an Egyptian diplomat." Pasikennae named this special passenger as "the representative of Pharaoh Sedwadjenre Nebiriau," identified in the Second Intermediate Period circa 1650-1580 B.C.E.*

*Pasikennae named a "sister" in Pylos, but on other stones she listed a "sister at the Crown [Horns/Gibraltar]" and another in "Cornwall tin country in Britain." Perhaps "sister" indicated a title of occupation, rank, or dynasty, as "merlin" did in Britain. Several stones also described Pasikennae's mother or older maternal relations as HER priestesses, "snake-armed." Pasikennae used a glyph to denote herself as a bull-leaper and captain/navigator, but these meanings were obscure. "Bull-leaper" might have also been a title, implying a family role associated with priestess. No mention of Pasikennae's paternity was discovered on any objects. The implication was that her family's status channeled Pasikennae into the roles she played. Possibly, as a bull-leaper, she moved into a life at sea, serving HER.*

*Many other objects and jewelry at the Pasikennae Find were validated when compared with the 2015 discoveries at Pylos. In the newly opened, untouched bee-shaped burial tombs (tholos) containing Minoan art, archeologists found a gold ring similar to one of Pasikennae's. It showed HER balanced by two swallowtail birds. On one of her stones, Pasikennae had told the story of HER descent from Sky, the birds functioning not only as ladies-in-waiting but also as HER wings.*

*Another Pylos object depicted the Bull of the Sun branded with HER sign, identifying Him as HER consort. An ivory plaque in the Pylos tomb depicted a mythological griffin, the lion/eagle, found in the older throne room in Knossos, Crete, on a Pasikennae bronze arm bracelet, and in her final words. A sixteen-rayed Sun icon appeared on an armor disk found at Pylos – its model had risen in an earlier era on agate and putty "genii" [insect/animal] stones buried with Pasikennae! Scholars newly argued that Minoans had long not only influenced but also lived in their foreign outposts.*

*3600 years ago, no one imagined 17th century discoveries by Anton Van Leeuwenhoek and William Harvey -- of blood cells and how they circulated around the body. It wasn't until the end of the 19th century, thanks to one 'Giulio Bizzozzero' that platelets became known. Even so, without knowing the word 'corpuscle,' Pasikennae believed she lived inside HER. Like a bee in HER hive, Pasikennae moved and breathed in HER breezes, sailed, drank, and voided HER water. Pasikennae didn't doubt any more than did a bird in a flock or a fish in a school. On distant journeys, Pasikennae must have known local divinities, but she remained identified by HER. Pasikennae was HER stamped passport. Who can explain a magic carpet ride?*


David was a light sleeper, especially when Alan was working late on a closed set. *HITTITE QUEEN* was filming at the TV studio across the East River in Queens. It was after midnight. David heard the front door open, followed by sounds of undress, then Alan's attempt to stifle a sneeze as he entered the bedroom. Instead of getting into bed on his doorway side, Alan came around to David who faced the window. The room was dark, but on the ninth floor, street light haloed Alan's nakedness.

Before David could speak, Alan sat down, lifted the warm covers and shoved David to the middle of the bed. Usually David took the lead, but Alan was taller and stronger, an athlete to David's intellectual. Alan pulled off David's pajamas. then lay above him, easily pinning him. Lips, tongue, teeth. Though dazed, David attempted the first steps in their familiar *pas de deux.*

"NO," Alan said, then less loud but no less insistent, "no."

Sliding off, he turned David over. He straddled him again, this time in thrusting penetrations to climax. Calmer, Alan rolled over to his side of the bed. David turned onto his back. Alan fellated him.

Finally, David spoke. "Who was I just then?"

Alan sneezed. He reached under his pillows for pajamas and put them on.      David was still lying naked on his back. "I tasted bourbon. In the town car?"

Alan spoke into the dark but not to David.

"Camera angles. Choreography. Hitting marks. King Hattusili hitting on me. Not to be outdone, the Queen of Hittites takes over the director's nighttime TV soft porn. Six feet tall, the Star *tosses* her SAG new-rules genital guard, orders closeup again and again. Everyone's terrified and turned on. It's surreal.  She's on top – the whole set comes together. Plenty of bourbon in the town car."

Alan stopped. He whispered to David. "At least you didn't taste *her*." Tears in his eyes, Alan laughed.

They lay silently for some time. Then David fished in the nightstand for tissues and witch hazel salve and put on his pajamas. Alan had turned over onto his side, facing the door. David spoke to Alan's back.

"How Diva. How *Deev-ine*. Two Golden Globes on her chest *and* shelf. Those Transformation Challenge wins, an Oscar, and now she's taken the Tapley prize. Some prefer the *domme*. Alan? I know you're awake. The erotic power you have? She just has more. Took you by surprise. I know it's humiliating, being ravished. Also, it is ravishing."

"Don't explain me."

"Like you, I'll do me. Long time ago, in college, I sat next to a girl. She was tiny. There was a big exam. I turned in ten pages to her two. I got an A. I saw on her returned paper a big A++. So then I knew."

Alan sneezed.

"Hope that's not a cold," David said. "Viruses are the smallest of all the microbes. Fungi rule forests. What's more delicious than a mushroom omelet?"

"You talk so much."

A familiar petulance in Alan's voice reassured David. Sirens dopplered in the distance. It was a bitterly cold January night.

"Ambulance, police, or fire?" David asked.

It was a game they played with the twins.

"How are the boys?" Alan said.

"Psyched for their birthday party on the 26th. Nanny Mercedes, I fear, less so."

"Four years old. I was four once," Alan's voice was fading. "On the day camp bus every day, a counselor kept me on her lap, inside her seat belt. Only me."

"You are one of a kind. I was sent to sleepaway camp at seven," David lulled Alan, "I thought the bus driver was the Pied Piper."


Many of the parents who either dropped off their children or stayed for the twins' end of the month birthday party observed "ruefully," said one, to general assent, that Arno and Dylan, as the January babies from their Calhoun School daycare class, were "the first of their four-year old cohort to have been born under an ominous Reality Show star."

Alan said, "O, you must wear your rue with a difference."

But there was so much confusion surrounding a living room of small children that spilled into the family room and boys' bedroom that Alan's mad Ophelia was lost in the melee. The parental guests were focused more on how successfully their children competed.

Grandparental stand-ins, the invited elders Pidge and Pearl chatted.

"Benchmarks and thresholds?" Pidge asked Pearl. "Did we worry about those?"

Pearl's expression was stony although rolling her eyes required some movement. Then her face changed, like weather.

"What?" Pidge said.

"I get it! The new *pithos* image at Akroteri they sent us. Its wine belonged to HER. The building owner was HER servant."

The Greek Ministry of Culture had recently invited them to explain a large urn whose inscription consisted of Linear A syllables and an ideogram written in ink.

The sun came out on Pidge's face. She lifted her glass of wine. "You're right! It was his prayer of gratitude and libation!"

Then she looked at the mountain of presents on the coffee table and couch. She had a fond memory of the Christmas party a month earlier. She missed the night and fire glow, tree and young Julliard musicians. It was a bright Sunday afternoon, but the light through the tall windows was cold. She held up her ribboned gift to show Pearl.

"I created a book about Pylos," Pidge said, "for little boys who have everything. I figured Bronze Age *tholos* and armor were up their alley."

Pearl held up two loosely-wrapped, long and narrow packages. "I know they're too old for stuffed animals, but I thought, maybe they'd like these blue monkeys ready to hang and/or swing. Which they'll probably use as weapons. I knew they'd get a fleet of trucks."

"Micheline will take the wheel on the biggest one," David said, joining his neighbors. "She looks like Dorothy among the Munchkins."

Micheline was the only outsider among the prep-school daycare kids. Her size, skin and eye colors, and "loopy black curls" had been a topic of some talk that caused James to cringe when he overheard the word *genetics*. Duly noted was Micheline's attendance at Rockefeller University's East 60's nursery-daycare from birth until "her current situation on West 97th." Her mother Susanna's defensiveness presented as an increased Arkansas drawl. But most of the parents possessed acute PC antennae that quashed even innocent ignorance, let alone audible bias.

"Whatever Micheline has over Arno and Dylan in height, don't they balance her, two against one?" Pearl asked.

"You'd think so, but she often plays them against each other," Alan said. "Thank god Mercedes can herd the cats."

They looked across the room at the slender young woman. Her straight black hair was cut short, her high-cheekboned skin, copper. She was a Latina born in California.

"I don't know what we'll do if she leaves us," David sighed.

"Is she making noises?" Pidge asked.

"Well," Alan began, "she's been with us since the boys were born, in LA. Her aunt had been our housekeeper, but no babies or New York for her! The boys are bilingual. They can be bi-anything they want. But Mercedes is young, and LA is her home. So. We worry."

Across the room, by the piano, another cluster of parents were chatting with parents new to the twins' daycare class. They wondered as politely as possible about the twins' origins.

One asked, "How many names on the birth certificates?"

Another of the newcomers observed, "You can certainly tell whose boy is whose. They are their fathers' images."

A class mother supplied, "Alan Tapley named his son Dylan for David's first initial, and David named Arno Rochester for Alan. Same maternal eggs, one surrogate. New York law still prohibits surrogacy, but all their names appear on the Connecticut birth certificate. She was a U. of Iowa humanities major whose father briefly played pro-football like but not with Alan's star quarterback Dad. So IVF. So twenty-first century! So the twins gestated together."

Another parent doubted, "How on earth do you know all that?"

The gossip was undeterred. She added, "It's quite a story!" which, unspoken, translated, approvingly, into *expensive*.

There was a crash in another room.

Later, as exhausted children and more exhausted parents left, the ninth-floor neighbors lingered together in the dining room. Mercedes had taken charge of Arno, Dylan, and Micheline, limiting them in Spanish to *one toy each, after Senora Shapiro reads you the book*! Pidge followed the quartet to the twins' bedroom. Pearl, Susanna, James, Alan and David sat around the big table. Caterers brought them more coffee and tea and cleared things away. Talk was about toilet paper shortages and surviving Micheline's birthday on March ninth. Her party was planned for Saturday the 7th the weekend before.

Before David could make another generous, co-opting offer, Susanna quickly added, "Their daycare, financial aid notwithstanding, does birthday parties better than most venues. And all the kids know where they are, how things work. We made plans months ago. I freed my schedule at the hospital. We can bring Arno and Dylan with us. We're all set."

In the twins' bedroom, Pidge was reading to the three children, sitting on an upholstered loveseat. It could move like a glider. Mercedes usually readied the boys for bed by gliding, reading, or singing to them seated on either side of her. But now, she had locked it still and rested beside Pidge. The children sat cross-legged on the carpet facing the professor, in the V created by the catty-corner of their beds. One was a bunkbed, and the other was a trundle.   Above the glider-loveseat on the wall was the large fresco painting of the blue monkeys that had been moved from over the living room fireplace. Each of the twins were hugging the stuffed animals Pearl had given them. Micheline was holding another soft toy she often chose, a reddish octopus. She had wrapped four arms on either side of her neck.

Pidge read to her rapt audience, *"Arnos and Dylus watched as great ships filled their harbor at Pylos."*

She paused between each sentence to show the trio the illustrations she had found online and pasted into the text. Some she had drawn herself, collaged, and scanned.

*"They had sailed from far away Knossos. The twins could see a girl they knew on one ship. Sometimes she came with her aunt and sailors. Dylus and Arnos waved to Mikelinae and could hardly wait for her to come ashore. They knew she was learning how to jump through the horns of a calf. She did not know that the brothers had been practicing. Sheep were easier than goats!"*

This last illustration was a coup: a former student, now a pop-up paper artist, had created two pages that opened in three-dimensions. Two boys vaulted over the backs of scalloped sheep, horned goats in the background, a Bronze Age sky above.

### *Chapter 10 March*

*Ring around a rosie, a pocket full of posies.*
*Ashes, ashes, we all fall down.*



The moon was bright over Isle Royale in Lake Superior on the vernal equinox. More stunning was the aurora borealis that shimmered and swayed in shades of green, yellow, white, underlined by a band of red. Millennia earlier, the glorious phenomenon had reflected in the faces of giant copper boulders and the same vast inland sea. But in the northern hemisphere this year, the misaligned hinge to Spring made a terrible grinding sound.

Micheline's fourth birthday party was celebrated on March seventh. Though they were invited, Pidge and Pearl stayed away. Micheline received, as requested, a book by Pidge.

"Another *Mikelinae in Noshsosh*, please," the child had asked.

"Knossos," Pidge corrected. "What's the oldest thing you can think of?"

Micheline just looked at Pidge.

Pidge laughed. "Older, even."

"The Statue of Liberty?

"Better guess. But older."

"Dinosaurs. Tyrannosaurus Rex.'

"Good. Younger than Rex, older than Liberty. Knossos was the first place where the end of the world began."

"Mikelinae's world's gonna *end,* Prof Pidge?"

"She lives."

"With blue monkeys?" Micheline suggested.

"Sure," Pidge said.

In Micheline's birthday book, Pidge focused on Pasikennae's earliest writing, possibly in her own childish hand, on the simple stone from a Mnkallis beach. It looked to her and Pearl like a lesson Pasikennae had to learn about her future role in Cretan society. The scholars had translated the Linear A in rhyme, apt for a girl's primer. Among the many astonishments of the Orkney *Find* was the implication that among all that was lost, Pasikennae had managed to save one homely etched stone and that it had been carefully buried with her among the other treasures.

*Listen more than you talk.*
*Observe more than display.*
*Follow one who knows the way.*
*Carry one who cannot walk.*
*Eat after sailors are fed.*
*Sing when mothers have daughters.*
*Sail to faraway waters.*
*Come home to sleep in your bed.*

That first weekend in March was the last one of open restaurants, theaters, and all the venues of the plagued metropolis. Instead, hospitals filled. HEPA filters were installed in ICUs to create negative pressure preventing infected air from escaping. *Ring around a rosie* increased in popularity only briefly before daycare centers also shut their doors. Yeast and toilet paper disappeared. David attended one of the last performances at the New York Philharmonic.

New plans replaced cancelled ones.

Esau Kimani and Dayita Persaud, Emergency Department doctors, had realized before most other New Yorkers the danger of exposure to their baby and Dayita's elderly parents. In early February, they had sent the trio to live in their brick three-bedroom Cape Cod upstate. After subletting their fourth floor Riverside Drive apartment to the next-door tenant who'd replaced the murder victim, Esau and Dayita moved uptown, closer to their West Side hospital, into her parents' Inwood co-op. Dr. Persaud got sick first; her ED director husband came down with symptoms after, for fewer days. But by the time March began, both were back at work.

Two weeks earlier, after midnight in late February on the East Side's upper Fifth Avenue, on duty resident in neurosurgery Dr. Susanna Duckett had been called to Mount Sinai Hospital's Emergency Department where an ambulance had rushed comatose *America's Sweetheart*, Veronica Drummer. Dr. Duckett's notes from that admission were not starstruck, but the Arkansas in her was. Though married to a scientist who worked with a MacArthur Genius and might one day become one himself, Susanna was hardly blasé about neighbors who appeared on magazine covers, like Alan Tapley or the Columbia professors. Now, from the Silk-Stocking district of Manhattan, stage and movie star Veronica Drummer faced mortal emergency – in Susanna's care. That night, she ordered a minimally invasive clot evacuation and days later assisted at the hemicraniectomy to reduce swelling.

Susanna was at Veronica Drummer's bedside when the actress awakened from coma. Those enormous brown eyes had focused first on Susanna's face, and then like a duckling, imprinted upon the young resident. Veronica "adored" Susanna and demanded her exclusive attention. The effect of those eyes, the braying Brooklyn accent that made fans adore *her* – but most of all, the star's vulnerable dependence – taught Susanna many lessons. Stardom was a mask that lifted to reveal a humanity as common as the anatomies dissected in first-year Gross – if less notable, than more noteworthy.

By March, Veronica Drummer might as well have been in another country since the hospital had become, well, Susanna's mother had called it, "a leper colony Jesus would shun" before the doctor snapped, "No, Mom, that's the White House," and hung up in exhausted fury. Patients like Veronica Drummer had been evacuated to a non-Covid hospital to accommodate the transformation into pandemic mode. Dr. Duckett along with a majority of personnel were "floated" to ICUs to treat the influx of infected patients.

Her husband, Dr. James Beekmans, saw a similar wrenching conversion to viral analysis away from his participation at Rockefeller University with nearly a hundred other genome consortium researchers nationally who had been deciphering the entire human genome. He heard random bits of information over lunch or on breaks.

"A stretch of DNA linked to Covid-19 was passed down from Neanderthals 60,000 years ago."

Pidge and Pearl would like that one, James thought. In his lab, genetic findings were being rapidly updated as more infected people were studied. James refocused on a gene coding for the molecule ACE2 that the virus attached to before breaching cell membranes. An international group released a new set of data that downplayed the risk of blood type.

A colleague at Harvard Med messaged, "The jury is still out on ABO."

James ordered his parents in the Bronx to stay indoors and arranged food delivery for them. He negotiated with David Rochester and the nanny, Mercedes, so Micheline could stay home from plague-closed daycare with the neighbor twins, Arno and Dylan.

Also in March along with so much else, *HITTITE QUEEN* halted production. Alan Tapley planned to move out to the eastern end of Long Island where his house was being finished.

"Maybe I can speed it up. We won't uproot the twins till it's ready," Alan said. David thought about toothsome carpenters. This ground felt as unfamiliar here as on Long Island. Palpable, how much he still didn't know about Alan.

"What about your parents?" he asked.

Alan sensed David's unease. "What about them? Except me, all descendants of Tapley Holland are in Texas as they prefer. *Barbie and Ken* can remember the Alamo together."

"It's never clear which you mean, your parents or siblings."

"Younger sibs Patsy Holland reads TV news, and brother is literally *Tad*. He was born to be a faceman: caddie/tennis/Pro Shop days, an MBA, country club manager married a (far)right girl. Straight pins all. I dropped the last name, and yours got changed. You've got your Rochesters to worry about."

Which was true. David's parents lived across town on Park Avenue in a building known to house Manhattan's wealthiest, which only increased its real estate cachet. When he had arrived from Manchester, England, David's great-grandfather's surname, *Rochas*, was changed at Ellis Island to *Rochester*, same as the small city in northern New York State, where *paterfamilias* was directed and settled.

After Lithuania, he had become fluent in British English, working for at least a decade in a Manchester bank. The great-grandfather for whom David was named had thrived in finance and sent his son to New York City where the family's rise in banking and real estate continued, creating the eventual hedge fund life that David inherited. Dynastic marriages along the way added to the family's fortunes. David's mother was an antisemitic Jew who would go no farther west on Manhattan Island than Temple Emanu-El on Fifth Avenue, and then, only on the High Holy Days because "one must be seen there."

As a small boy, David had been terrified by his mother when they were together in a cab whose driver had annoyed her. She had showed David the insulting ten cent tip she intended. She ordered him as they left the cab to, "Run!"

David knew he was an only child because his father was gay. His parents had remained married. There had been a great deal of money but no love to lose between them. David had grown up at 740 Park Avenue with a nanny from birth, kindergarten through fourth grade at The Calhoun School (on the intolerable West Side because his father was an alumnus) and then sent to Connecticut junior boarding, then prep school, always summer camp in New Hampshire, then college in Massachusetts.

David associated school breaks (or being himself) as his mother described him, "*De trop*," with the spacious apartment where the septuagenarians had lived with their old housekeeper Norma. In March, before they could escape to their Rhode Island summer waterfront Victorian, the three became mortally ill – too fast even for a private nurse to be called in. They all died in an ICU on upper Fifth Avenue, David's presence forbidden. So many seriously ill New Yorkers flooded into Mount Sinai Hospital that a field hospital was soon erected nearby in Central Park. David texted Alan not to return to the City.

Alan didn't argue. "How R U?" he texted.

"Angry," David replied, but as a columnist for the great Gray Lady, *The New York Times*, he knew better than to express rage against a sitting President. Earlier, in 2016, he'd recused himself from writing about the campaign because he had used a quotation that had gone viral from a favorite professor (now *emeritus*) from Wharton, a mentor and friend, who had said the candidate had been his "dumbest student, ever."

So David oversaw a fund, wrote about international politics, helped Mercedes with Zoom activities for the twins and Micheline, and played the piano when she took the children outdoors to look for signs of Spring. He'd put the small urns of cremains out of sight in his office downtown. His analysis of his grief was that it was unevenly divided, by far greater for his parents' miserable lives than for their calamitous deaths. He had some tears for his father, but David felt more in common with Norma as the other unplugged apparatus in the household. She was The Maid. He was The Son. Norma always had ready NYC-cliched soft black & white cookies when he came 'home.' Now, he turned to the piano for solace. He attempted the

Moonlight Sonata's *Presto Agitato* again and again. It sounded ferocious, but his lack of virtuosity only infuriated him more. A Juilliard associate suggested a *fortissimo* Chopin Prelude. He followed her advice to "Just bang away!"

Although other neighbors complained to the doorman Azul, who had to ask David to lower the volume on whatever device was thundering above and below them, Pidge and Pearl lied, he knew, assuring him they couldn't hear his baby grand piano. Columbia University had shut down classes and was converting swiftly to remote learning. The two professors had already been interacting with their students online most of the time so it altered their lives less than did Ginger's death. Going out for a walk now meant missing her even more. So they stayed in the apartment most of the time. Like everyone above the age of sixty-five in Manhattan, Pidge and Pearl wrestled with food delivery and cancelling appointments. David kept offering help they didn't think they needed but accepted out of concern for what he refused to call mourning.

The building's co-op officers wrote 'info-emails' that only echoed and amplified fraught news. Pearl's son Esa urged her to escape to Wyoming and stay with him.

She couldn't imagine how that would work.

"What did you tell him?" Pidge asked.

"That travel is a death threat second to how we'd be at each other's throats at close quarters. What did you say to Nina?"

"She's got a husband and twins to worry about. And her career. Now, add me? The one gift I can give her is distance. Also, what you said. Get on a plane now? Might as well go straight to a morgue – if you can get in."

Pearl was making toast. The kitchen smelled of warming rye bread. David had dropped off a fresh bakery loaf. Taking a deep breath without a ventilator had greater meaning now. Pearl felt grateful and breathed out, "Ah, carraway seed!"

Pidge took butter out of the fridge, "Might as well slather it on. Every meal feels like a Last Supper."

They sat down to breakfast. Classical music radio played as they read their daily-delivered newspaper that David had also brought from the lobby. Pidge looked up from the page. Pearl then paused, attentive. Pidge felt how good it was not to live alone.

"It's like musical chairs, isn't it," she said.

"What is?"

"I wonder if grandkids now even know that game," Pidge said. "I wouldn't allow it at Nina's birthday parties. I bet she doesn't know what it is. Was."

"Oh, Life, you mean," Pearl said. "When the music stops, sit on a chair or you're *out*. I didn't do that with Esa, either. You're right. What a lesson to teach little kids. Grab or die."

"Not many chairs left to us."

"Grab what we're sitting on. Our asses."

"Hold on and don't move," Pidge laughed.

Pearl pointed to the radio. "And don't stop the music," Pearl added.


The Muslim holiday *Isra and Miraj* began on the evening of Saturday, March 21st. Three stories down, in the sixth-floor apartment where Marwa was taking a late-afternoon bath, and John Donnelly was moving things around in the living room, distinctly different music played on their separate iPods. Marwa was listening again to a string quartet recording of her father's 2015 prize-winning composition. Her parents had divorced a decade earlier, after her father retired from Deutsche Bank. Marwa's mother had returned to Alexandria "to raise grandchildren since Sharif's wife has a *career* like *you*. Your older brother is a *real* father. He masks us outdoors and keeps us indoors." Marwa's (*unreal?*) father still lived in the Battery Park apartment of her teens.

Five years earlier, his new wife had been one of the prize judges. Marwa loved the low cello sound as one violin played the surprising tambourine. It always made her smile and wonder which one, father or stepmother, they also considered the prize. Maybe both did.

In Marwa's living room in a different mood, John moved a chair to the rhythm of Tracy Chapman singing the blues. So far, the FBI had kept a distance from the high-profile Luster case. As its lead case officer, John kept most of the details of his detectives' DD5 reports in his head. Moving furniture helped move minutiae around in his mind. October to March was too soon to cold-case the homicide, and his commanding officer was asking questions John still had no answers for. The new tenant was a person of interest. He had been a colleague of Elena Luster's. He'd bought her co-op asap. Then he also sublet the Persaud-Kimani adjoining apartment. Why did he want her apartment and the one next door? How could he afford either/both? What was he looking for they hadn't found? The second phone? Where was it?

The bathroom door opened, and John could hear the end notes of tambourine that punctuated, to his ears, though Marwa insisted *post-minimalist*, her classical music. Whatever. John remembered the Christmas party and the professors identifying the tambourine's Minoan ancestor …John remembered, yes, a *sistrum*. Made of local clay. Found on Crete. Marwa said ancient Egyptians also played them.

"The rhythmical shaking of the *sistrum*, like the tambourine, is associated with religious or ecstatic events, shaken as a sacred rattle in the worship of Hathor of ancient Egypt. Muslims don't have a winter solstice holiday. Ancient Egyptian religion did celebrate Hathor's return to her father Ra. That synchronized to the winter solstice. Muslims are taught to celebrate only two holidays: *Eid Al-Fitr* and *Eid Al-Adha*. In practice, well...people like parties. It would take faith for me even to be an atheist."

John stared blindly out a window above a low bookcase. He moved his tongue around his teeth. Only two holidays? Really? But what was tonight's … *Isra and Miraj*? Marwa had bought ropes of tiny LED's now strung around the apartment. Sun wasn't far from setting; she hadn't turned on the twinkling lights yet. Now, barefoot in the hallway, she wore a towel robe with a towel on her hair, and peered into the living room. Certainly turned *him* on.

"Whatcha doin'?" she asked.

His senses returned in a rush. He smelled heat coming up from a radiator and Marwa's fragrant shampoo. He felt in his right hand one of the five colorful Platonic solids he lifted unconsciously from an end table. It was the brown twelve-sided dodecahedron. He'd picked up the same one in early December, before the party, when they'd first considered living together.

Marwa had said, "Brown has no contrasting color. Which is why everything goes so well with it. It's a peaceful color. Wouldn't it make more sense for you to move here than for me to move to Long Island?"

Now, Beckett would turn ten in July, hidden away in the Caribbean redoubt with his ex, no longer Donnelly, Kirby Sloane. Her mother was a Beckett, family tradition of naming a girl for her maternal grandmother's surname. Would Beckett mother a Sloane one day? He put the manysided shape back down. Beckett was so far away. Remote learning via Google Meet at her Long Island private school had evolved into masked visits with a local tutor.

"Mamselle Reeshardo is Black. She wears cornrows. With *beads*," Beckett texted. "Her Mehmay worked here. Mom's family sent Mamselle to school."

John discovered that Mamselle Josette (aka Mimi) Richardot, twenty years old, on Covidleave from pre-med in Granada, was already a syndicated author. Her essay *Who Are the Working Class in St. Bart's?* had been circulated by the Associated Press. Kirby and Mamselle's mother (who now worked at the major concierge company on St. Bart's) were his age. Obviously, the tutor's mother had her right out of high school.

Though Spring had arrived two days earlier and Daylight Savings time the week before, John had begged his parents to keep hibernating in East Rockaway. The young Black blues singer began another lament. John went to his iPod and turned it off.

John finally answered, "Just thinking."

But Marwa had ducked into the bedroom. When she reappeared, she was dressed and toweldrying her hair. She took off the towel and fanned out her wavy hair. Then she walked around explaining the holiday, flicking on LED switches with the magnetic effect of beckoning fireflies and Night to follow her. Her voice, not the words, were also sorcery.

Marwa was saying, "In high school, I had the worst fight with my best friend Judy Yamaguchi over this holiday. Good thing it was over the phone because in person, I could have killed her. I know, *Things Not to Tell a Homicide Detective*."

John poured himself two fingers of bourbon. He sat down in the chair he'd moved. He waited. "Children are the point. We were given cartoon books when we were little and then real books as we got older, all en route to the Quran, Surah 17:1, which, of course, we memorized. When you're little, you celebrate at home. Then when you're older, at the mosque. We'd show off reading, memory, and there were candles, electric lights, and finally, the most delicious foods. Story goes: on a single night in 621, the Prophet," Marwa paused but did not say *praise be unto him*, "flew on a winged small horse named Buraq the 766 miles from Mecca to Jerusalem and back by morning – that's the *Isra*, journey, which includes the ascent, *Miraj*, up to heaven where Moses taught Muhammed how to bargain with Allah over *Salat*, the number of prayers to say daily. Allah had said fifty times. Judy said that since her mother was Jewish, it was all right for her to say that

Moses 'jewed God down to five.' I screamed, '*Blasphemy,* infidel!' and Arabic curses I didn't

know I knew. Teenage drama!"

It was dark outside. But later. Still getting used to the time change. John sipped his bourbon.

It stung. He had been biting his lip.

"I see you laughing over there," Marwa said. "Jonah in a whale like Pinocchio, Jesus like a

Navaho Skinwalker on water? A sexy dove descended on Mary? Zeus's golden rain fell on

Danae? Welcome Zeus-son, *Per,* soft z, *seus* patriarchal misogynist who lopped the snakes off

Medusa's priestess head? And you want me to believe any of *that*?"

"I'm not laughing. And that's not what I want you to believe."

March ended. New York media reported a forty-eight-year-old detective in a Harlem precinct

was the first NYPD officer to die from coronavirus. The last sick tally showed just over 11.2%,

or over 4100 cops calling in sick. So far, John Donnelly wasn't one of them.

**http://www.soul-alchemy.net/   at FB**
**https://www.pinterest.com/pin/480126010274419595/ actual source**

The end of March had seen *Megxit*, described in an April *New Yorker* issue as a "fractured fairytale." Pidge noticed the British no-longer-Royals had moved to southern California's Santa Barbara, hometown of Pidge's six-foot tall college classmate (whose father had been a Montana Governor). Half a century earlier, her giant friend had bellowed the BATMAN song from TV as her long legs pounded down the stairs outside of Pidge's Vassar dorm room. Pidge remembered last year's April Fool's Day when Alan Tapley and David Rochester had left Los Angeles for Manhattan, where now the masked population hid from plague.

Pidge sat with her laptop, scrolling back a year to escape into a pre-pandemic past. She found a photo she had saved – a possible cover for *Blue Monkeys*? -- of the oldest tree in the world, on Crete, estimated to be more than 3,000 years old. It still produced olives! But when Pasikennae had walked within labyrinthine palaces or along narrow lanes between multi-story stucco buildings and shops of *Mnkallis* and *Kriti*, that ancient olive tree hadn't been a seed yet. Not a bit. Not a pit!

Pidge browsed to another image from the previous April, of a shipwreck dated back 3,600 years, discovered loaded with copper ingots in the Aegean Sea. Archeologists had found it under 160 feet of water off the western coast of Turkey. The cypress-wood wreck was over fifty feet long, mostly intact and carrying its ancient cargo. In better times, before the ship and Mnkallis had sunk into the depths, Pasikennae could have walked that deck under wind-filled sails.     At the table, Pidge finally went to work reading Pearl's handwritten efforts at a translation into *Blue Monkeys* style of a Pasikennae tablet. She welcomed Pearl's gel-penned cursive words on the yellow legal pad, feeling how old-fashioned they would appear to younger eyes. It was the beginning of a new chapter.

***Pasikennae's Journey at Sea***
*This music is all strings.*
*The wind is rhythm, it beats*
*the waves like drums. Sea*
*birds are sistrum.*
*Call! Call! No flutes!*

Pidge combed her fingers through her kinky white hair. It was a nervous tic. She shared Pearl's anxious struggle with the original chapter stones. The syllabograms and words implied music, ocean, and birds, but they included a complex list of places, possibly harbors that formed a map from the Mediterranean north then west to America. Pasikennae's list began at Knossos, Crete, then Pylos, Greece, Cartagena, Spain, Gibraltar – those locations were recognizable. Thereafter, the chapter stones demanded jigsaw puzzle expertise. The list implied Lisbon, Cornwall, Dublin, the Orkneys, Faroes, west to "ice islands" (Iceland, Greenland, Newfoundland?), never more than six days out of sight of land at any time. One of the tablets ended with a 'sunstone' sign, a mixture of cloud and ship and sun.

Pearl opened the apartment door, her face flushed. She was breathing hard.

"You can't wait for Azul or the porters? You didn't try walking up the stairs again, did you?" Pidge said.

Pearl sat down, saw what Pidge was reading, and put the mail and two packages at the floor by their feet.

"I got off at seven," Pearl admitted. "To send it downstairs faster. People were waiting. I thought I'd see if I could increase my stamina."

"Lesson learned?"

"I don't like the elevator now. Either people defer to my age, or I'm one of two masked creatures pressed against opposite walls trying not to rhyme breath and death."

"I like that a dog counts as a person so I don't even have to get on," Pidge commiserated. "I miss Ginger."

Pearl's color and breathing calmed. She stood and read over her friend's shoulder, taking in the legal pad and the computer screen.

"Yeah, the sunstone. Find the sun through clouds. That always stops me between a *compass*, which Pasikennae didn't have," she gestured with crossing her two first fingers N/S – E/W, "and a *compass*," Pearl moved one hand onto the table, thumb fixed, the middle finger circling, "which she did possess, as did Egypt. The New Kingdom also bisected and trisected right angles with a compass and a straightedge. Try translating that into pop-speak."

"I think of Donne's *Valediction Forbidding Mourning*'s 'stiff twin compasses,'" Pidge said. She looked at Pearl's deliveries. "Amazon has replaced the mall."

Pearl said, "I'll see your Donne and raise you Heraclitus. The only law is the Law of Change."

Alan was on the phone, standing in the new house in Orient, Long Island. Work had ended for the day. One of the carpenters had thanked him for not choosing a factory-made modular that was overtaking the trade. Alan breathed in sheet rock and sawed wood with the salty scent of ocean beyond the wide cut-out space for the plate glass window. Before the walls went up, he was imagining the vaulted area where the five portraits would go above the stone fireplace. One for each portrait and one of the family together. Their colors, shapes, textures.

It was twilight. He clicked and sent David a photo of the window cut-out. It was like a frame. "You can't see the wide, old Japanese maple or the cherry-plum trees, all in bloom. They look like huge bouquets. There's honeysuckle, too."

"I don't think the poet had the fifteenth in mind when he said April was the cruelest month," David said.

"That's T.S. Eliot? But who said 'death and taxes'?" Alan asked.

Both knew that Alan was being generous and that David could not resist a question. David wondered what – who -- else was outside his limited view. He answered, "First recorded use was in 1716," he said, "'Tis impossible to be sure of anything but –"

"Death and taxes," Alan joined him.

"Defoe repeated it in 1726. Benjamin Franklin made three times a charm in 1789. 'Our new Constitution is now established, and has an appearance that promises permanency; but in this world nothing can be said to be certain, except --'"

"Death and taxes," Alan repeated. "It's good you incorporated me after the –"

"Alternative minimum tax," David supplied. "Well, your future earnings are a good bet."

"Well, I also have you."

David paused, took a breath.

"Yesterday, Micheline's mom told me an Emergency Department doctor committed suicide.

Hospital has next to no supplies and no Fed organization. They're keeping it out of the news."

"Jesus. I hope she told you out of the kids' earshot."

David could hear the shiver in Alan's voice. "Are you wearing a coat?"

Alan turned the phone and sent a selfie.

"I wish –" David said.

"You show me yours; I'll show you mine."


That midday, on the other side of the apartment, the children had been unusually subdued after the morning's schooling. While Mercedes prepared lunches, she left them alone to play. Four-year-olds, David said, didn't need a baby monitor anymore. So when she called them to the kitchen counter, it had been all she could do not to scream or laugh when they entered.

"We're starkers, not stalkers," Micheline pronounced the L. "Daddy told me."

Three naked humans, a girl and two boys, presented themselves to the young nanny.

"What is this?" Mercedes managed.

"Science," Arno replied.

Like his twin brother, he was the image of his own father buffered by similar surrogate maternal genes. Arno was pale skin, dark hair, and hazel eyes sometimes squinting myopically. Dylan, inches taller, was a mini-Alan, haunting light eyes in a perfect symmetry of features. And there was Micheline, the tallest of the trio, *café au lait* skin and loopy black curls framing her face.

"*Como se dice* 'circle-sized' *en espagnol*?" Arno asked, both embarrassed and flaunting his naughtiness.

"There's no circle," Micheline pointed.

Mercedes thought – *Qué haría Mamá y las tías?* – would Mama and the aunts make light of it?

"Circumcised," she corrected. "*Circuncidado*. You'd go to restaurants like that? Good thing they're all closed now."

Dylan was frowning. "Micheline has more holes than we have." He brightened. "But both of us have poles. *Circuncidados nosotros dos.* We can go fishing!"

"We can pee standing up!" from Arno.

"I can make a baby!" Micheline bested. "Like *Diosa, Senora* Pidge says."

"Well, *pequena diosa*," Mercedes concluded, "no one's getting any lunch *sin ropa*. Naked. *Diosa desnuda*," she pointed to Micheline, then at both the boys, "*dioses desnudos*. I will count to *veinte*."

The children ran to the bedroom, laughing and counting. That evening after the phone call and the twins in bed, Mercedes reported the merriment to David.

He laughed and said, "It's Spring, I guess. Sap rising everywhere."

Mercedes didn't mention her own yearning for Guillermo. Her *Memo* in Los Angeles. David thanked her, said he'd tell Micheline's parents and speak to the twins, but he thought of Alan.

From the 20th Precinct on West 82nd, Detective Donnelly headed home toward Marwa's apartment. But he had paused at the police station entrance, looking at the glyphic mural on the outdoor wall.

Had the NYPD commissioned it? John also looked at the building's date, *A.D. 1972*. Nine years older than he was. He realized he'd never paid any attention to either detail. The doorway mural was something the professors might decipher. The *Anno Domini* of the date seemed both a religious anachronism and a bell tolling something medieval, like the Cloisters uptown. Music in, on his mind. John was hearing the ringtone belonging to the associate of Elena Luster, Malcolm Ackerman, "Esquire," who'd played it for him. Today's follow up interview had raised more questions than it answered.

The two different versions of *Mack the Knife* replayed in the detective's head. He walked west past low-fenced squares in front of brownstone townhouses. Sycamore-like trees dangled ball clusters of tiny red or greenish-yellow flowers; some had daffodils and hyacinths planted around their base. The streets continued weirdly empty. The few other walkers, like John, wore masks and kept their distance. Ackerman's nickname and ringtone, the tall, bald man had explained, came from inheriting (selling to a conglomerate) a grandfather's craft tool company, Best Blade,

"The Kindest Cut." John knew the famous brand. This was a pretty familiar New York experience, to cross paths with the One Who Made It or their relative. He'd once had to question the Gulden's Mustard heir.

When John listened to the Bobby Darin version ringtone, Ackerman had impatiently gestured and taken the phone back to play an alternate recording of a tinny Lotte Lenya whining the lyrics from *The Three Penny Opera.*

"Personally, I like this 1928 one better, more authentic," Ackerman said, "There's also a *Mac Tonight* McDonald's ad one, from the 80's, 'bout when you were born?"

No shortage of gab from the cooperative Mack Ackerman. He'd eagerly repeated a DD5 report John knew about Luster's breakup.

"They never actually married, you know, though Elena wore a wedding ring. She was crazy about Ellen. *I know*. El and El. They sounded like AT&T!"

Mack the Knife remained a suspect. Against his lawyer's advice, the blustery guy gave explanations -- about bringing a bottle of wine and wearing painter's clothing (booties, hat, and gloves) to Luster's apartment where he'd found her murdered. He had a key to her apartment but had not reported the scene. He hadn't entered by passing Azul at the front door, but by a back entrance, "Because Elena told me to, so Doorman wouldn't hassle me as a housepainter and send me to the service entrance anyway."

His painter's suit was oversize, like his performance. Ackerman reprised a monologue enough to be consistent but questionably so. He liked repeating himself. He enjoyed an audience.

"I've lost a lot of weight since then. I keep seeing the … horrible. I can't eat. I loved Elena. Half a generation older, I'll admit to. We grew up in the same exclusive enclave, WASPY Howland Harbor, built on the South Shore (you could hear capital letters when he spoke) 'way before Kennedy *nee* Idlewild Airport was a glimmer in any Old Money blueblood's eyes. We didn't know each other growing up decades apart under the noisy flight path, both families New,

meaning Jew (who avoided temple) -- so add that to us both being gay misfits, we were locked

and loaded, aimed at Manhattan. You can imagine the fireworks when we first met – how

abandoned I felt when she moved to the West Side! El was my tiny best friend."

"But why were you there?"

"She asked me to help her paint the bedroom. She had painters for the rest, but it was a

Bonding gesture. And it was supposed to be a Hallowe'eny hoot, me showing up in costume at

her door. When she didn't answer, I thought she was hiding, to jump out and yell, 'Boo!' I had a

key. She did give me the shock of my life. Her death!"

John could almost hear the applause in Ackerman's head. He stopped at the red light at

Broadway, waiting to cross. He stood there for two lights more, lost in thought as traffic moved

in both directions on either side of the greening median. Ackerman didn't *report* the murder? He

covered himself in overalls and booties, painter's hat on his bald head, gloves on his hands? He'd

been married and divorced with an estranged adult son and an ex-wife who'd taken out a

restraining order against him. He wore expensive aftershave, but the fish stank from the head.

"I was in shock," Ackerman said.

Until we located him? John's skepticism and his legs took him across Broadway down a

treelined street. He turned onto West End Avenue and walked uptown to Marwa's building where

Azul's greeting jarred him back to reality. Entering the apartment, he saw her asleep on the

couch. He hadn't expected her back from overnight at the lab, another experiment "with fruit

flies' GPS," she'd said, "the ability of an animal to keep track of where it's headed."

Her mental compass hadn't gotten her as far as the bedroom. Twilight was coming later now,

at long last. He didn't turn on any lights and just stood by the door, grateful for and to her. He

saw she was wearing the same corduroy slacks and green cable sweater she had on when they'd first met in November. He didn't have faith, but Marwa was undeniably a gift from some

divinity. Good fortune was as random as bad luck, but it didn't feel that way. One felt like

reward, the other punishment.

A phone rang on the coffee table. Elena Luster's second cell was still missing.

Marwa woke, saw him, picked up her phone and turned it off.

Sleep still in her voice, she said, "You'll never guess what I found."

"At the lab?"

"No, right here in the apartment."

John took off his jacket and sat down. Marwa closed her eyes again.

"No," she said. "At Mecca. At the … the Kaaba. I was looking into the silver collar. But the

Black Stone wasn't there … the collar was a kaleidoscope … a tunnel …"

"A dream."

"It's *here*," Marwa insisted. "In Alexandria, I stayed with my doctor uncle and my mother's

oldest sister, fat Auntie Fatima. There was an old dumbwaiter in their kitchen. Walled in. They

said it was there. I saw through the kaleidoscope inside the dumbwaiter. There was an antique

telephone." She gestured, "The one like a candlestick, with a wire connecting the receiver you

hold to your ear? The phone was ringing."

By this point she was awake and shaking her head at herself.

"I never remember my dreams," John said. "Beckett does."

Marwa got up off the couch and stretched. It was dark outside. En route to the kitchen she

called back, "Some really young kids remember past lives."

John rose to join her. "You still dreaming?!"

Then he had the strangest thought, of his ex's pink and Marwa's brown nipples. That his

mother had breast-fed him.

Pidge and Pearl took a familiar early morning walk on the park side of Riverside Drive down to 76<sup>th</sup>, where overlooking the park's treetops, the low stone-walled sidewalk featured a minifountain and pool for canine succor and society. Ginger had loved it. It was lonely now. April's flowering gingkoes and cherry trees and young green leaves still allowed a view of tennis courts below and the Hudson in the distance. Then the women turned to look across the Drive at a budding tree and a still-winter-bare hydrangea in front of a 1901 turreted townhouse on the corner. It had just sold for ten million.

"Down from $26,915,500 in September, 2000," Pidge said.

Pearl gave her a look hidden by the mask covering most of her face.

They intended to stop at Zabar's for usual breakfast treats on the return trip uptown. They walked back in that direction.

"Let's save the *hegira* up to the French Renaissance on 107<sup>th</sup> for another time. Maybe in May, the gorgeous green tile roof and copper cornices," Pidge said.

"You see the news story that Schinasi stiffed his architect – who also did Carnegie Hall -- back in 1907 or so? Tuthill sued. I don't know if he ever did get paid. Schinasi sounds like Adolf Twitler's real estate M.O. Tuthill also built Schinasi a secret tunnel from the mansion's basement to the River. Sealed now, the *Times* said."

It was Pidge's turn to give Pearl a look, to equal lack of effect.

"Smuggling?"

Pearl shrugged. "Ironically, though a mogul *and* a Turk, Schinasi didn't inherit a hundred million from *his* Daddy like President Twit did. The obscene fortune came from inventing a cigarette rolling machine – and importing Turkish tobacco to roll into the cancer sticks."

"We'll have to find someplace else to aim for, uptown."

They continued walking without conversation for several blocks. As they crossed avenues

toward and onto Broadway, traffic and noise increased. At Zabar's, they navigated shopping and

meeting neighborhood grief for Xavier, an elderly employee who had just died of the plague.

*Zavy of Zabar's.*

They walked home with bagels and Novy, halvah, and chocolate rugelach.

Pearl said, "The pronunciation in the Proto-Indo-European was 'lox,' and that's exactly how

it's pronounced in modern English. It meant salmon then, and now it means smoked. That word

hasn't changed its pronunciation at all in 8,000 years. I always thought Zavy and Novy went

together. Zavy might be the first grocery worker in the City to die of this plague. We were crazy

to go in."

"You can't not breathe in deeply in there," Pidge defended. "Heaven should smell like

Zabar's."

"I guess now Zavy knows," Pearl said, abruptly adding, "This morning, I remembered my

dream."

"You never do!"

"My grandparents came for a visit. All four of them. They were younger than we are."

"How did you feel?"

"Not like they were coming to collect me. But to comfort me. Made me happy just to see them

looking so well."

"I saw my parents last night, too," Pidge said.

"Maybe it's a global phenomenon, pandemic-related. Or the heat was coming up, and we both

felt warm."

"I was in my mother's Spanish class," Pidge said. "But in reality, I only took Latin with her.

She was telling me her position at Brearley was *the*, she said, *lubricant* that would get me easily into *Alma Mater*. Then, my father was at the blackboard in *his* math classroom at what-were-they-still-calling CCNY then, CUNY now? City College. Do you remember *blackboards*?"

"You always remember your dreams. *Ad nauseum.*"

"Well, you brought it up. it's an odd coincidence."

They neared their apartment building. Pidge stopped by the flowers blooming under the curb tree.

"Look, the crocus are done," Pidge pointed, "replaced by daffodils!"

*Chapter 13*

**from Blue Monkeys by Shapiro & Feria… Pasikennae Obeys**     *With no modern clocks nor wristwatches, Pasikennae and Degw'Pwemanno nevertheless knew the lateness of the hour for them. Yellow, white, and purple crocus had bloomed. The northern lights again moved in giant green, purple, and yellow waves whirling in the April night sky. Degw'Pwemanno saw his gods above stirring up dust as they vied in a sport imitated below by his people. Pasikennae had seen him play with his friends, kicking a hard gourd up and down a meadow.*

*Pasikennae lacked knowledge of the tectonic collision of Africa and Eurasia over millions of years. The ocean floor had heaved-up the Alps, and Gibraltar and the Red Sea had stoppered the Mediterranean Basin to near-evaporated emptiness. Then earthquakes cracked opened faults that for a century refilled the Sea. So Pasikennae saw the aurora borealis as celestial dancing veils of fine Egyptian cotton. Pasikennae told Degw'Pwemanno that far away on Mnkallis, SHE never danced. There, HER sun and moon swelled much bigger than this far north, and SHE wore tall plumes of fire-jeweled smoke. When SHE stamped HER feet, buildings swayed, jars broke, and people fell. The skin of mountains cracked and bled fire.*

*Degw'Pwemanno was a young chief of copper mines and possibly of his people, a distant ancestor of the Eastern Shoshone in northwestern Michigan. A huge copper boulder on the Isle Royale shore was a sacred site where Pasikennae and Degw'Pwemanno mourned Many Smiles (Sueaysua), understanding their baby daughter's death as HER punishment for Pasikennae's disobedience. The ice of the Great Lakes was now melting. The season for travel had returned. So must Pasikennae. She was an 'ikwe' ordered to 'fly away home.'*

*The tablets that told this story were marked with glyphs of fear and sadness.*

April ended. The spring tide salted the air over the wide Hudson. Pidge and Pearl walked the riverfront greenway in Riverside Park, ignoring the breezy vista and low buildings of Guttenberg, New Jersey. They were discussing a syllabogram.

"It looks like *mother* and *guilt*," Pearl insisted.

"Guilt was human. It has to be Pasikennae's. Anything SHE did just *was*."

"Just unjust."

"This is news? Not to Pasikennae. Not until so much later when Job questioned his deity who – how could it be unintentionally? – had modeled revolution in Egypt. My Jewish father liked Jack Miles's take on the power dynamic. They heard no humility in Job's 'Now I get it.' Sardonic. '*Now* I get it.'"

So Pidge and Pearl translated, "*death as HER punishment for Pasikennae's disobedience.*"

"Was that an owl?" Pearl said as something flew over their heads to a nearby treetop.

"Do owls even fly in daytime?"

Pearl consulted her phone. She read aloud, "Despite what the common phrase may say, not all owls are 'night owls.' … two hundred fifty different species of owls … less than seventy percent … are nocturnal… Owls active during the day and sleeping at night are …*diurnal* owls. *Crepuscular* owls are most active during dusk and dawn."

"Crep-*pus*-cular," Pidge said, 'ugly word."

But Pearl was still reading to herself. Then she laughed.

"What?" Pidge asked.

"'What It Means When You See an Owl,'" Pearl read. "'If you see owls often, it could be a symbol that you've uncovered your own deepest knowledge. Strive to enjoy the wonder of life and discover your natural curiosity.'"

"I'm striving."

Pearl looked up again and shook her head carefully at the phone. "At Johns Hopkins they studied why owls don't get strokes when they swivel their heads so fast."

"They're obeying HER," Pidge said.

Three months was too long a time to be separated from baby Sandra, now ten months old, babbling and imitating her grandparents' voices. The baby was racing like a squirrel through the tent-and-tunnel toy Esau had ordered sent to the Cold Spring house. Videos miniaturized Sandra standing up in her crib and pulling herself along furniture.

"You walked and talked very early," Mam told Dayita.

She and Esau were missing everything. Did the baby recognize them at all on a phone or tablet?

The Emergency Department had gotten worse. 'Pre-Morgue' wasn't even *gallows* humor. It had become *ED humor*.

The police contacted Dayita and Esau with more questions about their fourth-floor apartment. So did the building management and realtor eager to sell/buy it.

Dayita's sense of smell had returned; she bought pots of hyacinths for the north Manhattan apartment windows. She could taste rum. Would she recognize Sandra's scent? She remembered nuzzling the baby's neck. It smelled delicious, like vanilla cookies. She couldn't hold other babies. They stank to her. Dayita recognized the biology – and the emotional overlay. Esau had had the milder Covid case, but hadn't regained his olfactory sense. Overwork and separation contributed to his weight loss. Dayita supposed they couldn't go on like this, but they had neither time nor energy for more than surviving routine. Dayita delighted in a perfumed breath of pink hyacinth but knew – its stem, leaves, flowers, and bulb were poisonous. The bulb was its most toxic part.

John Donnelly questioned Malcolm Ackerman about the OPLA (Office of the Principal Legal Advisor) associate he and Elena Luster had had in common, the man who bought her apartment and now was knocking down walls, joining it to the one next door. OPLA was the largest legal program with more than 1,250 attorneys serving as the exclusive legal representative of the Department of Homeland Security. OPLA also provided legal services to all ICE (Immigration & Customs Enforcement) programs and offices. OPLA attorneys supported the DOJ (Department of Justice) in the prosecution of ICE cases and in the defense of civil cases against ICE. In addition to headquarters in Washington, D.C., OPLA operated in more than sixty locations across the country. John was gagging on the alphabet soup of government agencies.

If Ackerman was Mack the Knife, then the real estate buyer was *Cagey*. For all his obsession with the Luster apartment location, Philip Cage, Esq. was rarely in it, and then only to make enough noise that building management received repeated complaints. Cage avoided meeting John anywhere but downtown in the Federal Plaza OPLA Field Office.

He was forty, two years older than the detective. Cage was Black and red-headed, like Malcolm X. John thought he was a Rorschach test of a man. People at the Field Office actually called him "Cagey." Intellectual Property Unit. And no one would talk about him. Detective Donnelly speculated that Cage might be a front for the kind of foreign/criminal/corporate syndicate Cage's own department investigated. And/or a plant/spy for them. A double agent. Wheels within wheels were spinning.

Phil Cage was divorced. His sons, ten and twelve years old, lived in Oklahoma City, where his ex-wife worked at an OPLA Sub Office. When questioned, Cage was quiet and calm. But what was he doing, making all that noise in the Luster apartment and the Persaud-Kimani's sublet next door? Cage had never been rich, but after early life, never poor. Who had paid for the

Luster co-op and the purchase of the rental? What was Cage looking for so loudly -- that Donnelly's NYPD team hadn't found? And Luster's other phone? Where was that?

Cage had a good alibi. Last October, he'd been at a hospital in Oklahoma City where his older boy had been rushed for an appendectomy. So how had his fingerprints been found in Elena Luster's blood?

A clear May dawn. The sheetrock had been primed, ready for painting. Now it was easier for Alan to imagine where his canvases would hang on the widest, highest wall above a working stone fireplace. The eclectic architecture cued the harmony and dissonance Alan wanted. The house was a chimera: Pollack-Krasner weathered Hampton farmhouse, angular modern Philip Glass, plus some gothic Romanesque arch. There was nothing of Texas in or around it.

Alan turned away from the vaulted wall and walked to the kitchen area. Its lower ceiling was a comfort. His thoughts settled. He listed: his teens as *sensation*, his twenties as *sensuality*, and now his thirties as *sense heading toward sensibility*. Brian at Decker & Penny, the Greenport hardware, paint, and art supplies store, would be a real help in color choices and layout. Brian Penny. There would be no mirrors on these walls, either, but Alan couldn't help seeing the frog in the well, three steps up, sliding down slippery two.

His phone rang. It was David. Early for him. Twins okay? Mercedes, breakfast. Alan paced as David spoke. When the workmen began arriving, Alan went outdoors. He focused on the sound of David's voice, not the words, translating the lengthy monologue into summary: Dayita and Esau were in "Manhattan north." That news via Micheline's mother, Susanna, reporting also James's description of a crosstown bus ride from work with Marwa: the medians along Park Avenue and Broadway were in bloom, Detective Donnelly had questioned someone "cagey," and asked if Alan's new house next door to a mansion was "Gatsby *redux*."

David hesitated, not explaining.

"I get it," Alan said. "But not *redux*. This is next door to -- what's the one that collapses?"

*"Fall of the House of Usher."*

Both of them could hear, over the sound of carpenters, what neither was saying. Nothing to do with mansions or English majors.

Brian Penny and his wife, Abigail Decker, were descendants of Greenport's earliest seventeenth century British settlers. The Corchaugs were the peace-loving displaced Indigenous, leaving their name on an avenue in another Long Island town. Local lore had Walt Whitman teaching one semester at Greenport High School, Brian and Abigail among its graduates. They were a year younger than Alan. They looked more like siblings than husband and wife, slim and pale, watery blue eyes, English Longhead faces. They'd been classmates since kindergarten, scholarships to college in Massachusetts at Mount Holyoke and Amherst. After, they lived in lower Manhattan for several years while Abby got a degree in Early Childhood Education at Bank Street, and Brian worked as a gofer for artists and galleries. His family in Greenport owned North Fork Nursery. His brother ran the family business alone after Brian "abdicated."

Brian described his marriage as "two halves of Plato's unity. There are five sexes, and Abby and I are at least three of 'em." They had a four-year old son and a two-year old daughter. Abby's mother minded them. She had retired from the Greenport elementary school where Abby taught second grade. Abby's father was a licensed electrician, jack of all trades, excellent woodworking craftsman, "thereby a major asset at D & P."

Brian had been an art history major/philosophy minor at Amherst. Returning to Greenport when Abby was first pregnant, Brian had worked at the store he now owned. He was not an artist himself – "manque" – but his knowledge and contacts in the City and Island art scene gained gallery owners' and collectors' trust and commissions. His first conversation with Alan over paint chips had led to a long drive to the Jackson Pollock and Lee Krasner Museum/house in East Hampton, and a lingering drive back to Greenport.

By mid-May, Alan, Brian, and Abby were a transparent triangle. Though little shocked Alan, he'd been surprised by Abby's bedroom monologue:

"Two marriages threatened? Not at all! Art is Imagination. Sex is sex," she gestured, "better between ears than legs. And we're not promiscuous, just imaginative. I'm as likely to strap on as any dyke, climb Mount Brian, as he is to mount me."

"Even after two kids, no hips and flat chest, Abby looks like a teenage boy," Brian praised. "It's a genetic gift," Abby took a bow. "When we were little, we began with curiosity… and grew into virtuosity."

"Virtue, like Beauty, is in the eye of the beholder," Brian concluded a practiced speech.

Outdoors, in May, they became what the plague called "a pod." There were afternoon get-togethers in the Penny-Decker backyard, evenings around a stone firepit. Like his pro-football father and cheerleader mother, Alan was a good athlete. He had played football as expected in high school and in college as a left-hander, first base. He taught Brian's two-year old girl to throw and four-year old boy to dunk a basketball in the same adjustable hoop/set he'd bought for the twins back in Manhattan. Brian had been enthusiastic about Alan's sketches of the cherry-plum trees, so much so that he was already agenting in Hamptons galleries for these backgrounds along with the big canvases. They had conversations with Abby about the five-portrait series for the new house.

"Where will you put the sixth one, of us?" she said.

"Is that a request or an order?" Alan asked.

"Yes."

Abby and Brian laughed.

At his store, Brian wore a mask. Some customers didn't. This county at the eastern end of Long Island was a microcosm of the country's division about the pandemic. Vineyards vied with anti-science.

"Some people call mask-wearers "the w(h)ine crowd," Brian reported, "but they keep buying. Politics + Business = Politics. So at D & P, P stands only for the penny."

Windows open, Alan drove west on a narrow road from one of the wineries along North Road back to his rental. The flowering vines perfumed the salt air well after dawn. He made coffee and sat outside on the small back porch, facing the Sound, the view similar but wider at his new house. He needed art supplies, which meant seeing Brian at the store. He wasn't clear on Abby's teaching schedule these Covid-ridden days.

He imagined her dominating a remote classroom of seven-year-olds, while her own younger kids were somewhere in the house with their grandmother. When contacted, Alan Zoomed with people at *HITTITE QUEEN*, but he was uneasy about it. The new triangle he found himself in was too loud an echo of the TV storyline. Alan hated mirrors. He was a manipulated lover back in the Bronze Age; what was he now in an Information one? Though Brian had made the first move, he took orders from Abby. Alan pictured Abby bossing Brian around when they were in kindergarten.

In the car that first time, returning to Greenport from the East Hampton house/museum, Brian had pulled over on a nowhere road bordered on both sides by empty farmland that awaited furrowing and planting, stretching flat for miles. Brian was babbling about shadows on the wall of Plato's Cave, sounding like David. Then he turned and reached for the back of Alan's neck, pulling him into a kiss. Finally taking a breath, Brian refocused below Alan's belt.

"You are all-that and a bag of chips," Brian leaned over, "and wow, what an all-thing!"

"In Iceland, the *Althing* is parliament," Alan had actually said.

Brian laughed, caressing, "Says who, Jane Eyre, your Mr. Rochester? Mister 'All the news that's fit to print?' Are you the crazy wife in his attic? All delicious, unprintable you?"

Alan shut out the rest. As he swallowed now-lukewarm coffee, he shifted to Abby's, what could he call it, induction. Not seduction. *Incubus. Succubus.* David's voice in his head. Abby had been spouting some philosophy about pregnancy and God-given free will. Example: is involuntary kidney donation to a virtuoso violinist justifiable? Something else about the Greenport church that their families belonged to forever.

"It has to be a choice, or it's illegal forced occupation for nine months in a house."

Brian had added on cue, "Like the British billeted soldiers in Boston and New York in the American Revolution."

"Obedience isn't a choice," Abby concluded. "It's fear, manifest. Don't be afraid, Alan."

Abby was another director. Alan was an actor. Let self-loathing be his character note. And, *scene.*


Mercedes had given up trying to sleep. It wasn't the usual street noise of the City that kept her up, it was hearing over and over again her best friend Anayeli's voice – her *best* friend! – telling her Memo belonged to her now.

"We decided I should tell you, not Memo," Yeli said.

*We.*

Yeli had cried. What did they call them, *crocodile* tears?

She and the twins had watched the Disney PETER PAN many times. Mercedes heard the song in her head. "*Never smile at a crocodile… you can't get friendly with a crocodile… Don't be taken in by his welcome grin… He's imagining how well you'd fit within his skin.*" Mercedes would never watch that movie again.

She walked into the dark, empty living room. When she had phoned Memo, all he would croak was *Verdad.* Not even *Lo siento. Nada.*

She wanted to go home. To what? Her mother, her aunt… they would say *te lo dije!* And the worst was, Mercedes knew they were right. No, the worst was she couldn't even cry. She felt like … like after the appendicitis five years ago when she was fifteen and missed her *Quinceañera.* How her stomach ached. But she had cried then. Cried and cried.

Mercedes heard sobbing. It wasn't hers. It came from the other side of the living room, in Senior David's bedroom. She had a magnet for crying that would take her to the twins, but this time to their father. Nothing made sense in this world. *El corona. Memo. Yeli. ¿Ahora que?*

Though the room was darker than her own, she was familiar with the master bedroom since she'd replaced the housecleaning service to minimize the family's exposure to the virus. As in the twins' bedroom, blackout curtains covered the windows, but here, they were thicker material that went to the floor. There was a masculine, musky scent in the room. Senor David still sobbed. He didn't seem to notice she had entered the room. She made out his shape under the covers, tucked into himself like a baby on one side of the bed only, leaving Senor Alan's side empty. This brought the first tears to her own eyes.

Mercedes got into the bed and put herself in the empty space. David went rigid, like a child. She soothed him. Like a mother? Not his. He was exhausted. He could feel breasts against his back. Her body held him like a shell. He was crying. So was she. They slept. Later, Mercedes turned over and stretched her legs. Her movement drifted David from sleep into a waking dream. Alan's back was to him. Arm over waist, David translated the differences of scent and soft, size and strength, dreaming Alan. Only then did an erection begin, but rather than arouse, it reassured. David slept more deeply. In the morning when he woke, the young woman was gone.

Even with the drapes closed, there was light in the room.

***Chapter 14  June***

**from Blue Monkeys by Shapiro & Feria...**

*Pasikennae's year began at the autumn equinox. She knew the sky maps that directed navigation. SHE had taught HER people both a lunar and solar calendar, even including a day to be added every fourth year. What we call Orion's Belt, its brightest stars, centered a constellation that formed a double axe. Often HER image's two outstretched arms also assumed that angular shape. No tablets found thus far have described Pasikennae's return from Lake Superior to the mouth of the wide St. Lawrence, hugging shorelines north to Greenland, Iceland, and the Faroes.*

*She did leave a kind of map, headed by the sunstone glyph, that resumed at the Orkney island where her tomb was discovered. It showed one or more ships never more than six days out of sight of land at any time, sailing south through the Irish Sea, across the Channel down France, Portugal and Spain. Pasikennae met with 'sisters' again at Gibraltar, the Great Horns ('Through HER Crown'). Here, she inscribed a monkey glyph with a symbol for 'welcome', reminding us of her lost pet langur and the imaginary blue monkeys leaping in Mnkallis murals she must have yearned to see again. We felt her homesickness.*

*At Gibraltar, Pasikennae was sternly warned to go no further into the Mediterranean. SHE had gathered them like seeds and scattered HER people far and wide. Old walls had fallen. People moved broken stones out of their path. The largest pithoi were set under doorways. They took silver, treasures, and animals when they sailed away. As far as Gibraltar, 'We heard HER voice!' HER roar and poisonous darkness forbade their return. But Pasikennae carved glyphs describing the copper inside the ships with HER insistence to go on. Sueaysua's name repeated.*

*Then other, deeper marks impressed a catastrophe so inexplicable to Pasikennae that its syllabogram remained undecipherable to us. We could only guess at 'approach' or 'arrival'. Now with only one ship, Pasikennae's voyage east reversed its beginning. She stopped again at Pylos. Summer was ebbing into autumn. On this chapter stone, the 'sister' at Pylos was gone, and the harbor nearly empty of ships. Fire-breathing monsters accompanied more warnings to go no further. The strange tablet included glyphs for 'green' and 'light' – possibly Pasikennae reporting on a phenomenon known to occur briefly at sunset in the Mediterranean. (Scottish legend echoed a belief that 'a green flash' conveyed power mightier than invisibility, to see into the souls of other people.)*

*Pasikennae continued east to Crete. Words and syllabograms of rain and tears, tsunami, smoke and death cover an entire stone in Linear A on both sides – its usual Egyptian translation absent. This read like CAPITALIZATION ... or shrieking. The presence of human and animal terror and unutterable absence of any reference/invocation to HER was palpable. In a smaller vessel, Pasikennae sailed (alone?) north to Mnkallis. At first, she didn't recognize or believe what she saw: the image showed hands covering eyes. She contrasted an earlier syllabogram of the tri-circular concentric island that again identified it as a kind of [Minoan] Vatican, HER center, with a glyph that looked like a letter, shaped like modern-day Santorini, a left-facing C with three dots.*

*Meticulous inscriptions that had appeared on an earlier tablet, a map of heliographic links (functioning like smoke signals), were now missing mountaintop bronze mirrors around the entire Aegean Sea. We understood this to mean, in the present day, as if the internet and all telecommunication disappeared. Also listed missing were birds and animals, juxtaposed with an unusual sea monster, all mouth and heart, as if It had swallowed everything, and all Pasikennae could hear was the systole/diastole of the sea.*

It was hot in June in St. Bart's. Beckett Face-Timed her father tearfully. John Donnelly tried to explain to the nine-year old that even if she came home, their separation would continue until there was a vaccine. Adding to John's anguish, Beckett cried about what her mother allowed her to see online.

"Breonna Taylor was asleep in her bed! The policeman stepped on the man's *neck!* He couldn't *breathe.* Daddy, you would never do that!?"

John winced at the question mark in Beckett's voice. He tried reassuring the little girl, "You can ride your bicycle around a beautiful island," but it came out wrong because he had to explain there was a shortage of bicycles in New York because so many people weren't taking subways or buses.

"Anyway, Daddy, it's too *hot* here to ride even a horse! It's boiling!"

John couldn't make it better, and Kirby had also been watching the protests on TV with their daughter. Then she had Beckett's long red hair cornrowed with beads. He wondered what Mamselle thought. Was there a statute of limitations on cultural appropriation? He could only divorce the woman once.

His anger shifted him to the memory of the Luster crime scene. Red blood splashed, soaked all over the white space. That rage. He thought of the recent flare up in the lobby when the Columbia professors were thanking the doorman for delivering groceries right to their apartment door. The doorman had looked bluer than usual. Then Pidge began scolding Azul about taking his medicine in rapid-fire Spanish. She matched his anger. John knew Azul was upset about a just-deported relative, and another had become a *"persona de interes!"*

John took the stairs.

It had been three weeks of racial protests nationally and internationally. Even little Rhode Island had taken *Plantations* out of its seventeenth century charter name. On the Friday in 2020 that began the *Juneteenth* Weekend commemoration of the 1865 Texan proclamation, the Senate Leader's 2019 insult went viral online: "We paid for the sin of slavery by electing Obama." A mask-less Presidential campaign rally in Tulsa had to be moved to Saturday, the twentieth.

"Come for the racism, stay for the plague," said Drew Burgos, David's agent, phoning about a contract detail, but more as an excuse to hear a friend's voice.

"A million tickets sold, they said?" David added. "For a venue for nineteen thousand that only sixty-two hundred attended? What's bigger, the lie or the failure?"

Drew suggested, "A new title for the Bloated Orange Tick? He's the *Pathetic Phallus* form of the *literal* plague."

David laughed. "Prick's indeed the apotheosis of fallacy, pathetic or otherwise. The other infection in the body politic. How do you like *Adolf Twitler*?"

"I favor the double entendre of *Cheeto-in-Chief,*" Drew paused, then asked, "Is there anything you're actually looking forward to?"

David heard too much backstory in that question. He didn't want to ask about Vera. He sighed.

"I can only *listen* to Daniil Trifonov at Carnegie Hall at the end of the month. Online only."

"That's a nice memory," Drew said. "The seats you gave us for the Philharmonic opening two years ago. The four of us together."

Still, David didn't bite. "I keep trying to do his Liszt. Three minutes of *Paysage* at least. Truly least. My study will never be their *Transcendental Etudes.* Liszt could stretch a tenth, even an eleventh. Trifonov plays like he has not only four hands but at least two brains. I was there in

March at Carnegie for his Bach *Chaconne* and *Fugues* before they closed for the plague."

"Before your parents –"

"Yes."


"There's a strange message for you on the landline message machine," Pearl said when Pidge emerged from the bathroom. "Look at you. Everyone else is turning on air conditioners, and you're taking a hot bath. You look like a red potato."

Pidge was wrapped in a towel. Walking to the phone, she mumbled, "Who called?"

"Vera Mifeng?"

"Drew Burgos's young wife?" Pidge echoed surprise.

They listened to the message.

"Professor Shapiro, I hope you don't mind I've been reading the pages you sent Drew. I just love **Blue Monkeys**! When you said Pasikennae's Sueaysua died, I cried. I cried and cried. I just had a miscarriage."

Pearl looked at the machine. "She's still crying."

The message snapped to a stop.

Pidge tightened the towel across her chest. "Oh, dear. I guess I have to call her back."

"Call Drew?"

Pidge turned to her bedroom. "Oh, god. Let me get dressed."

"Talk to David? He knows Drew better."

"Oh, David," Pidge shook her head.


Days later, Pidge and Pearl, both wishing they were walking with Ginger instead, missing the respite from each other she had afforded, walked down the tree-shaded steps beneath the Joan of Arc statue in Riverside Park.

"I always feel like I'm looking up her nose," Pidge managed.

"Glad she's up on her high horse," Pearl also made the effort. 'Wielding her Excalibur. I'm glad she's not being burned at the stake right here."

"In Rouen, she is."

They found a bench. It had been a half mile walk north of the apartment. The sun dappled their bare arms. Both women wore masks and sunhats. Pearl was in faded madras Bermuda shorts, Pidge a loose yellow dress. They heard traffic sounds both from Riverside Drive and the river, but at distances that felt secure, like walls. Also masked, a young Black mother pushing an empty stroller walked by with her toddler. The little bandit wandered toward the two old women. The mother sang out, "No!" and kept walking.

"They can't see us smiling at them," Pidge said.

"We're smiling at you!" Pearl called, waving.

The mother paused, turned, and they both waved back.

"What I can see, she's a beauty like -- Bess Waters -- at college," Pidge remembered. "She was a Miss Black Texas who married a white Yalie ministry student. She was a freshman when I was a junior. I met her when Tereze Sedgwick and I heard her sobbing in her room because her religion professor had told her to go home, 'You don't belong here.' She begged us not to go the college president or report him to any authority. Couple of years later, we went to their wedding."

Pearl was quiet.

"Ready to walk back?" Pidge said.

Pearl stood and breathed deeply, grateful for working lungs. Being alive in June was a gift. She looked down at her still-seated friend.

"*You don't belong here,*" Pearl echoed.

Pidge craned her neck at St. Joan's sword. "Vera Mifeng said Drew insisted on an abortion.

Then she miscarried."

Pearl sighed and went up the steps toward the Drive. As Pidge joined her, they walked side by side.

"We can go down to Zabar's and pick up some halvah," Pearl said. "You like the marbled."

They waited at a light to cross to buildings' shade from the western-arcing sun. Pidge shared conciliation.

"The *Times* Science section said this morning that your under-Yellowstone supervolcano might not be so bad. It's a '*cooling* hotspot.'"

"So may they all," Pearl said.

The light turned green.


James and Micheline ate breakfast at the small table. Standing at the kitchen counter, Susanna gasped at her phone.

"Sues, what?" James asked, getting up.

Susanna was shaking her head. "A patient. Veronica Drummer. That lovely star. Her husband didn't put her in hospice." Eliding for Micheline, Susanna quoted, "'In the care of two nurses at home, last night.'"

But the four-year old had also moved from her chair to her mother and put her arms around her waist. "I'm sorry, Mommy."

Susanna put a palm on their daughter's head and looked up into her tall husband's dark brown eyes.

### *Chapter 15  July*

If Dayita and Esau were ever going to get out of the City, it would have to be as the pandemic

curve lowered in July. One evening past eight o'clock, they walked in Inwood Hill Park. It was

hot and humid. As twilight darkened, they saw fireflies. In the distance, a bagpiper wheezed like

a bizarre oracle. They walked within the rare, small island of time they had together. Manhattan

Island surrounded them and was Itself encircled by rivers and ocean. They sat on benches

overlooking the water and lights of The Henry Hudson Bridge that crossed Spuyten Duyvil

Creek to the Bronx. They talked about a nasal spray that blocked the virus in the nose and lungs,

was inexpensive, and needed no refrigeration -- developed at the Medical Center.

"Next step is applying for a patent," Dayita said.

"And beaming up Columbia's researchers to Operation Warp Speed."

They reviewed their own plans next week for their transfer to the hospital's Hudson Valley

'campus' south of the Cold Spring home. They would finally move in before Sandra's first

birthday in early August. They walked more, to Shorakapok Rock, whose plaque said the park

was where Peter Minuit had bought Manhattan from the Indigenous Lenape. The bagpipe music

grew louder until they saw the piper in Highland Dress kilt and ostrich bonnet beneath a tall tree,

performing for a small, masked/spaced audience. They kept their distance.

"Only in New York," Dayita said.

"Or Scotland," Esau laughed.

Walking back to Dayita's parents' apartment, the couple was silent. They held hands, then

released them, then held them again. Dayita imagined a future summer night walking home from

a park upstate in Cold Spring with Sandra falling asleep in a stroller. Home to an icy smoothie

rum mango *lassi*. Esau, who was calmed by lists, thought of the one he'd written recently in a

notebook he kept for the purpose. He thought of sitting 'on benches *overlooking* the water.'

*Overlook* meant to watch – or fail to notice. Esau thought of moving from Manhattan to Cold Spring. From Kenya to America. *Bolt* - to separate by fleeing or to hold together (as with a bolt); *Bound* - going toward a destination or restrained from moving; *Buckle* - to fasten together (with a buckle) or to bend or collapse from pressure; *Fast* - firmly fixed and unmoving or able to move rapidly; Most of all – *Left* - departed or remained behind. Esau sighed.

"What?" Dayita said, as if waking.

"Contronyms. Words with two meanings the opposite of each other. *Wear* means to endure or to deteriorate. *Weather* means to withstand or to be worn away. I don't know if there's another term for a whole sentence I just thought of: *If anyone can do it, you can.*"

Dayita took his hand again. "I like that. Verbal equivalent of those optical illusions where you see a crone's head, then a maiden's. The vase/face. You're not anyone. And *you* can."

He flinched. Dropped her hand.

"Esau?"

He looked around into darkening woods. He sniffed. Breathed in deeply.

"What is that?"

"You can smell it?"

"Can you?

Dayita started laughing "Stink, yes! I just stopped mentioning smells months ago. Your first smell again? Skunk!"

Esau pulled Dayita close and put his nose in her neck, breathing her in.

John Donnelly received the report about their move upstate both at the precinct and from Marwa who heard it from Azul, who wouldn't even look him in the eye let alone share building gossip with him. Cage's purchase of the doctors' adjoining apartment still gnawed at the detective. The familiar I've-missed-something feeling made him more irritable than the July heatwave and the distraction of a high-profile burglary case. He wasn't the lead on it, but it put everyone on edge.

Meanwhile, living in Marwa's apartment since the end of March, under the increasing duress of Covid confinement, they'd had their own graphed (by Marwa) highs and lows. Her logic clearly outweighed yearning for his Oceanside condo: staying together in the one-bedroom apartment in Manhattan meant no extra exposure for his parents, and John had no reason to travel to Long Island since Beckett remained "trapped in St. Bart's" according to her birthday text. Having always relied on reason, John sometimes had to admit (though not aloud) that Marwa's skill surpassed his. And her dreams! She (too) often retold them in detail precisely in the waking moments when he wanted quiet.

The lowest point was the morning of the primes. John had slept badly after a cough sent him for a test whose outcome he awaited. The cough was gone, but anxiety would remain even if he tested negative. Marwa was home from the lab that morning. He didn't ask why. He tried to focus on her nightie as she made breakfast. She launched into a cheerful description of yet another dream.

"I was at a party of primes! No formula predicts the occurrence of prime numbers—they behave as if they appear randomly. Euclid proved, in 300 B.C., that there is an infinite number of primes. Twin primes are two apart. Cousin primes are four apart, sexy primes are six apart, and neighbor primes are adjacent at some greater remove. An absolute prime is prime regardless of how its digits are arranged: 199; 919; 991. A beastly prime has 666 in the center. The number 700666007 is a beastly palindromic prime…"

John's mind wandered.

"… circular… cycles… Cuban… Cullen… curved numerals… deletable prime… emirp –"

John startled, "Prime spelled backwards."

Marwa wouldn't be interrupted, "– is prime even when you reverse it: 389, 983."

She went on and on. The sound of her voice implied it was finally ending.

"Titanic primes; Wagstaff primes; Wall-Sun-Sun primes; Wolstenholme primes; Woodall primes; and Yarborough primes, which have neither a 0 nor a 1."

Marwa paused, he supposed, for breath. Coffee fragrance filled the small kitchen. John poured them both mugs.

She took a swallow and said, "There is a distance within which, on an infinite number of occasions, there will always be two primes!"

John said, "You think we're those two?"

She was happy. "It's like thinking that the universe is infinite, unbounded, and finding it has an end somewhere."

"Is that a good thing?" John said, but he did test negative.

Dawn was early in the summer. Pidge and Pearl chatted in their familiar *steganographic* way.

"*Hidden writing,* crossword clue," Pidge said. "Who does the *Times* think it's messing with? The thing about July – is hot. Heat."

She was watering herbs on the narrow kitchen windowsill. She rubbed some of the leaves and sniffed.

Pearl could smell whiffs of rosemary and oregano. "It's good to be in a kind of pod with David and the twins, thereby Micheline and her 'rents. And Mercedes. She sounds happy when you speak Spanish with her. Did you sleep?"

"We're a new genus of *pseudopod*? That clue? 'A temporary protrusion serving as an organ of locomotion.' James tells me we have five senses. Plants have fifteen more. I don't know if I sleep anymore. I wake from dreams. James said genetic engineering restored corn. A gene borrowed from oregano was put back in. But now his lab is frantic with virus."

"Frantic?"

"Well, he's frustrated away from his research," Pidge said, sitting down, sipping milky tea, idling with the *Times* puzzle. "*Linnaeus!*" she pounced and wrote in the word, looked up, grinning. "Linnaeus planned a garden where you could tell time by observing plants. Leaves close around flowers. Some fold and hang upside down like bats. They literally sleep like babies – assume the positions they had during germination. Also, they sleep better when they're young. When they're old, they're awake longer and don't sleep well. I'm one old *ficus*."

Pearl shook her head. "You're no fig. I see you as… garlic! Bulby under, hyacinthy above. Can't cook without garlic! However, it's hot enough by ten to start simmering, so turn on the AC soon."

She stood up, pulled her robe away from her body. "Sticking to me already… I wish we could just march right over today to the transplanted Strand on Columbus. It opens at eleven. A new bookstore. Balm in Gilead. It has a neon sign! Mercedes is taking the kids, masked like bandits, to the new Children's Room in the basement. This first month, spending seventy-five dollars gets you a free branded tote bag."

"Cool in every way, but we're *stranded* here," Pidge said.

Pearl groaned appreciatively.

"Can we send Mercedes with money?" Pidge said. "She can get books for herself and the kids, and we can be 'left holding the bag!' We're already incarcerated."

Pearl had walked to the windowsill. "I read that plants' roots -- root tips communicate via chemicals. They move like flocks of birds, no collisions."

Pidge refocused on her crossword but nodded. "If you look down from rooftops or planes at people walking in cities, we don't bump into each other, either. Except tourists. Only," Pidge sighed, "none of their *murmurations* in the plagued City this summer."

Alan was disturbed when Brian unexpectedly appeared at the barn studio near noon that July morning. Black-lensed aviator sunglasses under his white Decker & Penny logo cap. Arms filled with canvases and stretchers, a can of paint. Carpenters in the new house on lunchbreak.

At breakfast that morning, Alan had a better phone call with David than in a long while. Now standing in the hot sunshine, Alan had been reliving it.

"Where do you want your *Yamaha Clavinova* digital grand?!"

"My what?" David had said.

Arno and Dylan were jumping around, demanding to be included.

Alan had been showing David the living room panorama that now featured the shiny black instrument. "I'll have an outlet installed in the floor. No need to worry about the ocean effect on an electronic piano. Two world class concert grand pianos are in it! It won't need to be tuned. Isn't it a beauty?"

Then Alan told David the rumors about *HITTITE QUEEN* resuming in September or by November, and – *piece de resistance* - "New film. For theaters and/or streaming. Agent overnighted a great script, THE FIRST END OF THE WORLD. They want me for one of the three leads. I'm neither straight nor a stripper. Evidently, *HITTITE*'s made me 'Hollywood's go-to bi.' *HITTITE* diva thinks she's one of the trio, but," in a flawless impression of a famous Midwestern actress, Alan said, "'don't tell-or-I'll-have-to-kill-you' star greenlighted the project. Her accent's as thick as mine will have to be -- Scottish. Younger love interest played by a 'too-hot-to-touch' who also signed on. They both asked for me, I don't die, 60's setting 'way before

HIV. I'll have to wear contact lenses that give me neon yellow irises outlined in dark brown. The shoot could start in like, maybe, October, 2021. After the plague."

"Where?" David asked.

"Okay, take a breath. On Crete. Also Santorini. Pidge and Pearl will love this – I'm an artist for an archeological dig at Akroteri. A Greek government official has stopped it."

"The movie?" David asked.

"No, no, the dig. In the script. A real Greek actor will play the part. The locals have seen ghosts. "The Greek word for yes is *nay* and no is *oh-hee*. You shake your head opposite."

Alan demonstrated for the twins, who tried to imitate him. Laughter followed.

"See, it's great for the boys! Just the four of us – and Mercedes – together."

"Together," David repeated.

Now, standing shirtless in the sun, breathing in honeysuckle, Alan turned to face Brian who had put down all the paraphernalia, staring at him.

"There's a bee on your shoulder, drinking your sweat," Brian said. "You, mistaken for pollen? Nectar? Understandable. Don't move."

Alan's eyes crossed looking down at the tiny pool between collarbone and shoulder. Reliving the phone call, he hadn't felt the honeybee.

"Allergic?" Brian asked.

"I was stung once. Long time ago. I won't know till a second sting?"

"I don't know, either. But you're standing next to honeysuckle, midday. Tempting Fate?" In a British accent, "Mad Dogs and Englishman, Alan, what?"

The bee kept to Alan's shoulder, rising, then returning.

'You're tempting *me*," Brian said. He stepped forward and palmed the insect away. He grabbed Alan's hand and pulled him into the barn-studio, added, "Stay!" while he brought everything indoors.

Because building the new house would take more time, the barn had been renovated first. North and south walls of paned glass, open for ventilation. Mini-split AC high up on a wall. Light, pickled hardwood floor. Well-stocked shelves above a long wooden worktable with high stools. Deep sink and kitchenette. Special touch, architectural metal-and-wood spiral staircase to the loft and bathroom.

Alan watched Brian take off his cap and sunglasses and pull Alan's old pink polo shirt over his head. Set down the wooden stretchers against a wall. Laid out canvas on the open floor. Went to the worktable. Opened the half gallon can of pale green paint he'd brought. Held it up.

"Benjamin Moore, *Scenic View.*"

"These walls are *Simply White*, as you well know," Alan said.

"Washable latex," Brian said, lifting the can onto his palm, balancing it. "A bee sting is a lightning bolt. You see stars. As a kid, I was too stunned to cry. Pain and crazy itch. Then you scratch – ecstasy! Still ranks up there. Bliss."

Alan frowned. "But when you stop scratching – the pain is worse –"

Brian crossed the wide space. He set the paint can on the floor and faced Alan. He stood no more than an inch above Alan's shoulder, exactly where the bee had sipped. He licked the sweat, put his hand on the back of Alan's neck, and they kissed.

Then, in swift moves, Brian stopped, crouched, picked up the paint and stood back, splashing on himself, pouring some on the top of his own head so it ran down his face, then did the same to Alan.

"What are you doing?" Alan sputtered.

"Wha'dya think *Pollack* was doing?! Brian laughed.

Brian covered them both, "like bees smothered in pollen," finger-painting circles over their bodies, pulling off his shorts, then Alan's. He lay down on the now-spattered canvas and rolled around. Reached up and pulled Alan down.

First there was Alan's spitting out the paint, then Brian's harsh laughter. Fast, it became a schoolyard fight -- jest until the blow that roused fury. It ended in predictable mess, two green men listening to their breathing slow.

Brian snarled, "And – *scene*, that's what actors say, isn't it?"

Alan was still.

"No words without a script?" Brian insisted.

"Not my scene," Alan said. "Yours."

"Ah. I know a last time when it stings me."

Alan sat up, looked around at the green canvases. At their bodies. His paint-crusting hands.

"So," Brian said, staying on his back. Looking up at the beams in the barn ceiling. "You're not *doing us* anymore, any *way*? Your best impression may be your last. I loved your Abby. She loved your me. She'll be so disappointed. Albeit validated. She said you were just a bourgeois in denial. You avoid their rejection with your flawless breeder impression. Why do you want to be their 'normal'? Abby and I live without labels. We write our own dictionary. Our kids are our mortality, replacements, usurpers – nails in our coffins. Why let anyone else define you?"

Alan stood, picked up one of the drier sheets of canvas, and wrapped it around his waist. He shook his head.

"But I should let you tell me who I am. I need a shower," Alan said, going to the staircase. He gestured around the room. "I'll clean it all up."

Brian still had not moved. "I bet you will," he said.

By the time Alan returned downstairs, Brian was gone, cap, sunglasses, shorts, several pieces of canvas. He'd left the pink polo shirt behind, thick with the pale green paint. On the floor, Brian had dragged a paint-soaked canvas near the door, where with a finger he'd drawn a large heart and inside wrote, 'I TESTED +.'

"Christ!" Alan bit his raw lips and ran a hand through his wet hair. He heard the carpenters across the lawn in the new house. Loud reggae blared from speakers that one of the crew always had around. He couldn't make out but knew the words. *I wish I never met yo' ass/Sometimes it be like that.* [https://www.azlyrics.com/lyrics/kanebrown/belikethat.html](https://www.azlyrics.com/lyrics/kanebrown/belikethat.html)

*Chapter 16  August*

*from Blue Monkeys by Shapiro & Feria...*

*Though it has long been London, much longer ago -- four millennia, in fact -- the cultural center of the British Isles was in the northern Scottish Orkneys. Evidence remains of pavements and painted houses. Fired, decorated pottery was made, and the first stone henges were built there. Though Pasikennae used no word for 'concept,' ideas clearly spread to the rest of Neolithic Britain. Some perhaps from a Minoan outpost?*

*Where her burial site was unearthed, what we called her 'Summertime' tablets included one of black, weathered sandstone that seemed a jigsaw puzzle missing so many pieces, glyphs, letters, words, and syllabograms that we speculated it reflected Pasikennae's fragmented mental state after arriving at the Orkneys. The Egyptian hieroglyphs on its reverse side were similarly distorted. We arranged the tablets chronologically from stone through the fired clay ones, guessing that the latter implied Pasikennae's stabilized situation that allowed the building and/or use of a kiln.*

*No tablet found so far reported on Pasikennae's long voyage north from the traumatic Mediterranean. The first Summertime tablet carved in Orkney stone astonished with glyphs of bull jumping, then of a child's death, then a series of witch-like images we further guessed implied Pasikennae's review of her life as Maiden, Mother, Crone. She could not have been an old woman – by modern standards – when she sailed north, but perhaps the earlier two stages of her life had been vaporized with her homeland. Perhaps she imagined herself buried in the steep cliffs of ash on Mnkallis as she made the final journey to her Afterlife.*

*Or the trinity of references could have been an invocation of the awe-ful divinity that Pasikennae never again mentioned as SHE or HER, out of fear or obedience or some other motive we could not imagine. Pasikennae did mark the absence of the trees she had known in the other far north of Lake Superior, and the contrasting presence of an aurora borealis which she did not inscribe as dancing veils or Indigenous game-playing. She carved only the syllabograms for night sky, clouds, and their identifying colors green, purple, and yellow.*

*Pasikennae may have been sick for some time; medicines and medicine women and men appear, who, upon her survival, Pasikennae apparently joined since another Summertime tablet is entirely devoted to herbals and plants, fauna and flora recognizable in the same location today. Yet another presented signs for some sort of religious role for Pasikennae. The bull leaper reappeared. Images of tribute were listed along with other valuables: grain, pigs & cattle, metals & jewelry. These gifts were offered to a high-ranking female.*

*Three clay tablets and one obsidian were carefully set into copper sleeves, indicating their importance. The three looked like enlarged-lettered children's primers of Linear A language on one side and an unknown (Orkney?) script on the other, a stunning discovery in themselves with no other examples thus far. Was Pasikennae teacher as well as healer and religious figure? The three clay tablets appeared to be stories she told about white-winged birds and the constellation Orion, brown & blue monkeys, and a green flash of invisibility. The obsidian fourth became for us an object of mystery and speculation.*

After yet another thirty straight hours in the lab, James tried to clear his mind by walking uptown to East 79th to the crosstown bus stop. Susanna had also been on duty all night at the hospital, Micheline again sleeping over in the Rochester-Tapley apartment's trundle bed. Instead of waking him, the walk lulled James nearly blind along York Avenue and cross streets, dozing with dream-like thoughts about genes for arms and legs that first appeared in organisms that had neither, of fruit fly genes for gonad development that worked to develop human brains, and of genes used in different tissues for entirely different purposes at the same time. The August sun had been up for hours by nine a.m., though to James felt it still felt like night. He was frustrated; he knew there was something he'd failed to do, to imagine, but he couldn't quite --.

He didn't notice anything as he sat in the long accordion bus across the Transverse through Central Park, but he jarred awake, drooling, at the wide avenue of Central Park West. Confused, he got off the few blocks too early. He walked south in the wrong direction to the Museum of Natural History. Sabrett umbrella'd stands and other concessions awaited visitors unlikely to arrive in numbers during the plague. Half a dozen police officers were protecting the bronze Teddy Roosevelt 1939 monument from a potential "cancel culture mob" before the museum removed the statue as planned.

James woke up at the familiar insult of a naked African standing on one side and slightly behind the President's giant steed, Roosevelt in regalia astride, high above the statue. Through Pearl's eyes, he also saw the half-naked Native American statue on the horse's other flank. Avoiding eye contact with the police, James retraced his missteps. He thought, *so may we all.*

He walked irritably toward the Hudson River west on 81st Street, pausing at Broadway to look uptown at the trees on the median, tempted to sit down on an end bench. But he forged onward and stopped at the light on West End Avenue. He looked at the wide-screen glass face of the Calhoun School. Its pre-K through second grade building was down on 74th Street. David Rochester, an alumnus, was on its Board; the twins were already registered for kindergarten, and David had invited Micheline to join them, implying he would help out.

James had demurred; he and Susanna could, if pressed, manage the exorbitant tuition. But why? His path from Bronx Catholic school salutatorian to Presidential Scholar at Fordham had seen him to a Rockefeller lab. His mind's eye saw numbers: kindergarten, first and second grades: $52,600; third through senior year: $54,680; Parents Association dues, $100 per family –

the next thing James knew, Azul was opening the apartment building's beveled door.

"*¿Está suficiente caliente para Ud?*"

Translation foggy, James nodded at Azul's tone. Then he was lucky -- the elevator door

opened as he reached it. Finally inside the apartment, hotter than outdoors. Shoes off at the door,

then clothes off his body as he aimed for the bedroom. Naked, he moved past the high dresser,

catching a whiff of Susanna's gardenia cologne. Good, no anosmia nor headache. Even this close

to collapse, checking for symptoms. Pulled back the light summer cover, lay down. Really felt

like *falling* … to sleep. Let dying be like this.

When Susanna entered the apartment, she thought, was Arkansas ever *this* hot? She smiled at

the shoes and path of James's clothes. She turned on the living room AC, got a cold beer out of

the fridge – beer for breakfast? Yes! In the bedroom, Susanna looked at *Whole Lotta Man*

sprawled akimbo. What a time to hear in her head her mother's first appraisal of James! Only a

DaVinci artist-anatomist could do James justice. The scent of his healthy sweat against the

disease of her last twelve hours, all the months before, all the years of her career to come – what

a wonder James was! His length, muscles, strength, brilliance – how deep and how very dark

was – *hey, Mom!* – this original image of the Almighty.

Susanna took off her clothes and turned on the bedroom AC to its lowest hum. James moved,

then stilled. She looked at him, and as if she willed it, his erection rose. Then – what she wanted,

how it would go -- everything became clear. Worry about missed pills, choices, change – gone. It

could be next April. Spring! James didn't awaken when she lay down beside him. But when she

straddled and fixed him inside, his hands reached, clasping her hips. His eyes opened.

He saw her the fantasy of white marble come to life, alabaster skin, pale hair, pale eyes. Never the Holy Mother, but maybe one of Her saints. James swelled with humor as he filled Susanna. Was there a patron saint for sex that his parochial education missed? He laughed.

"Sues?"

"Who else?"

Her laugh caused ecstasy.

Sometime later, as the room and they cooled, she pulled the light cover up over them both, and they slept. Before noon, James awakened first. Slowly, Susanna opened her eyes.    He was dressed, in the bedroom doorway. "I'll just go pick up Micheline. We can have lunch together before I have to go back."

Susanna raised onto her elbows. "I have next shift off. All those hours."

"I was stuck," James said. "I think you solved my problem."

"I think you did mine as well."


August was never easy in Manhattan. Skyscrapers, sidewalks, and avenues created a concrete/asphalt heat island. Overworked trees tried to convert $CO_2$ into oxygen. But well north of the City, the Perseid meteor showers could be seen in Cold Spring where Sandra Persaud-Kimani celebrated her first birthday. The elderly professors on the ninth floor suffered over having to imagine Pasikennae's feelings. Agent Drew Burgos had demanded "creative speculation." The White House ordered its Post Office appointee to remove sorting machines and who knew what else in obvious efforts to slow the mail to suppress votes all over the country. Pidge and Pearl worried about receiving their mail-in ballots on time or at all. Thank goodness their income was direct deposit and what medicines they needed were reliably delivered by the Starbucks of pharmacy chains in Manhattan, Duane Reade.

Over a hundred miles east, on the north fork of Long Island, Alan Tapley had consulted his phone and lived through two days of rain before driving the near-twenty miles to a testing location across what felt like a continent past vineyards and towns. The Urgent Care in Cutchogue ominously faced an old cemetery across Main Road. Though he had no symptoms, he tested positive. Alan phoned David.

"I'll take care of everything," David said.

At first, Alan hoped his tightening chest was just nerves. David FedEx'd supplies overnight and sent a private nurse two days later. "They" arrived masked. Like Alan, they were early thirties. They wore colorful scrubs, Rainbow Race Hi Tops, and a yellow gold wedding band. De'Lynn Yu had taken their husband Alex's surname.

De'Lynn gave a practiced introduction as they examined Alan, "Alex and I are trans. He is 38-year-old Chinese rooster to my Black hen though I was born D'Lion, a tall drink of water in Alphabet City, and Alex was just a short sip in Chinatown. Now we sing the flip sides of our original demos. Surgeries deleted Mama Nature's wrong notes. We never met till nursing school, but we transitioned together after."

De'Lynn took a breath. "And you don't play Scrabble with *us*! We're RN's. LGBTQ-BIPOC. Alex has an MS, too. He still nurses ICU, but I went private during Covid. Never expected to be sent out here to *you* in Timbuk*tu*!" they rhymed. "Alex and I both caught it when it first hit the City, in February. Alex got us into antibody trials."

Alan heard the nurse's affectionate repetition of their husband's name. A chill shuddered the length of his own body.

De'Lynn then chattered about a small greenish bronze statue they placed on Alan's dresser.

It was about nine inches high, a narrow, haloed Mary sitting straight-backed. Her crossed legs five inches or so wide held in her lap a similarly-haloed slim line of child Jesus standing, His arms out, palms open. Her crossed hands held Him upright. Alan saw its circles, straight lines, and triangular base. Stylistically, it looked Rodin-influenced, but it shared iconography with Cycladic and even more primitive madonnas worldwide. It was a beautiful piece, likely quite valuable.

"I bring Her wherever I work now," De'Lynn said. "After a patient survived illness, the ancient white lady on the Upper East Side gave Her to me. She just patted my hand and made me accept Her. 'Blessed Mother said She wants to go with you.' I just love the way old ladies talk."

Though his head hurt and he'd started a fever, Alan recognized De'Lynn's intention to distract him. After those first efforts, they became quietly professional. The nurse ordered groceries, organized, and disinfected. Several days later, Alan couldn't smell the spicy Jamaican chicken soup De'Lynn prepared nor the VapoRub they spread on his chest. They had a good singing voice. At one point, Alan thought he'd gone deaf. He saw De'Lynn's mouth moving behind their mask, but could hear nothing. Maybe they were praying? For him? Alan's headache got much worse; his fever rose. He felt riddled with bee stings. The pillow felt hot as a heating pad. De'Lynn turned it over or replaced it frequently. Gave him alcohol rubs. Momentary blissful cool, but the alcohol burned to breathe. Alan wore a finger sleeve that monitored oxygen.

He had never been so sick in his life. Nausea, vomiting, diarrhea. Fever dreams. De'Lynn woke him with cool compresses. Pink eye was another symptom, gluing Alan's eyes shut.

De'Lynn bathed them open. Alan's lungs turned to glass that threatened to cut him to pieces. Each cough a stab wound. He imagined he looked black and blue, muscles bruised even without stiffening them against a cough. So little strength even to try.

He lapsed into dreams. A giant Queen Bee landed on his bare chest. She was hot. So heavy. Six hairy legs gripping his skin – he shuddered with disgust. Chills. He was too weak to defend against the huge head swaying above him. He was painting Her portrait. He couldn't smell the paint. It was thick, hard to apply with a brush. Needed a palette knife. He saw Her ghastly multieyes and two pulsing movable jaws – Her royal antennae buzzed the word *mandibles*. *Those black claws could swing in and out instead of up and down.*

In the dream, Alan's right hand held the brush. His wrong hand. His left hand was -- gone. The horror! He couldn't make a sound. *Howl! Howl! Howl!* Who died? Madness. He was too young for Lear. So much black paint, so many shades. David would know; David had written an article: *She had simple and compound eyes*. Five of them. On the front of Her head were three dots in a triangle. Her *ocelli* eyes. Her compound eyes were huge, one on either side of Her terrible head. They had tiny hairs to find the direction of the wind. Y*ou see, David, I did listen.*

De'Lynn bathed the delirious, beautiful white boy. They held the phone near Alan's ear when David called. They overheard the story of a junior boarding school infirmary stay when David was ten years old. His mother continued *"en vacances"* in France. Only his father drove up from the City to see him. Silently, De'Lynn altered one word in a Southern expression, "We were *rich*, but we didn't know we were poor."


By August's end, both presidential conventions were over. These were days of illness, slow recovery, and quarantine.

Alan asked, "Mom… text me?"

"Yes," De'Lynn assured him.

"David?"

"No, she phoned him. She just had a feeling. Mothers," De'Lynn touched the bronze statue on the dresser.

"Not Dad."

De'Lynn made a face behind their mask. "You should be Jewish, Alan. They say *dayenu*." Alan laughed, then coughed. The next breath still hurt and terrified.

De'Lynn talked about the second presidential nominating convention, Zoomed from Delaware.

"Better fireworks than Macy's July 4th! That's how they should do it from now on. And Kamala! If Joe doesn't win, I don't know. Right now, more than 170,000 have died from this thing."

Alan touched his chest. "Almos' in … number."

De'Lynn began singing *When the Saints Come Marching In.* They stopped and added, "Biden said, 'It didn't have to be this bad.'"

Trip to the kitchen, then De'Lynn returned to Alan's bedroom, carrying a lunch tray and rapping a different song, "*Everybody, every goddam body...*"

They had prepared a new soup. Alan couldn't smell it. He sipped fresh-squeezed orange juice.

"Sweet…sour."

"That's the name of your soup, too. Has tofu in it. Protein. Eat 'em all up. Your sense of smell will return," De'Lynn said.

"Or not," Alan said, energy and breath allowing only brief speech. He sighed.

De'Lynn said, "It takes a real breath to do that. A good sign."

"Song… *goddam?*"

De'Lynn took out their phone and scrolled *Thought Vs. Everybody*, handed it to Alan, who shook his head. "Can't –" deep breath for three more syllables, cough, "con-cen-trate."

So De'Lynn quietly performed the words to the rhythm. Alan fell asleep before De'Lynn hit the end-rhymed *imperative…narrative*.

They took away Alan's tray and closed the blinds.

Marwa brought up the mail that included a big envelope for John from *Beckett Anne Donnelly* in St. Bart's. He was in the small kitchen making their dinner. He looked up from a pot of simmering chili.

"Open it for me," he said. "Read, please."

A lined note was paperclipped to a bright yellow booklet, another of Beckett's handmade stories.

Marwa read, *"Dear Daddy, I had to change Dr. Anne Solver from the city coroner to an actual detective. And I made Anne into Andrew. I named the Fry leader Anne. Detective Andrew is still the only human who can see and talk to Small Fry."*

John tasted and stirred more tomato paste into the chili. The kitchen was fragrant with peppers, onions, and spice.

*"Anne finds a missing cell phone. 'Portables' on Barts. Pronounced Por- TAH-bulls. You'll never guess where!"*

"Uncanny," John said. "Where?"

"Inside a wall," Marwa said. She read, "'*We Small Fry can of course run up and down inside the walls like mice only we use ladders we make out of string and hair. Only we are of course much q-u-i-t-er,* crossed out,*"* Marwa said, then, *"q-u-i-e-t-er than mice – they have big feet! We know how to reconize and avoid traps,' Anne told Detective Solver."*

"*Recon,* no *g*? Her illustrations are improving," John said, glancing at the page Marwa displayed. Her mother was an art major."

But he was thinking about *inside the walls,* niches and dumbwaiters, and Marwa also glimpsed a remnant of dream, a candlestick telephone. The image was sheer – then gone.

"I hate when that happens," she said.

John thought she meant any reference to Kirby.

She saw his expression. "No, no," Marwa said, fingertips at her temples. "Memory. How it comes and goes. Among the hippocampus – 'seahorse' shaped – and the gyri."

John stirred the chili. The scent of bread warming also filled the kitchen.

"Turning and turning in the widening *gyre*/ The falcon cannot hear the falconer;/Things fall apart; the centre cannot hold," he recited Yeats.

"Gyrus. Plural *gyri*. With the sulci – sulcus – make the folds of the brain."

John turned off the flame. "'Where sits our *sulky*, sullen dame, /Gathering her brows like gathering storm, /Nursing her wrath to keep it warm.' Bobby Burns. There was wine in Luster's stomach. One bottle, but no glasses."

Marwa tapped John's forehead. "What's going on in there?"

"I wish I knew. I need the Small Fry."


Pidge and Pearl sat in their living room, both suffering Ginger's absence, which felt like a presence. It was September, and they were not returning to the campus they had left back in March. They were also not traveling to Crete or Akroteri. Labor Day had passed. So would the Jewish New Year and autumnal equinox. They had to get flu shots before the end of the month. An outing in doubled masks. Fear increased. Plague filled anticipation along with the election and winter.

"I hate the days *dwindling down*," Pidge remembered Kurt Weill's song.

"Like ours," Pearl agreed.

"I don't like making up Pasikennae's life."

"Imagining it," Pearl said.

"I like translating. That's hard enough."

It felt like an effort to both of them to speak aloud.

Pearl rose from a soft club chair. "We need coffee."

Pidge watched her walk into the kitchen. It was easier to speak when they were not in the room together.

"How odd," Pidge said.

"What is?" Pearl called.

Pidge could hear her actions in the kitchen and translate them into images in her mind.

"Us. Do you ever really wonder about Pasikennae? Getting inside her as she was inside HER? And failing."

"What a September song," Pearl said.

Pidge stood up from the couch and paced. Maybe they should have the room painted white. But couldn't have painters – anyone – in now. Wait till the Spring and open windows. Would the plague be better in the Spring? The walls were all bookcases, filled with years. The windows were darkening with twilight. More often these days, she thought of silently screaming. How it would it be finally to snap like an old dry branch in a gust of wind? She felt like she was always losing an invisible race. Talk about vaccine tormented. Pidge ambled into the kitchen. Pearl was pressing the coffee. It smelled rich. Pidge went to the fridge for milk and poured some into a little pitcher.

"Use the carton. No need for that," Pearl said.

"Want? Need?" Pidge mused. "Another song? Rolling Stones?"

"Wasn't that *Satisfaction*, 'I can't get no?'"

"Not what you want, but what you need. Did Pasikennae ever get either, or expect to? I doubt it." Pidge heard the song in her head and swayed. "We danced. I danced. Did you?" Pidge asked.

Pearl handed Pidge a mug of coffee. Pidge breathed in its rising steam.

Pearl watched her. "Pasikennae flew through the horns of a bull. She trekked to Lake

Superior. *Kitchi-Gummi.* Now she was a dancer!"

Ceremonially, Pearl used the pitcher to pour milk into both their mugs.

Pidge sipped, then walked back to the living room and sat at the round table where they worked on their book. "All her years north of Scotland. Living to our old age? Did it feel like the Afterlife, for her? Not heaven, a kind of hell." She set down the coffee mug and opened her laptop.

Pearl followed but went instead to a window. She looked out at a sycamore now creating a shadow cast by a streetlight.

"Pasikennae lived in HER bubble. As we live in what we call universe, space. Spacetime? I doubt all our projections. I doubt she separated creation from Creator. Does a finger question the Hand?"

Pearl held the coffee mug in her right hand and wiggled her left fingers.

Pidge shrugged. "Maybe Pasikennae identified her loss of her child, *Many Smiles,* Sueaysua, not as punishment but with some divine grief expressed in the volcanic explosion of HER island."

"What?"

Pidge looked around. "Maybe that's why I don't like projecting. This plague. My Nina. Your Esa. They haven't been mine nor yours, if ever, for a long time. The grandchildren don't know us. Pasikennae's bubble also burst."

Pearl hmm'd. "Drink some coffee."

Pidge sipped.

Pearl said, "Who – what -- are any of us, to contain the grief of the Cosmos? What are human options?"

"Hamlet's *interim?*"

Pearl sat down at the table and gently toasted Pidge's mug with her own.

Tropical storms and hurricanes came earlier and more often than ever before. This unprecedented activity was fueled by an ocean-cooling La Nina that had developed over the summer months. The greatest number of storms – ten -- occurred in September. John and Beckett kept track of their names – and tracks. Maximum winds for *Nana* on September first (John thought of the Auden poem) were exceeded by *Teddy* two weeks later at 120 mph.

Beckett texted, "*Yu shuda seen the waves in the infinity pool! We hid in the safe space under my room!*"

The day after a rally in campaign battleground Ohio, the autumn equinox poised the momentary "*climacteric*," Pearl noted. "Greek *klimaktēr,* literally, *rung of a ladder.*"

"Whether we *climb* or fall remains to be seen," Pidge agreed.

That Monday evening, the President that Pidge called *Twitler* had declared that "the virus affects virtually nobody. It's amazing." On Tuesday, America reached the grim milestone of 200,000 COVID-19 deaths. For many months, the U.S. had had the highest number of infections and deaths in the world, with more than 6.8 million confirmed cases. By the end of September, with more than two months left in hurricane season, the Atlantic had already spit out twenty-three named storms — roughly double its long-term average for an entire season. For only the second time in its history, the National Hurricane Center exhausted its regular list of names. Pidge and Pearl noticed when it began using the Greek alphabet.

Alan was recovering. De'Lynn, dispatched to the art store for supplies, learned about the Covid deaths of Brian's parents and Abigail's father. Her mother was still hospitalized. Alan took photos of De'Lynn's Madonna statue. He sketched it repeatedly until De'Lynn insisted he sit outside in the sun.

On a Friday in September, David met Drew for lunch. Part of the adapted urban landscape, the Ale House offered a makeshift outdoor space on Amsterdam Avenue. The Open Restaurants program was supposed to end before Hallowe'en, but the Mayor said it would become yearround and permanent for eighty-seven streets around the City with plans for expansion. Before the plague, pedestrian and traffic noise and exhaust would have kept the entitled men from eating outdoors on benches at picnic tables. They much preferred the view looking through paned, wallheight windows from a table for two inside the restaurant with its Old Manhattan tin ceilings, stained glass top lights, shining wooden bar, and shelves of colorful liquor bottles.

"Though New Amsterdam never looked like this," Drew said.

Both wearing masks, they sat at a diagonal distance across a whitewashed table.

"At least now it's obvious we're a city of bandits."

"David, I can't tell if you're smiling or not. You notice how some people's eyes smile? Yours don't."

A masked server brought their drinks and took their orders. David: tuna steak burger with fries; Drew: grilled vegetables and goat cheese wrap with onion rings.

The server left with the menus.

Drew said, "I'm allowed nothing fried at home."

"Onion rings?"

"Is food cheating?  I can't do any more marriages, David. Four and done."

David removed his mask and took a long swallow of strong gin and tonic. The server knew them as big tippers.

"Mannahatta. New Amsterdam. New York," he said. "I wonder what it will be renamed. Maybe a meteor will hit us like the Yucatan Peninsula." David waved his arm in a wide gesture, offering, "Chicxulub crater. Here, underwater, New Atlantis?"

Drew looked up at the cloudless blue sky over the wide avenue.

"I feel enough like a dinosaur most of the time as it is. What am I going to do about Vera?"

He plucked the olive from the skewer in his Bloody Mary, then lifted the right loop of his mask and let it hang off his left ear. Using the celery stalk as a swizzle stick, he ate the olive, then swigged his drink.

"Are you going to leave it like that?" David reached but was too far away to grasp Drew's dangling mask.

David mentally kicked himself under the table. Would Drew mistake his comment, mask for wife, pursue the question David wanted to avoid? Let the food arrive! Not that he was hungry although the drink helped. Of course he knew about Vera. About Drew's June demand for abortion followed by miscarriage. As in most long relationships, more was unsaid than said. He knew Drew's father was Miles Burgos, scion of not only a Jewish family in New York, but also long before as one of the seventeenth century founders of the Touro Synagogue in Newport, Rhode Island. In his practiced expression, "The family that flees together, stays together," Drew had described his family's escape from Europe. Once in the Americas, Drew always apologized, they were likely part of the Triangle Trade.

The food arrived.

While throughout childhood David had always been sent away to camp in New Hampshire, Drew had summered in Newport. Drew was five years older than David. Born into different buildings on Park Avenue, they'd been at early elementary school at Calhoun in New York, college at Eliot House/Harvard, but crossed paths only between, at Hotchkiss. When David entered in fifth grade. Drew was in ninth. At 'the Kiss,' David had been teased for being gay, but not bullied because an understanding existed at prep school: seriously-moneyed Jewish students were "future assets, not assholes. At least Burgos and Rochester don't look *y'know*."

Drew removed his offending mask and made a face. "Okay now?"

An M11 bus gassed by. David waved exhaust away with a crisp potato baton.

Drew looked up, thinking David was gesturing at someone on the sidewalk. "Who?"

David looked at the french fry and thought of Drew's older sister.

"How's Andrea?"

Drew laughed. "She's a celibate, vegan Catholic intending to vote for Dump for a second time. She named her dog *Rove*, which makes people ask *Rover?* So she gets to flap her mouth and right wing characteristically *No*. She'd like to weaponize all the feral cats on the tiny Maine island. I do not exaggerate. She's the ombudsman."

"So you're close."

David knew the Maine house came from Drew's maternal side. His parents had left New York for the more isolated northern island instead of the paternal Rhode Island property. For her obsession with social rules, Drew called his mother 'Super-Couth Ruth' – her surname, *Tripp*, had been translated from the early German-Jewish immigration of her *Fahrt* family, an unceasing source of mirth at prep school.

"Andrea and Andrew," Drew considered sibling names. "No one can blame my parents for being imaginative. Super-Couth baked her *To Die For* brownies all summer. An unfortunate gaffe, given the plague. Chocolate and peanut butter chips, marzipan Royal icing. A direct cause of Type 1 diabetes. Which fortunately does not run in the family."

"Oven on all summer?"

"Air conditioning. She has a miner's carbon footprint."

"How are your kids?" David asked.

"Ah, Wife #1, the real estate merger. *Sara* retaliated by calling me *And*rew and the children by their whole names, while I passive-aggressed with nicknames. I never remember whether she was a 2nd or 3rd cousin how-removed from Super-Couth's side. *Madeleine*-Maddy is twenty now,

Barnard. *Edward*-Eddy is seventeen, another Kisser, hoping to be a legacy, if Harvard still does

that. As *if* they don't. I pay tuition, and the nicknames Zoom. They're both Sara's with my

surname. 'Remote' is the word of my undoing," Drew shrugged.

David waited.

Drew looked up at the blue sky. "It was like this, a perfect September day. I was scheduled to

show a downtown property on 9/11. Appointment changed at the last minute to 72nd Street."

"You were at The Edgewater down the block from Sotheby's that morning."

"Right across the street from George Plimpton's old *Paris Review* red door in a gray

townhouse. I was Alan's age, early thirties. Fabulous building, wraparound terrace on the

nineteenth floor. Looked east and south. An early appointment -- the husband was a surgeon. We

were all on the terrace looking at the Towers when the first one fell. Remember the sirens? Then

the silence. No planes overhead for how many days? And the horrifying stench in the air? I was

sure they wouldn't buy, but they did. Thus endeth my mortgages to religion and real estate begun

at a Plaza spectacle. My father used to say, 'Bigger the wedding, shorter the marriage." Then

came my two California blonds, one with dogs, the other, cats."

David remembered. Years after 9/11, he'd been surprised to cross Drew's path again at a

party in LA. Drew was an agent for writers on the TV series co-starring Alan. David was a

deputy editor in LA for the *New York Times*. Drew introduced them. David had no intention of

pursuing the young actor delighting guests like a parrot by instantly imitating them, but after the

party, Alan had sent David a flattering pen and ink portrait. Which was now framed, discreet on

his office wall downtown.

"Your family lost some buildings on 9/11," Drew rambled on. "But all rebuilt bigger, air rights! And then Highline adjacent. A coup. Still not selling that heart of the Cast-Iron Historic District pre-war filled with art lofts? Neoclassical 1903 John W. Stevens? Eleven-foot barrel-vaulted ceilings, keyed elevator access? Floor-to-ceiling windows flooded with natural light? It would sell itself."

David woke from his reverie. He blurted, "You saw George Plimpton's ghost."

Drew switched gears fast. "Or whoever Plimpton was pretending to be at the time. I think I did see a ghost at the Harmony Club. Probably one of our cousins or aunts and uncles who intermarried over the centuries. Maddy the English major could join me coddling authors. Eddy's heir apparent to the real estate realm. I'm fifty-one, David. I don't want pets or kids. I can't lose Vera. Look at me. I can't wife-hunt anymore."

David looked at his longtime associate. A friend? The weird diagonal distance between them at the picnic table had angled their conversation as well, making it more intimate than any previous face to face.

Their server had taken away dishes and brought coffee, Drew's iced, David's hot.

"I see before me a dapper, urban mover and shaker coddling this writer," David said, pouring cream into his cup. "I'm no one to give advice."

"Bull. Don't tell your investors… How's Alan?"

"Recovering."

"Jesus. David. You let me go on and on. I am a selfish SOB."

"Aren't we all."

"He coming back – when -- from – the Hamptons?"

"North Fork. Remains to be seen. He already had the studio I gave him in Soho 'Cast-Iron *Historic* District," David shrugged.

"Is the house out east finished?"

"I hope that's all that is."

The bill was presented. Drew picked it up.

"I'm coddling," he said. "We talked about your next book, right?"

For the first time over lunch, David laughed.

## Chapter 18  October

### *from Blue Monkeys by Shapiro & Feria*
### *The White-winged Bird*

*See HER pour! Honeyed drink, divine song!*
*See HER pour! Honeyed drink, divine song!*
*Blue owl has white wings wide as clouds.*
*Wings' beat, the sound. We are afraid. We are amazed.*
*How sweet the drink.*
*How strong the song.*
*Round eyes see through night's black curtain.*
*Round eyes see through night's black curtain.*
*Wings fly between the bull's wide horns.*
*Wings slow the bull's sharp hooves.*
*Wings' beat, the sound. We are afraid. We are amazed.*
*How sweet the drink.*
*How strong the song.*
*HER song stops black angry bull.*
*HER son is brave. He raises his arm.*
*HER white wings lift him into the sky.*
*Wings' beat, the sound. We are afraid. We are amazed.*
*How sweet the drink.*
*How strong the song.*

*As an ocean-crossing captain, Pasikennae knew as much about the stars as anyone except perhaps for the priestly proto-astronomers of her era. But she likely perceived and named the stars differently from our modern day. On this one of the copper-sleeved tablets, she appeared to relate the cold weather-signaling constellations of Orion and Taurus to a white-winged blue bird (also seen in a Cretan fresco) which Pasikennae also conflated with a white owl and/or Hen Harriers, white-winged birds familiar at Orkney cemetery mound hills.*

*Whether Pasikennae was retelling a Minoan story or adapting it for her Orkney listeners – children? – wasn't clear. But its outlines were. The tablet, characterized by repetitions, described an unnamed Divinity or winged messenger who appeared, saving a youth who was being attacked by a bull. The bird flew through the horns of the giant bull and carried the son into the night sky, placing the bull at a permanently safe distance. Archeologists have found apparently-related ritual vessels shaped like a bird-headed and/or breasted woman. Liquid could be poured out of its beaked mouth or from dual nipple-like spouts. Out of the bird's mouth/breasts pour both song and as a spout, libation.*

There was no scent of coffee brewing. Morning twilight before the sun's rising found Pidge already at her laptop.

Pearl entered the living room and murmured, "*Tsaangu beaichehku.*"

Pidge looked up. "*Bonjour* to you, too."

"Frowning?"

"Are you happy with *amazed*? Kept me up all night."

"*Awed* was just awful. Can't win that wrestling match with the angel. I've got the new name and dislocated hip to prove it. *Call me Israel.*"

"That's *Ishmael*, Moby. Go ahead and appropriate the Old Testament, but it's too early for Melville. I had nightmares all night about making something from nothing."

"Sounds divine to me. I'll make coffee."

Pearl turned toward the kitchen.

"No, really," Pidge said, closing the laptop. She stood up and paced to the window. Pearl exhaled through pursed lips. "Again? This? The Translator's Lament? In your nightmare what did something from nothing look like?"

Pidge sighed. "Misshapen clay pots flying off a wheel. Clay everywhere, clay drying, my skin cracking. Bleeding."

"You and your dreams!"

"A container shapes what's in it. Thoughts and feelings become vibrations of air. *All* language *is* translation. We compound distortion. 'Awed' *was* just awful."

"But now, look, sunrise. Coffee."


It had been a year and almost a month since Elena Luster's move into the building, then her murder. There would be no Hallowe'en trick-or-treating parties this year. What created more dread, pandemic or impending election?

Pidge said, "We're counting the days till we -- and democracy -- live or die."

Declining summer Covid numbers were rising again. The unmasked, infected President was rushed into Walter Reed hospital on October's first Friday. Many called it *karma*, but the very medical science he'd mocked saved his life. By Sunday night, an exhausted doctor witnessed two Secret Service agents accompanying the Presidential SUV as he rode waving to his cheering supporters who had gathered outside the DC hospital.

"Every single person in the vehicle during that completely unnecessary *Cheeto Benito* 'driveby' just now has to be quarantined for fourteen days. They might get sick. They may die. For political theater."

Family forbidden from his bedside, Vera Mifeng's father did die in a Queens County hospital. In uptown Manhattan's Mount Sinai, Dr. Susanna Duckett reported more deaths of medical personnel. One was a suicide. The air was filled with grief and fear, lies and insults. Voting polls made promises that had broken hearts before. Dining, where permitted, was chilly outdoors even in the heated bubble pods, trellised sheds, and LED-lighted yurts that looked like the Jewish harvest holiday was being celebrated citywide in boughed-covered *sukkahs*. Door fronts were boarded up in graffitied plywood. Theaters remained closed. Masks covered unsmiling faces.

The streets were empty, the mood grim. Day to day, small routines tried to reassure, but the autumnal equinox meant increasing darkness.

David had good intentions when he told the twins (and Micheline on a sleepover) about the imminent Orionid meteor shower. It was the lead-in he was writing to a *Times* column about political omens. But he saw he'd paved more of the way to hell when the four-year-olds understood that the meteors would streak across the night sky well after their bedtime and be obscured by City light if not by predicted fog.

Arno, Dylan, and Micheline wanted to stay up (this time) because they "knew *everything* about Orion from the professors' *Passykennay* stone."

Arno agreed with his twin. "Orion started their calendar with the equinox."

Dylan knuckled a table with one hand, then the other. "See, equal knocks."

Micheline competed, "They had a special *room*. He's carved on a wall. His stars *made* the double axe."

Arno said, "Like two letter C's –"

"Facing *away* from each other," Dylan interrupted, shaping his hands down and backwards.

Micheline did the same, adding, "*Mena* was the Moon's name!"

"It looks like the Moon, *waxing,*" Arno's right palm, bending, "and *waning,*" left palm.

David tried to distract them. "What causes fog, anyway?"

Mercedes assisted, "*Como se dice* 'fog'? *La niebla.*"

Micheline pounced on the word, "Nibble? That's hilarious. *Como se dice* 'hilarious?'"

"Fog's said to walk on cat feet," David said, demonstrating with paw-hands in the air.

David described to Alan later, "That was all the trio needed to fall to the floor and 'fog and nibble' their way back to the family room, looking more like hamsters than cats."

Alan had awakened from a nap and was sitting up in their bed, a bamboo lap-desk angled over his legs as he worked on a drawing. His concession to David's hyper-solicitude was wearing pajamas, but he wasn't under the covers.

"I'm not cold," he said defensively. "*Hilarante?*"

"*Si, carino.*"

David approached and saw Alan's latest sketch. "That's coming along," he praised.

Alan smiled, which brightened the room for David. "Content free statements. Gotta love 'em."

He saw David glance at the *HITTITE QUEEN* script removed from its delivery envelope on the bedspread.

"Back to work next month? So soon?" David said.

"They're more worried about production safety than you are. The writers are keeping us so socially-distanced, maybe they'll write a plague into Queen Pudu's reign, too. Fans won't be happy with the absence of the soft porn, but lust translated into anxious pity works well. Also, our star isn't happy sharing the royal bed -- spotlight -- with me anymore."

"Triangles inevitably have sharp points," David said.

The actor's face revealed neither thought of Brian and Abby nor acknowledgment of his husband's geometry.

"It's what Diva demanded. I'll be out of sight, out of mind. From the Hittite palace, I'll be sent as an envoy to Egypt. And that will become a good out for me for filming on Crete a year from now. This season, I'll survive episodes being poisoned by an Assyrian spy. Very *General Hospital* soap opera without the IV and nasal cannula. I can do mortal illness; it's not a stretch. De'Lynn should be written into it. Helluva nurse. And 'they' even look Nubian."

David listened as he located something on his phone. He showed Alan the small screen.

"Your powerful Queen – a *Tawananna* -- Puduhepa signed the first known international peace treaty, sixteen years after the Battle of Kadesh, 1274 BCE. Here's her seal," https://women-make-history.jimdofree.com/2013/06/02/puduhepa-great-queen-of-the-hittites/

He scrolled to another image. "Here it is with the glyphs explained." https://travelatelier.com/blog/queen-puduhepa-great-king-hattusili/

Alan laughed.

"Lungs still hurt?"

Alan had pressed his hand against his heart.

"Not much, *carino*. I just missed your -- information."

David hesitated, then asked, "You back for good?"

"Not for ill."

"For Sale out East?"

"Compromise… *Tawananna*? Vacations. Summer place. Escape plagues. Not as far from the City as the celebs who fled to Rhode Island."

"Drew's 'rents flew to Maine." David suppressed relief. "And he's found you -- a new gallery rep, Island and City. If you --."

Unsurprised by David's understanding, Alan returned to sketching the bronze statue.

"I do," he said.

The virus had reached Egypt back on Valentine's Day. In Cairo, the fatality rate was nearly six percent. In Alexandria, Marwa's mother stayed indoors with Sharif's children. There, in March, people stayed away from mosques to pray from their balconies; others who had taken to the streets to chant prayers to alert people (but instead spread the plague) were now forbidden. Marwa's fear for her family in Egypt was superseded early one October morning before she could leave for the lab.

Hildegarde Wentworth, her stepmother, phoned. Hilly had forced Marwa's father into a cab from their Battery Park City apartment. They were "on 33$^{rd}$ and 1$^{st}$, at the NYU Langone-Tisch Hospital."

"Is he on a ventilator?"

"No, Anam's in a huge room with three other men and two nurses. He's receiving antibodies. He'll be here for a few more hours. They see only eight people a day."

"Monoclonal antibodies. How did you get him in?"

Marwa could almost hear Hilly shrug. "If you can't pluck strings from Juilliard – then where?" Her cough was muffled by a mask.

"How are you?"

"Positive. Symptomatic. Fever. *Anosmia.* Don't offer."

Marwa was equally assertive. "I know the perfect private nurse. He – goes by 'they' – just brought their patient home."

"In a box?"

"Alan Tapley *lives* three floors above me. David Rochester had the nurse for his husband."

"The actor? The *Times* David Rochester? Okay," Hilly said.

Marwa texted her lab assistant, then David Rochester. By the time John had awakened, showered, and dressed for work, he was surprised to find Marwa still home. She held up one palm to keep him quiet while her other hand held her phone to her ear.

He waited. Watching Marwa raised the thought of the lost Luster phone and – why? – then he remembered the three little kids in the lobby clustered around their nanny, Mercedes, in the window seat. The twin boy who resembled the *Times* journalist had bounded toward John, snatching an obviously new book they'd just opened (its torn delivery envelope on the floor by the young Hispanic woman's feet) to show him. It was a Hallowe'en paperback, its pages designed like an advent calendar.

Holding the book open, showing and telling, the child riddled, *"Why do ghosts like to ride elevators?"*

"You got me," John said, trying to remember the kid's name.

"I'm Arno! Because *it lifts their spirits!*" He put the book in John's hand.

John had appropriately chuckled and looked at the tiny, numbered windows the kids had already opened. He touched one closed, then opened, then returned the book to the boy who ran back to impatient demands.

The opening/closing paper *niches* - the word appeared and niggled at John's mind. Just the month before, hadn't Beckett's Small Fry and mice run inside walls around dumbwaiters and telephone *niches* sealed over in building renovations? Hadn't Azul echoed the building manager's reports of increased noise complaints against Phil Cage? Taking down the wall between the two apartments had triggered a new search warrant. John felt like he'd been smacked on the back of his head.

Marwa's phone call had ended. She had to repeat his name.

"What?"

"My father's in the hospital getting antivirals. Outpatient. Hilly's also sick. Not as bad. I got Alan's nurse for their return to the Battery Park apartment. Good thing they have three bedrooms."

John refocused. "Two weeks ago Friday, they pumped those elite meds into Dump. Sunday night, he was limo'd around Walter Reed to be hailed for surviving what he called a *hoax*? The illogical liar --" John stopped. Abruptly, "Remember the old-fashioned telephone you dreamed about? Stuck in those wall niches?"

"What? Candlesticks? Telephone *nooks*, they called them."

John kissed Marwa's cheek. "You okay?"

"*Inshallah*," popped out of her mouth. "Go," she insisted.

She knew what a breakthrough looked like. After the apartment door closed behind John, Marwa sat down. She reviewed: (1) Hilly's strained voice; (2) arrangements for De'Lynn done; (3) she couldn't go near *Baba* and Hilly.

It used to rankle Marwa that her stepmother's favorite (expropriated) expression was *Inshallah*. Hildegarde Hathaway Wentworth. Vassar Yale Juilliard. Triangles! Hilly had never been Marwa's atheist father's instructor. Five years earlier she had been one of the judges for his first winning composition. Anam Al-Halimi's surprise triumph had begun a new career for the retired banker. Now, Marwa knew, her father hadn't yet completed *Opus Inshallah*, commissioned for a Lincoln Center debut – whenever the Juilliard orchestra would be allowed to return.

In her sixties, Hilly was a decade younger than Marwa's father. She was old New York railroad money, Wentworth mansions on Madison Avenue evolved into a modern National Historic Register hotel, finances recovered after a Stock Market scandal. Hilly had never married before. Possessing the serenity of sure status, she had no need of vanity. Her blond hair was turning gray. Her face looked like a thumb. Marwa looked at her own thumbs and imagined them

texting. Now she was calm, ready to go to the lab. *Inshallah.*

## *Chapter 19 November*

James was already in his lab at Rockefeller, relieved to return to the pre-Covid genome consortium study. Susanna was uptown at the hospital as well, back on neurosurgery rounds although a post-holiday rise in infection was predicted and feared. Micheline was with the twins and Mercedes, but plans for kindergarten next year had to be made. Plans to move. Susanna was due the first week in May. James had promised Micheline he would provide "evidence" of her presence in his lab, so he took a photo to prove her new creatively-spelled poem was taped to the cabinet door above his screens.

> *I am for. I want mor. Let me por on the flor.*
> *Do not glare. Do not stare. I will rore at a bare on a chare.*
> *I can fly if I try. I don't cry. So, goodby!*

There were five Mondays in November that year, dominated by its first Tuesday, Election Day. James fumed over the Incumbent's claim that he had done more for Black Americans than anybody with the "possible exception" of Abraham Lincoln. Voter turnout was higher than any election in the past century. By noontime, even Fox News had called Pennsylvania for Biden. It was an unusually warm sunny day. All around Manhattan, people were yelling joyfully out of open windows, honking car and truck horns. On the sidewalks, happiness momentarily overwhelmed social distancing for the masked citizenry.

Some good news also appeared re the plague: a nasal spray had been developed that blocked the virus in ferrets. James heard about the study funded by the NIH and Columbia University Medical Center. He quickly texted former neighbor MD's, Dayita and Esau; though neither was part of the research, they reported the celebration at their ex-urban Columbia satellite hospital. Patent applications and human testing awaited in the future.

Happy to hear about a sibling expected for Micheline, the couple answered James's questions about moving to their previous neighborhood in Manhattan's north end. Characteristically, Dayita and Esau had thoroughly researched Inwood schools for baby Sandra even though it had been as premature as unnecessary since their move well out of the City. Esau sent updated links. There was a kindergarten lottery to enter starting December 10th, deadline January 22nd. Wouldn't hear till April. More likely was the public school where kids wore white polo shirts and gray pants.

Esau texted, "Kindergarten applications there also open Dec. 10th, deadline January 19th. Make sure you're in district parameters."

Susanna took over what she called the *Application Watch & House Hunt*. James, in charge of *Mortgage & Movers*, heard the italics. Then Dayita contacted Susanna; settled in the Cold Spring house, her parents were ready to sell the condo. To James and Susanna! The closing/move-in dates could beat those deadlines.


Detective Donnelly's cold case was warming up. Probable cause, warrant in hand, he'd joined a forensic team at the Luster/adjoining apartment. They stopped the demolition and examined the exposed wall. Cage didn't have to be present. But John was. A specialist called his name, and with a gloved hand outlined an arched niche, reached in and pulled out, not Jack Horner's plum, but Elena Luster's cell phone! It revealed a person of renewed interest.

Beckett texted him a riddle that couldn't have been more apt:

*Where is happiness made?*

*Where?*

*In a satisFACTORY!*

Two weeks later, Pidge and Pearl tried to see the Leonid meteor shower. They had taken a

hopeful walk in Riverside Park to a lighted, circular ornamental temple whose plaque "also

seemed to celebrate the election," Pidge told Alan Tapley, "declaring it had been "ERECTED

BY THE CITY OF NEW YORK TO COMMEMORATE THE VALOR OF THE SOLDIERS

AND SAILORS WHO IN THE CIVIL WAR FOUGHT *IN DEFENSE OF THE UNION*," she

emphasized.  "New Jersey glittered across the Hudson River, but we managed to see only one

flash of a meteor, if that."

Azul had held the door for Pidge and Alan, all masked against Covid, wearing coats and

gloves in the now November cold, The duo waited in the lobby for the elevator to come down

empty. It was dark again, early.

Alan was quiet.

"Return to Standard Time, my eye," Pidge said, "no concession speech, plus expected holiday

*superspreader events*."

Smiling, Alan reminded, "A *neologism*?"

She had recently taught him the word. She blushed, glad the physical mask covered her

reddened cheeks. She wrestled a professional one back in place.

Pidge praised, "You're a quick study."

"I have to be, back at work. Scripts to memorize!" Alan shrugged the backpack over his

shoulder.

"Trip out to Queens? How are you feeling?"

"They send a car. Window-separated from driver. I'm in an antibodies' trial. May be of some

use. My RN is now caring for Marwa's father. Her stepmother's in the hospital."

"I thought she was better."

"She got worse."

"How's the new house out on the Island?" Pidge asked.

"East End realtors so bombarded Builder with offers from plague-fleeing urbanites that he convinced me to rent/lease. Through mid-May, I think. David handled it."

"I wash my hands as soon as I get home," Pidge said.

"I carry hand sanitizer," another shrug of his backpack.

"Who doesn't?"

Pidge retrieved a small gel container from her coat pocket, as if to join in a toast.

Then the elevator door opened. They stood in distant corners. Alan pressed the button. They remained silent for nine floors.

Pearl was already home, preparing dinner.

"Alan seems different now," Pidge said.

"He's alive."

"Gaunt but heavier somehow."

Pearl sliced cucumbers. Onions were sauteing. She spoke slowly.

"I always thought he was understandably spoiled. But Beauty – what's the saying, *When the gods wish to punish us, they answer our prayers*? Now, after a tryst with Death ..."

"Anyway..." Pidge said, turning.

"...he still makes you blush."


John Donnelly recognized the familiar ringtone music on his phone. Bobby Darin was singing *Mack the Knife.* Ackerman had been wrong; a DD5 update showed that Elena Luster and Ellen Grenley had been legally married. Separated, not divorced. Luster's heir. A Duane Reade pharmacist. Maybe Malcolm Ackerman hadn't been invited to their wedding? Much wasn't entirely kosher about Mr. Ackerman, John thought. He listened to the emotional message.

"So, Detective, *November?* We un-celebrated an un-happy deathday a month ago already. *Any* update on my best friend's *murder?* Thanksgiving upon us, not feeling so thankful. Call me or else -- I may just show up -- masked!" He ended the recording with a comedian's vocal drum, "Buh dum *dum.*"

Consistent with John's assessment of Ackerman, his bluster didn't translate into action. But along with increasing evidence re Ellen Grenley, the investigation had identified who *was* behind Philip Cage's fingerprints at the crime scene. His Oklahoma alibi remained solid. What Luster's packed phone revealed was how deeply a crime syndicate was involved in the OPLA office. The mob secreted Cage's fingerprints into Luster's bloodied apartment to blackmail him into moving in to find and destroy her damning phone. Cage's failure turned into a double plus for the DA. In protective custody and deal-making, if Cage backed up the evidence on Luster's phone? Maybe more. If and maybe. Questions for the DA's office, not the detective.

Who was Ellen Grenley? Tall and muscular, Black, thirty-five, separated, but still wore a wedding band. Though Ackerman had repeatedly phoned or texted over the previous months, John had heard nothing from the grieving widow. Because she already had the answers? Grenley had agreed to appear for an interview (with lawyer) on the second floor at the back of the precinct. Equally imposing, they both wore dark suits.

Police radios, phones, and monitors filled the space with noise. November light came weakly through the windows but enough to cast shadows as the duo walked through the squad room of old, gray, shared metal desks characterizing their owners by order or disorder, past the Captain's closed-in office and holding cell to the relatively quieter back area where the detective awaited them in an interview room.

Grenley said, "Laney taught me – never speak without counsel."

John was relaxed. He began the digital recording. They went through the usual dance. The conversation was more face than fact for Donnelly. This long year later, Ellen Grenley was not in shock. Comparison and contrast created a *bas-relief* of the suspect. Award of life insurance awaited the investigation's outcome.

"I don't need the money," Grenley said.

The year earlier, before masks, she had appeared stiff and still. Grieving. John remembered her eyes. At the time, marital status had been unclear. She called Luster *Laney.* An office manager had identified the mangled body.

Now, Ellen Grenley was calm. *Blunted affect.* Pharmacist/self-medicated, now? Then? Neither eager to help, nor anxious about progress in the case. Not even curious to be questioned? John's mind's eye saw a recent report of a black hole in space. Whatever fell in wasn't coming out. Now when he looked at the suspect, he saw the photo of 'Hawking's soft hair' – the part of the black hole story proving that no information was ever really lost. Might be irretrievable, but left its impressions in the halo of *event horizon.*

"You visited Ms. Luster at least twice in October. Phone records show you phoned Ms. Luster repeatedly in the days before," the detective said. "Some long conversations."

Ellen Grenley agreed. "Laney had moved out. There was a lot to discuss. I liked to listen to her."

John thought of Lear's Cordelia. *Her voice was ever soft, /Gentle, and low, an excellent thing in woman.* He said, "She had no safety deposit box?"

"An octopus, Laney said, can get in anywhere. Tentacles everywhere."

"Did she tell you about a second phone hidden in the wall?"

"Yes."

"Why didn't you tell us?"

"You didn't ask."

But the detective knew he had.

After, John sat thinking about the uncoupling couple. His probes had been evaded, but soon it might not remain a matter of opinion whose idea the breakup was. Motive. Means also required further forensic review. Knowledge and access to an undetectable poison/drug plus more subtle means than bludgeoning -- suited the pharmacist's profile. Pre-meditated passion wasn't necessarily an oxymoron. He tried not to think of Kirby.


What a change from the holiday party a year earlier. Only seven ninth-floor neighbors sat at the Tapley-Rochester Thanksgiving table. Her stepmother Hilly was isolated on a ventilator in the hospital. Sixth-floor Marwa was Zooming-calling with her father and De'Lynn downtown. John was cyber-celebrating in St. Bart's with Beckett and his parents on nearby Long Island. Pidge and Pearl hardly left their apartment.

Mercedes had Skyped LA, as had Susanna via the boosted WiFi in her mother's Little Rock trailer park. Now the nanny sat at one end of the table with the twins to her right, flanked by David; Alan sat beside him at the table's other end. On the facing side, Micheline sat between her parents. Mercedes sat at the end closest to the kitchen, and she insisted on serving though James and Susanna were up and down nearly as much. It was pot luck, not Norman Rockwell turkey, trimmings, and pumpkin pie.

James had brought iron-pan baked black-eyed peas and sweet potatoes along with the kids' favorite, "slap-yo-mama-mac-n-cheese." Susanna contributed Arkansas spaghetti-with-turkey ragu. Mercedes made oven-fried turkey *taquitos*, and Alan's green beans were heaped with bacon and stewed onions.

He drawled, "We just call 'em 'green beans' and it ain't Thanksgiving without'in sweet tea and pecan pie," he pronounced "pah."

"Which I had delivered from Wolfgang's," David amended.

There was no talk of the election. Susanna frowned when Alan asked about shortages of PPE at the hospital.

"What's PPE?" Micheline asked.

As the adults reacted, Dylan ceased mixing spaghetti and mac-n-cheese together. Arno stopped lining up picked-out sweet potato cubes on his plate. They waited.

"Personal protective equipment," Susanna answered.

James intervened, not only taller but also talking over everyone's heads. "The phase III vaccine trials are moving fast. The positive cases in the control groups given placebos rose so swiftly, it's easier to see the vaccines' success. Pfizer has ninety-five percent and Moderna's not far behind."

"Light at the end of the tunnel?" – David.

"Helluva tunnel…" – Alan.

"Holland Tunnel doesn't go to Holland. New *Jersey*," – Dylan.

Arno punched his twin.

Mercedes moved their sweet tea glasses out of danger.

"I wish the profs were here," Micheline concluded.

***Chapter 20 December***

"Christmas won't be Christmas without any *people*," Pidge altered Jo March's opening

sentence in LITTLE WOMEN. She was wrapping a gift as she sat on the couch, not "lying on

the rug." The couch was weathered brown corduroy, the carpet even older Persian.

Also wrapping a package, Pearl sat across the room at the round table now cleared of laptops.

"When I was given the Alcott book in school, it was science fiction to me," Pearl mused.

Pidge looked up. "You never said."

Pearl shrugged. "I was Pearl *Pinhavayqia* then. Means 'honeybee'. They tried sending my

mother away to missionary school. Even less successful with my Kuchun-deka, <u>Buffalo</u> Eaters,

Wind River stinging Pinhavayqia father," she hmphed. "By the 50's – 60's, we were in 'public'

schools. You can imagine how *Silas Marner* fared in my teenage hands. I never considered

school a place to learn, which was truly liberating. I put whatever book I wanted to read *inside*

old Silas. I'd been spreading, breaking book spines for alternate inserts since elementary school.

I can't remember what I hid my turtle book inside of, but the number thirteen was *ours*. My

birthday. My grandmother taught me that every turtle shell has thirteen segments for the moons

of the year. The smaller segments along the lower edge of every shell? – twenty-eight for each of

the twenty-eight days between the new moons. Oh, I remember the *Nimerigar*, aka *Nunumbi*."

Pidge had stopped gift-wrapping. "Who or what ---?"

"Little people. Ours were homicidal, not helpers.  I went from Shoshone legends to – how on

earth did a book about French bull-jumping find me in Wyoming?"

"*La course Landaise?*"

"Led me to French, to Latin, to Greek, Sacajawea to Pasikennae. And acrobats. Gymnastics

… declension, yoga."

"You miss yoga class a lot."

"I'm so stiff, if I sneeze, I'll snap."

"Do you suppose it's these months of confinement, the season, or age that prods our memories?"

"Whatever, we're getting down to our nubs."

Pidge nodded. "Marwa once said that we have 'only' eighty-six billion neurons in the brain and thousands of synapses per neuron up here." Pidge tapped her forehead. "Cerebral cortex. There's been only enough evolutionary pressure to generate enough synapses for the memories making up a typical lifespan. By our seventies, we forget names and confuse words. If we could live two hundred years or more, there would have to be major forgetting to free up synapses for new memories. So. Choose long life with a personal memory or ultralong-life alternative?"

Pearl laughed. "What is that, Hobson's or Achilles's choice? -- as if we choose. Evolution – including AI now – will make whatever of us all."

Pidge lifted a finished package wrapped in shiny candy cane foil. "No trips to the Post Office this year. Amazon is sending Charlotte's and Clarissa's gifts to Whidbey Island. Nina's twins are eleven. I got e-advice via Marwa/John's ten-year old Beckett. She makes up stories about mouse-size people in walls."

Pearl admired her own work. "In grad school, I wrapped for Macy's."

Pidge groaned merrily. "That annual chestnut? Well, no going out even if vendors are roasting 'em – and the incessant song, ceased. Is Jack Frost even in the air if you can't see him? Are unheard trees falling in forests? What-*ever*."

"How do we get a tree this year? Do we get a tree? The numbers are worse now than April's. Field hospitals again to cope with overflow. We can't budge outside. Grump can't concede. Some Amazon serf will deliver Pinaquanah's 'Cool LEGO Stem Toy, Boost Creative Toolbox' – whatever that is that Esa put on the seven- year old's Wish List."

It was afternoon and already dark. 'Whatever' was the word of the shortest day.

Before the solstice, a blizzard had blanketed New York. Awaiting Marwa, along with holiday giftwrapping, was a pile of stamped postcards she'd agreed to write, to get out the vote for the Georgia run-off election in January. Just a year since the party on the ninth floor! What a year. In just the five days after the Thanksgiving weekend, close to a million positive Covid test results in the U.S.

December, always a summary and visionary month, also chronicled: neither Marwa nor John had been infected; ditto Susanna, James, and Micheline, David and the twins. After her fourth relative, a cousin her own age, died in LA, Mercedes needed a long phone call with Pidge *en espagnol*. Covid also killed Hilly. Talk of vaccine increased but so did record-breaking plague numbers, fatigue, and political polarity.

Marwa told John about a nightmare – turning the pages of the 2020 calendar – its boxes for every day of January to December numbered – but blank, white, empty.

The detective thought of George Orwell's *Ministry of Truth* when he remembered two years earlier when the loser – what nickname had he heard recently at the precinct, *Fuckface Von Clownstick* – had explained why he kept attacking the press.

"I do it to discredit you all and demean you all, so that, when you write negative stories about me, no one will believe you."

The attack on the press was a subset of the Big Lie. David wrote a column about it for the *Times*. He referred to a new Wikipedia entry: "*große Lüge* is a gross distortion or misrepresentation of the truth used as a propaganda technique. The German expression was coined by Hitler when he dictated his *Mein Kampf* to describe the use of a lie so 'colossal' that no one would believe that someone 'could have the impudence to distort the truth so infamously.' Hitler claimed the technique was used by Jews to blame Germany's loss in World

War I on German General Ludendorff. The Nazis used the idea of the original big lie to bring about the Holocaust. In the 21st century, the term has been applied to [the incumbent's] attempts to overturn the 2020 election. 'The big lie' in this instance is the false claim that the election was stolen from him through massive fraud."

Alan created a game with Arno and Dylan: *What I Want* – after asking David that question.

David answered, "*My cup runneth over*. At prep school, all I remember reciting is the 23rd Psalm and the Lord's Prayer."

Pressed, David conjured a memory from "summer camp in New Hampshire on Lake *Winnipesaukee*. At least five different meanings for its aboriginal name. There's a shorter, Hiawatha-like poem, not by Longfellow, that explained one translation. 'The Spirit's Smile' by J.E. Hurlbut. *Hurl butt*." David rolled his eyes. "You can guess what boys did with that. We lived in cabins, but there was a big house with a big stone fireplace. I liked to see, smell, hear the fire crackle in that fireplace. I stared into it for hours."

"There's a fireplace in the new house," Alan said.


Apartment buildings' open summer windows were closed, and the seven-p.m. nightly applause and cheers for medical workers had gone quiet. In Times Square, the New Year's crystal ball would descend before an invisible cyber-crowd.

But since Thanksgiving, the rising five-year-olds, prompted by Mercedes and their parents, had been creating and leaving "arty-facts" at Pidge and Pearl's apartment door. Among crepe-paper and mini-poster boards were, in modeling clay, two blue tempera-painted 'monkeys' by Arno and Dylan and a white-brown pied bull (horns) with a girl jumper pipe-cleanered above its back.

This inspired Pidge to make Christmas gift books for each of them, continuing the adventures of *Dylus, Arnos,* and *Mikelinae* as the hero/heroine of their individual books. As Susanna, James, and Micheline began packing, in *Mikelinae's Journey North* Pidge conflated their move from the Upper West Side to northern Manhattan with King Nestor's Pylos-to-Patra and epic Pasikennae's *Mnkallis-to-*Orkney-shore. Pidge cut out colorful images from magazines, included glue sticks with the books, and left space for the children to create their own illustrations in those blanks. Work on **Blue Monkeys**, worry, and winter gripped the elderly professors.

Looking out the frosty window, "Agoraphobia," Pearl said.

"*Loimos*phobia," Pidge amended.

"A *plague* on both our houses."

Neither spoke aloud their plans for retirement, an *emeritae* Spring, if it should arrive with them alive.

There weren't many gifts to wrap. From its shape, Pidge guessed that Pearl had heard the hint about replacing her nearly empty Chanel No. 5 spray. Pidge had already hidden her surprise for Pearl. A friend, Andi, a retired art professor at Columbia who still consulted at the Brooklyn Museum – plague-Zooming from home – had been able to have a photo taken of *Painted Elk Hide* by 19th century Shoshone Cotsiogo from the fifth floor America's First Peoples gallery.

Pidge had been able to order the jpg transferred to spacious canvas for Pearl's bedroom wall, or for the living room if she preferred.

For Pidge and Pearl, the winter solstice cooking required mortar and pestle. They each owned personal ones. Along with the rent-control apartment, Pidge had inherited her mother's wooden *pilon* from unknown earlier Puerto Rican generations. Pearl insisted her Shoshone relic, a white-veined black soapstone, was much older.

Like her mother, Pidge never made latkes for Chanukah, though a dulled brass menorah on a kitchen shelf evidenced her father's presence in the past.

Tradition included a Spotify accompaniment, the flute music of the Shoshone Warm Dance. https://open.spotify.com/album/1OjdyrmxNze26wAfT5d4t3. And as usual, the old stories needed repetition.

"I was neither baptized nor bat-mitzvahed…" Pidge began.

"…but your parents 'liked borrowing God' from different houses of worship where non-membership saved dues –"

"and educated me on—"

"-- the 'Shapiro Spiritual Scholarship," Pearl concluded. "Pasikennae lived inside HER as we live in Manhattan. SHE was the world, a temple. Topography *was* worship."

Pearl paused to listen to a particular flute passage.

Pidge said, talking to herself, "Winter wants fat. Frying in oil, whether potato pancakes or my mother's *mofongo.*"

She breathed in the crushed bacon and garlic as she added the fried plantains to her *pilon.* Similarly, Pearl was mashing together pemmican ingredients she had oven-dried: cranberries from Massachusetts bogs with bison meat and backfat from a farm in upstate New York.

Following food preparations, Pidge and Pearl returned their laptops to the round table and set to work on Pasikennae's second copper-sleeved primer tablet.

"Do you imagine she wrote the stories in the winter?" Pearl said.

"For the Orkney children? The kiln could have been a good place to be."

"Maybe they had a Warm Dance, too. What a long, cold night the north must have been."

"After Pasikennae's bronzed, bare-breasted Cretan life," Pidge agreed. "Though she knew winters at Lake Superior."

"With her hot copper chief. Did you write stories for Nina when she was little?"

Pidge leaned back from the laptop screen. "No. Then, all you and I did was work."

"Competed. Divorced. No wonder Esa headed for the hills," Pearl frowned, examining the *Blue and Brown Monkeys* tablet image on her computer split screen, beside its translation page.

Pidge was studying the same two pages. She was shaking her head.

"It always asks more questions than it answers," she said.

Pearl sighed. "So now we know the monkeys were Hanuman langurs (genus *Semnopithecus*) from the Indus Valley, a world away, their tails curving up as an S- or C-shape towards the head, not African vervets whose tails hang down."

"But grey, tan, not blue," Pidge added. "*Blue* monkeys. Someone had to imagine them blue. What does *that* imply?"

"What *does* that imply? Can you live with eliding down to *Death did not end their pain?*" Pearl asked.

Pidge thought aloud, "The labyrinth under the Knossos palace implies belief in afterlife. Where every nine years, fourteen of Theseus's Athenian *korai* and *kouroi* were sent to be 'sacrificed' by a Minotaur priest. Motivation for later Mycenean revenge? Who knows? We've got *blue* monkeys for sure and *brown*. Immortals versus mortals, racism not the issue."

*2021*

## Chapter 21  January



***from Blue Monkeys by Shapiro & Feria***

### Blue Monkeys

*Blue monkeys danced with Sky.*
*Down the steep mountain Sky*
*sent Sister and Brother*
*blue monkeys. They could tell*
*truth from lie. Blue monkeys*
*offered gifts to brown ones*
*for answers to questions:*
*fire, music and dance,*
*and a golden scepter*
*to measure everything.*
*Some brown monkeys answered*
*truly they did not know.*
*Some thought it smart to lie.*
*Truth tellers won the gifts.*
*Gold scepter killed the rest.*
*Death did not end their pain.*
*Sister and Brother climbed*
*back up the steep mountain.*
*Blue monkeys danced with Sky.*

*The blue monkeys reveling on the muraled walls of Akrotiri may or may not be the same as these celestial messengers. What stands out is how boldly colored, how brightly painted the Minoan murals were. From prehistoric times, iron oxide and other clays varying in color (white, red, pink, yellow) had been used decoratively – and religiously. 'Egyptian blue' was made from a copper compound or powdered lapis lazuli, and pigments used for fresco during this time included saffron, iron ore, and indigo. A mix of Egyptian blue, natural iron, or powdered malachite created green, carbon or manganese the darker colors. Lively fauna from land, air, and sea along with glories of flora ornamented Minoan walls. Fish, dolphins, and octopuses rode Aegean waves. Blue birds and red-headed swallows filled the skies, and colorful crocus, papyrus, and lilies bloomed.*

*Throughout the very Old World, color was the norm for buildings. The temples and palaces of Crete, Egypt, Persia, India, and China – and in the Americas! – were riots of lively pigment, nothing like the pallid cemetery stone of modern cities that imitated ancient models only after their old rainbows had dissolved and been long forgotten. Even the architecture of Gobekli Tepe in Turkey – whose causes and effects are more deeply lost in time 6000 years before Stonehenge, 7000 before the pyramids – likely was brightly painted, a passionate veneration and mirror of Nature.*

Drew Burgos praised the translation and commentary, but he wanted *a map*. Pidge thought maybe Andi their friend who had helped her with Pearl's Christmas gift (now framed on their dark green living room wall) might devise one. Drew was eager for them to focus on Pasikennae's *life* rather than language. He saw a publishing date for early 2022. Vera Mifeng saw a contract as her breakthrough to senior editor. She called and texted.

"How do you say *noodging* in Chinese?" Pidge said. "If she's hocking us, can you imagine Drew with the miscarriage and her father's death in October?"

"And he's *our* agent? No conflict of interest there," Pearl added.

Vera wanted their book. Pidge and Pearl wanted a vaccine.

Taking a break from trying to write about Pasikennae's journey from the Mediterranean to Lake Superior, Pidge read news from her laptop.

"It's *America First*, all right, in *deaths*, nearly a quarter million of newly-infected US a *day,*" Pidge spat out. "Israel is unsurprisingly vaccinating the most, the fastest. Quarter of their nine million were vax'd in one month, and all we've got here is the phone frenzy I've been battling for days. Don't get me *started* on Duane Reade online scheduling. It's easier deciphering Linear A. Let's hope Susanna can get us into Mount Sinai."

Pearl silently rose from her chair on the opposite side of their round table and took Pidge's coffee mug into the kitchen.

Later that morning, they walked together in Riverside Park. It was sunny, not cold for an early January day. As Pearl squinted at the glittering Hudson, she thought of Pidge's news reading about the pilgrimage to the Ganges as part of --

"What's the Hindu bathing ritual?" she asked.

Pidge followed Pearl's line of sight to the river. "The Kumbh Mela?" and added, "India has recorded more than 150,000 dead, the world's third-highest number, but hundreds of thousands of Hindu pilgrims' are still en river route. One entire zodiac year into this pandemic, two million dead globally. More than 400,000 Americans. Deaths per day 3,300. More than the 9/11 attack."

"Well, today we celebrate Georgia. The Senate. Your postcards helped."

Pidge did smile behind her mask. "I am happy. It's a Georgia peach pie of a day!"

A teenager skateboarded near the two elderly women, reading his phone.

"Can they Zoom their classes like that?" Pidge asked Pearl, who shrugged.

Though he had not heard the question, the boy expertly stopped and held up his phone to show them.

"You won't believe 'sup down in DC," he yelled through a black mask. "There's a *riot* – they're *storming* the Capitol! To overthrow the election!"

The youth flipped down his board and sped away.

Pidge remembered looking south as the second plane hit its Tower. Now she gazed south again through the park's bare trees that seemed to be raising their arms to the clear blue sky.

"Peach pie… and hemlock."

Pearl said, "Let's get indoors."

Micheline and her parents had moved to Manhattan's northern end, Inwood, on the first Monday of the New Year. It was the day before the Georgia election, two days before the attack on the Capitol. They beat the kindergarten application deadline. The black ceilings (Susanna asked the new Super who liked having a doctor in the building, "Why, just *why* paint ceilings black?!") had been freshly repainted (Super said, "Ivory, like the soap") before the *Wall Street Journal* advised the ex-President to resign. There was little media coverage of his and Melania's vaccinations before departing the White House. His second impeachment began one week before his term expired. The U.S. surpassed twenty-four million Covid-19 cases. On Inauguration Day, a new big screen TV brought Lady Gaga singing the National Anthem into the Duckett-Beekmans living room. https://www.youtube.com/watch?v=HezPdHTwdGA

Micheline marched around the room, to-the-beat pressing her hand to her heart and her forehead, saluting.

James asked Susanna, "You think she'll remember this? Whenever she smells fresh paint? Glad your morning sickness is over. Glad you got vax'd."

At the anthem's crescendo and ending, Susanna's eyes filled with tears.

"First time I think I've really heard it. This *is* still the home of the brave. We survived the perilous fight. So far."

Micheline's delight also turned to thoughtfulness. "Do we still live in Manhattan? Or *on* it? How can you be *in* and *on* at the same time?"

James laughed. "Do you want to handle quantum linguistics with a five-year old?" he asked Susanna.

"Daddy," Micheline said, "The twins were just five. Dylan got *Equal Knocks for Dylus,* and Arno got *Arnos Sees a Green Flash.* Prof Pidge promised me another *Mikelinae* book. But I'm not five till March!" She turned to Susanna. "Am I?"

"Yes. March ninth. We live on Manhattan Island, and people *say* 'in' – it's just the way people

talk. Let's find maps and see where we were and where we are now."

They found an Etsy site where an artist's print showed the island's neighborhoods in different

colors. Micheline chose one in *Rainbow.*

"We can order it for your new bedroom. Where did we live?" Susanna asked.

Micheline pointed and read the map's upper middle. "Upper West Side, green."

"And now?"

This was a new game. Micheline moved her finger to the top of the image on the phone.

"Blue!"

"Inwood, *aqua* blue," Susanna said. "Like tropical water."

Micheline frowned. "*Agua.* Wood is not water," she said, but she ran to her room to find

*Mikelinae's Journey North*, the Christmas gift Professor Pidge had created with its map of

Mnkallis. While Susanna and James returned to unpacking, Micheline was busy drawing and

coloring in her *own* map of the Minoan island.

When free from his TV schedule, Alan went to the Soho studio. David had arranged shipping his canvases back from the Long Island property and renting it at incredible profit. City-distanced locations were in desperate demand.

Alan's portrait paintings were outlined, but at the moment, he was absorbed in De'Lynn's bronze Madonna foregrounding a cherry-plum trees background. Her green, greys, and black dominated the painting. She was haloed in pink, red, and white. Further background sky in blue. Angularity had taken over, nearly abstracting the forms. Rodin gave way to the Cyclades and Duchamp. Often asked, Alan said his current favorite artist was <u>Njideka Akunyili Crosby</u>. He'd met her in LA. He liked saying her name. Sounded like conjuring. He liked that the studio was *on* cobblestone Crosby Street in a Cast-Iron Historic District building.

In this studio, Alan slowly ground his own colors. The work was penance. It differentiated the paints from the summer's debacle and aftermath. After adding the oils a few drops at a time to the pigments, he held the muller on top of the paste, the heel of his left hand down and thumb up. That he could smell the scents of linseed and walnut oil --- deep breaths were further benedictions of mercy and forgiveness. Alan moved the tool in a circular motion outward from the center of the paste, spreading it in a thin layer with a spatula on the clean, flat surface.

Some pigments, like lapis blue, needed a small amount of beeswax added to the oil. What was at first dry and stiff became wet and soft. A metaphor. A prayer. A memory of honeysuckle and nightmare Queen Bee. His left hand gone! Here it was now, hard at work, and he was as filled with gratitude as he had been then with fevered horror. Alan removed accumulated paint from the sides of the muller with the spatula. Sometimes the muller stuck to the grinding surface. Using the spatula as a lever, he raised the muller's edge, then slid it off the surface. Next step, storing the paint in tubes. It accumulated at the open end. He had to tap to settle it away from the tube's opening. He cleaned the tools with odorless mineral spirits, then warm water and soap. No ritual could have been more religious. Christ died in his thirty-third year. 'According to Thomas Aquinas,' according to David. Was resurrected.

Alan returned to the apartment in time for dessert. It had started to snow. David sat at the table with the twins and Mercedes. The boys were scooping up spoonfuls of warmed apple pie and vanilla ice cream. Alan breathed in the delicious scents. The nanny quickly moved her chair, but he stopped her with a palm up.

"Not hungry yet," he said.

David explained that it took time to wind down.

"Who wound Da up?" Arno asked.

"Where's his key?" Dylan said.

Alan picked up a spoon and stole samples from the boys' bowls. They both protested.

"Key to a man's heart is through his stomach, don't you know anything?" Alan said.

"I know that's a cliché," Arno said.

"What is a cliché?" David demanded.

"You know," Arno answered.

"Yes, I do. How do you?"

"How do *you* do?" Arno again.

Dylan was laughing. "Doo doo!"

Mercedes took them in hand: "*Salgan de la mesa!*"

Suddenly obedient, the twins put down their spoons and raced to their room. Mercedes followed them.

"You hungry?" David said.

"Yeah. A little. It's cold out."

"It's January."

They cleared the table together. In the kitchen, David put together a plate and microwaved it. Alan ate at the granite counter. As David watched him, he thought of Drew's phone call.

"I've got news. 'I think Vera's pregnant,' Drew said. 'She got me.'"

Pidge and Pearl became officially Professors *emeritae*. But it wasn't a time for in-person retirement festivities. There were, instead, local, then national and international Zoom celebrations, many closeups of wine bottle labels and various glass shapes and sizes sometimes photobombed by unmuted animals, birds, and children. The libations were often accompanied by screens of food platters that the women began classifying geographically. Because they were obsessed with *maps*.

"Our agent wants to see Pasikennae's journey from Crete to Lake Superior and back," Pidge explained to well-wishers.

"I feel like I'm making the trip," Pearl added. "Exhausted!"

By the end of January, Andi the art professor had come through. Following Pidge's directions, she had Googled the long route, and for clarity's sake had decided to create two maps, one for the European part of Pasikennae's journey and one for the North American. On both, she'd indicated Pasikennae's direction and location with a customary broken line that in no way captured the challenges and dangers she'd faced.

On the first map, the line began where Pasikennae had, from (Mnkallis) Thera and Crete – then she'd sailed west, across the Mediterranean, through Gibraltar, and then north up the Iberian, French, between the British/Irish coastlines, to the Orkney Islands. From there she'd travelled north and west to the Faroes, Iceland, and Greenland – and then across the Atlantic to Newfoundland. On the second map, the broken line entered the mouth of the St. Lawrence Seaway … travelled down it and the Saint Lawrence River – into and through Lakes Ontario,

Erie, Huron, to Lake Superior, *Kitchi-Gummi*, to its western end, Isle Royale.

Drew was glad to get this news.

Pidge and Pearl were gladder to get their first of two Pfizer vaccinations. Susanna had gotten them onto a list at Mount Sinai. At first, vaccine ran out there, but enough arrived in time before the hospital was overwhelmed yet again. At first, relief and gratitude crowded out all other emotions.

"Maybe we will live a while longer."

Both were surprised by little reaction to the vaccinations. A degree rise of their normal low 97's just up to 98.6 the next morning, and fatigue hardly different from a too-long walk or online overwork. Good dreams came to both of them in afternoon naps. When they woke, the world felt new.

### *Chapter 22 February – March*

On February first, *Aurora Borealis* was dancing in her green veils over Lake Superior. NASA announced its replacement for the Hubble telescope readying for a Hallowe'en launch; the new Webb Telescope looked like "a giant sunflower riding on a surfboard." A Neolithic/Bronze Age site even older than Pasikennae's was discovered eroding in the Orkneys. After Valentine's Day, the rover *Perseverance* landed safely on Mars, upgraded from its predecessor, *Curiosity*. It carried seven primary payload instruments, nineteen cameras, and two microphones along with a mini-helicopter named *Ingenuity*.

Covid deaths neared half a million in the US. A huge snowstorm caused a power crisis in Texas and blocked vaccine delivery from the Midwest to the East Coast. A big wind was blamed for twirling a massive container ship into a blockade of the Suez Canal that dammed up worldwide shipping and froze nearly $10 billion a day in worldwide trade. But Pidge and Pearl finally got their rescheduled second doses – and headache, low fever, joy. They had to wait two more weeks to be safe, not entirely from infection, but to survive it.

On a surprisingly warm 62$^0$ day, still masked, they were walking in Riverside Park down at the boat basin where the Café had closed. Though the grass was still brown and the trees bare, the sun glittered on the Hudson River, evaporating white caps into ocean-scented breezes.

"Do bears feel like this after hibernation?" Pidge asked.

"I think they're just hungry," Pearl said.

Pidge, exasperated, "Really. Do bears – or you – ever rejoice? I miss the Café's blue umbrellas."

"Where are the houseboat folk?"

"*Ou sont les neiges d'antan?*"

"Where, indeed," Pearl agreed. "Do you remember the Mole People who used to live in the Amtrak freight tunnel under there?" She pointed toward the water's edge.

"I remember that friend of Andi's, Margaret Morton at Cooper Union. She created a collection of her photos of the underground people. She graduated from Kent State when they killed the kids in '70. I wouldn't part with her book. Small fortune now that the paperback goes for $150. Margaret died last June. Seventy-one. Not from plague. Leukemia like my mother."    They retraced their steps from the riverside walkway through a tunnel to broad stairs that led several blocks north, arriving at a wide plaza. It was centered by a fenced circle of shrubs around a flat plaque, a Warsaw Ghetto Uprising Memorial. Still on a rising incline, they walked past a playground and up another hill to the sidewalk at Riverside Drive.

Pidge pointed north.

"I know the way uptown," Pearl said.

"*Duh*, cranky Sacajawea. I meant that Susanna and James and Micheline are 'way up there in Inwood. Right now."

"Well, *duh*, right now, she's about seven months pregnant and still working crosstown at the hospital," Pearl nodded direction, "and he's down at Rockefeller, Micheline returned to its daycare."

Pidge took a few steps and paused. "*I feel the earth move under my feet.*"

Pearl looked up. "Let's hope the sky isn't tumbling down."


Almost four months since the detective's follow-up interview with Ellen Grenley, no confession, but she had admitted the existence of a Luster safety deposit box. *Location, location, location.* A real estate mantra. Which had become something of his own. The Luster murder/Dayita-Esau fourth floor conjoined apartment was up for sale. Room for Marwa's father and Beckett. An extended family. If they could get it all together quickly, they could avoid a mortgage altogether by combining the liquidation of John's Long Island townhouse, Marwa's apartment, and her father's Battery Park three bedroom -- plus the Wentworth-widower inheritance. It was Anam Al-Halimi's expert idea. Move-in early June?

Marwa's slowly convalescing father said, "A good investment. Your daughter can call me *Jid.*" He pronounced it *Je-duh.* "It means Grandpa. Kids say *Jiddo.*"

Although St. Bart's had just closed its borders due to a surge in Covid cases, Kirby, and more importantly, her fiancé, could manage the return of one ten-year old freckle-faced redhead who would turn eleven in July.

Beckett had sent him a volley of upper-cased texts beginning months earlier when her mother had revealed plans to send her to Kirby's Connecticut prep school alma mater in the fall.

*I will NOT run, fly, or WALK to Walker's!*

*They want me OUT of the picture? GREAT. YOU take me IN!*

*Only good thing about Jean Le PUKE is his palomino. White mane and tail.*

*Mom and Puke are GAGA over each other and I don't mean LADY!*

Leave it to a ten-year old, John thought, to put a stake into the matter's heart. Including his own. Kirby was marrying Jean Le Pieu, a St. Bart's old money scion, part of an island-ruling cabal in the process of selling off prime island real estate.

*He calls me SEXY-ON. SAXON? That's GERMAN. Gramma says my face is the map of IRELAND.*

John wanted Beckett out of there asap, vaccine or no. Kirby was insisting if not Walker's, then she and scion "would certainly pay for Calhoun," but John intended half somehow. This just left *Gramma* and *Pop* in East Rockaway not that far away. Beckett liked the canal in their backyard "*BETTER THAN VENICE.*"

The plague's first anniversary in New York City in March included a Zoomed from Fifth Avenue Temple Emanu-El memorial for David's parents. Micheline turned five on March ninth. Pidge sent her a new story booklet to illustrate and color in, *Mikelinae & Moon Goddess Mename*. On its cover, it had an outlined double-axe shaped sail on a Minoan ship (more of art professor Andi's work). James's parents drove across from the Bronx for "drive-by gifting" – waving at a distance. Susanna and Micheline watched through the lead-glass window lighting the 1925 greystone's lobby. The senior couple left presents (balloon attached) at the curb to be picked up by James. He waited outside at the building's beveled-glass double-door entrance. In Manhattan, all but Micheline had been vaccinated; the Bronx was scheduled, but still waiting. When they got out of the car, his parents wore masks. James knew, via Marwa at Rockefeller, that it was worse for John Donnelly's 'rents on Long Island; their appointments had been cancelled when doses ran out.

Micheline put the balloon under her shirt to imitate her mother's pregnancy. Baby due in April. She had begun drawing pictures of *him* inside something that looked like Santa's sack. Various stuffed animals had been her models, carefully positioned on her new desk. Her grandparents' birthday gift had been the easel and paints in her new room. Now on a big, spattered mat.

At breakfast, Micheline announced she was going to be an artist.

"Arno and Dylan's Da is an artist at home and a prine-in-ster on TV. What's a prine-in-ster? What's he *in*?"

"Prime minister. Like a president," Susanna answered.

"On TV, he's old, but his wig isn't white. It's like real, dark and wavy. He says his costume is heavy. Like Hallowe'en."

"Ancient, not old," James suggested.

"What's ancient?""

"From the distant past."

"Where?"

"It's not a where so much as a when."

"When? When's the past?"

"Yesterday is the past. And every yesterday has a yesterday."

"Do think that helps?" Susanna said.

James shrugged. "You try."

Susanna said, "Wait a sec. She returned moments later from the bathroom with a hand mirror and James's shaving mirror removed from its wall holder.

Susanna showed Micheline the two mirrors facing one another. "Look, honey. See the tunnel? That's how far the past goes."

"And the future," James said.

"The future is tomorrow?" Micheline asked.

But the child didn't wait for an answer. She frowned and spooned oatmeal into her mouth. She swallowed.

Then Micheline said, "I don't like mirrors. Their Da doesn't either."

"What's wrong with mirrors?"

"Things go backwards. They make tunnels. I don't understand. The baby is going to be very confused, and I won't be able to explain it to him."

Susanna stroked Micheline's wavy hair. "You'll try."


Marwa was on the bus home, crossing town on the 79th Street Transverse. Central Park was greening and blooming, daffodil buds swaying. Pregnancy was normally thirty-nine to forty weeks. Her period was late. Breasts' heightened sensitivity, but different from pre-menstrual.

Harder. Hotter. The test had found the chorionic gonadotropin (hCG). She couldn't remember exactly when, three weeks earlier, she and John had folded into one another, but she smiled at the thought. That's how it felt with him.

His humor was a steady gyroscope that nevertheless could send her spinning. His confidence and expertise felt like the ease of sliding inside sheets and under blankets, under the comforter, dissolution in the dark and cold of winter, warmed by arousal. Until the detective, no real competition since James. They were both *real*. Springing ahead -- clocks, light, vaccine – reality. They were moving to the big apartment downstairs -- with her father and Beckett Donnelly. Now, somewhere around Thanksgiving, a baby.

Marwa had never imagined becoming a mother (like *Ummee?*). It was an existential question she'd avoided. So, how could she let it happen? Blame it on stress, both of them unthinking, relying on the pill, too tired to bother, she'd be thirty-seven next month, so decreasing probability. But truth be told, the luxury of just letting go, not caring, neither believing not disbelieving. Just being. So, welcome, Little Being. Marwa had loved Latin in high school. Her teacher quoted Aristotle, "*Horror vacui*," 'Nature abhors a vacuum' Not scientifically true, but this was: If you relinquish control, it'll get Taken.

The accordion bus swayed like the budding daffodils. Marwa felt a twinge. Not menstrual cramp. The blastocyst had swayed across the fallopian tube and was rooting in her uterus. Six to twelve days after conception. How did anyone ever do this? She remembered a Rockefeller classmate walking across the stage, accepting her doctorate diploma – nine months pregnant. Now, Marwa recognized an increased sense of smell as a cool whiff of scent, the day's rain in the earth, came through a nearby slightly-opened window. A symptom the opposite of Covid's anosmia. Marwa saw ahead that the clouds had cleared for a spectacular sunset-painted sky. The bus headed to the West Side. *Inshallah.*

Once again, around the oak table on a late March morning, Pidge and Pearl wrestled with Pasikennae's tablets. Pots of flowering white, pink, and purple hyacinths on the kitchen windowsill sent their strong fragrance into the living room. Both scholars were split-screening the green flash tablet with the two previous specimens about the white-winged bird and blue/brown monkeys. They both guessed rightly that the other was procrastinating, sneaking to random sites. Pearl said nothing about the *New York Times* article she read about the "neo-New Deal, American Rescue Plan," but evidence of her wandering appeared when she looked up and asked, "What would you do if you were invisible? Would you pass or fail Plato's Ring of Gyges test?"

Pidge looked up. "Could I green flash-see into the souls of other people? I'd have to be entirely immune, too. Can I fly? Time travel?"

Pearl considered rules. "Use your *dayenu.* Don't be greedy."

"Greed is one of the temptations. But okay. *It would be enough* if..." She looked at her split screen. "In the present, I'd fly to the dig at Akrotiri and then go behind the scrim 3600 years to when Pasikennae walked those narrow streets. I'd bump into her."

"Invisible?"

"Oh, right. Well, I'd follow her around. Walk around her ship with her. See the harbor, the square sails. If they were brightly colored. I'd speed up time and travel with her all the way to the Orkneys. Watch her talk to herself as she inscribed this damn tablet. See what she meant."

"You'd have to understand what she was saying."

"Translation goes without saying."

"That oxymoron. If only."

"And you?

Pearl was ready. "I always look west, not east. First thing I'd want to do is see the black tides of buffalo flooding *urheimat* homelands. Fifty million before the Europeans – a thousand now. Smell original home like I can the hyacinths," she pointed to the kitchen. "Hear a stampede like a tornado across the plains. Arch my neck up at the Rockies. Taller, vaster than skyscrapers. See the Pacific Ocean with ancestral eyes. Then I'd wheel around like an eagle to Ohio and Louisiana, to the ancient mound builders. See where *they* were living in cities of ten *thousands*. Where artifacts from Pasikennae's people have been found with their haplogroup X2 genes. Hear their voices. Their songs."

"Would you want to see Pasikennae?"

Pearl considered. Closed her eyes.

I'd like to see her face. And where she lived on Isle Royale. The deep mines, copper gleaming in the sun. See Sueaysua and her copper-skinned father. He's a shameless erotic fantasy I enjoy.

"I feel guilty," Pidge said, looking back at her screen. She was quiet for several moments.

"You may have a gene for guilt from your father."

"Really being invisible is creepy. Dis-orienting. What would the brain do with such strange signals? See the world around you but not your own arms and hands when you look down? Turn into one total phantom limb?"

Another longer pause.

Pearl had been expecting, awaiting this.

Pidge said, "Even invisible, I wouldn't go to Ben's funeral. '*Mami,* ' Nina texted. 'you're my only parent now.' She can't fly east to New York. Char and Clar aren't vaccinated."

Pearl listened to repetitions and news as Pidge needed to unwind.

Her daughter Nina and husband Chad Satriano had met at Stanford, computer science. They were "data scientists, whatever. Nina's heroes are Hypatia of Alexandria and Ingrid Daubechies of Duke who says, 'I don't get even. I get odder.'"

They lived on Whidbey Island with eleven-year-olds Charlotte and Clarissa. Nina had phoned from Seattle to say that her father, Ben Abes, eighty-five, had died the day before, "but not from Covid. Like a salmon, Ben had ordered his burial in Saratoga Springs," where he was born, after a lifetime that included Columbia in NYC, University of Chicago (after the divorce where he met and married Brenda, ten years younger than Pidge), and Cal Tech in Pasadena "where *Miha's* half-siblings Bobby, Bonnie, and Billy were born and raised."

Pearl said, "You feel guilt unlike our unrepentant Governor, a tragedy of his own entirely visible making. Why would you go to Ben's funeral upstate now? You've been divorced longer than you were married. I don't even know if mine's alive or dead. I'm sure the feeling is entirely mutual. I know, you didn't hate Ben. But I married a racist anthropologist. That oxymoron. Skip the *oxy*."

Pidge returned to staring at the green flash tablet filling her screen. Linear A on one side, the unknown Orkney markings on the other.

"Invisibility," she said. Her professor voice. "And/or the ability to 'see through' someone as if unmasked. Timely image. What must that be like? Like observing animals, babies, and small children? In her 'after' life, Pasikennae likely was a teacher and healer. Believed powers came from HER?" Pidge shrugged. "Why wouldn't she after the voyages she'd captained? A teenager jumping through the horns of a bull?! Born into a family and society where SHE was the First and Only Cause of everything. SHE dragged Pasikennae back from Isle Royale only to send her to the Orkneys? The locals certainly buried Pasikennae as revered. Reverenced."

Pearl also returned to her work screen. She read aloud about the solar phenomenon that reappeared as a Scottish legend.

*"A green flash is a phenomenon in which part of the Sun appears to suddenly change to bright green for about one or two seconds. The brief flash of green light is seen on the horizon more often at sunset than at sunrise, more often at sea than on land... If you see the green flash, you gain the power to see into the souls of other people."*

"I'd like to see that," Pidge said.

**Chapter 23 April**

**from Blue Monkeys by Shapiro & Feria**

*Cypresses watched Sun journey across the sky.*
*They called to Sun, 'Let us be ships to follow*
*and worship You!' Sun heard their prayer,*
*pitied the trees. Sun sent a great green stork*
*at sunset on the sea. It spread wide green wings*
*just for a moment to guide them. It turned*
*the trees into ships, their trunks into masts,*
*their roots into keels, their leaves into sails.*
*The ships followed the Sun into the harbor of night.*
*They sailed with the Sun as day began,*
*bringing with them secrets of sights and sight.*
*If you see the green wings of the stork*
*beat against the sea at dawn or dusk*
*you can become invisible and see into souls.*

In April, lines of cherry trees transformed into pink-gowned bridesmaids leading Spring down the aisle. *Ingenuity* flew on Mars. NASA called it a "Wright Brothers moment." On Earth, everyone in the flight control room wore masks. As a tribute to the Wrights, *Ingenuity* had a postage-sized bit of fabric from the brothers' aircraft, known as the *Flyer*, attached to a cable under its solar panel.

David and Alan had lived in the Upper West Side building for two years. David wrote about the anniversary in one of his *New York Times* columns whose name "had been changed to 'Guest Essay' because 'Op Ed' didn't relate to online reading, only to print copy. *The Times*, they are literally a'changing," David said.

He watched Alan shaving-without-looking in the bathroom mirror.

"I don't know how you do that without cutting your throat."

Alan smiled. To an old melody he sang, "*Seems like old times... la la la ... whatever ... Seems like old times, la la la some more ... Seems like old <u>times</u> being here with you.*"

"1945, Guy Lombardo's younger brother Carmen wrote that song with John Jacob Loeb. Recorded in the 1940's by Vaughn Monroe and Kate Smith, in the late 60's by Ella Fitzgerald. It was Arthur Godfrey's radio theme song."

"*Annie Hall.* She sang it. Ten years before I was born. I auditioned with it once. That's enough history for me."

Alan rinsed his razor.

David hesitated, then asked, "How's the shaving cream?"

"Doesn't smell like cabbage."

There was a loud noise in the living room.

"Mercedes is taking the boys out before it rains," David said.

Alan perfectly imitated Nina Simone singing *Just in Time.*

David restrained himself from mentioning renditions by Dean Martin, Frank Sinatra, and Tony Bennett, plus two films with the same title, the white one from 1997 and the Black one streaming from Netflix in 2020. Alan had smiled. *Dayenu.*


Anticipating Beckett's return from the Caribbean, John was glad that as NYPD, he'd been vaccinated. Once his daughter's arrived, Marwa's apartment was crowded with people, schedules, and morning sickness. Real estate had changed hands. Also vax'd Anam Al-Halimi (De'Lynn found him a part-time aide) would crowd in, mid-May. Neither Marwa nor her father observed Ramadan's April beginning. Beckett had landed at JFK *sans* cornrows in her red hair. Again through Kirby's influence, Beckett entered a Calhoun cluster as a fifth grader, middle school to begin in September. Half of her classmates attended in masked person; the other half was virtual. Beckett did a hybrid bit of both around the adults' schedules.

Marwa had told John, of course, but no one else. *Pregnant. Expecting.* It was odd not to be alone in her body. She felt *lived in*, like her apartment. Like the building. She thought of her anatomical windows, elevators, basement and penthouse.

"Where *are* you?" a graduate student asked.

Marwa sat at a round table in the new dining hall at Rockefeller University, architecturallypoised above the FDR Drive along the East River, with a bright, expansive view of the 59th Street Bridge. Their trays, china plates, bowls, and coffee mugs were *green*, meaning *reusable*, though through Marwa's synesthesia, those words evoked a *utensil* pale yellow, Crayola *Canary*. She had drifted away from the conversation about a reported physics breakthrough. Something about a *muon*, "one of the seventeen (so far) fundamental particles in the universe."

Like an electron, but two hundred and seven times heavier. Swollen? Was *it* pregnant? She'd tuned out to, "Why is there matter in the universe at all?"

Someone said, "Brookhaven."

Marwa rejoined the conversation.

"Twenty years ago, I was at Brookhaven Labs on Long Island when that research was early days."

Someone else was eating a BLT; a whiff of bacon made her gag, breathe, and swallow. "I mean, *I* wasn't there, but a Stuyvesant classmate of mine was a summer intern just as I was at Stonybrook then. He drove up to get me, and we rode bicycles around Brookhaven before we went to the beach. I had to learn right then to ride a boy's bike, leg over bar! And there were wild turkeys crossing the road. My friend talked about 'measuring the magnetic moment of muons.' It sounded like poetry."

Marwa didn't mention that it was the summer of 2001, just before Prix and everything.

"Well, it looks like they've got confirmation after two decades. If it holds up, it'll break the Standard Model.

"Why did a wild turkey cross the road?"

Marwa laughed in unison with the rest of the table: *"To get to the other side!"*


Micheline's baby brother Carl Cooper Beekmans was born on April 21st. James phoned Esau up in Cold Spring to share the news along with hearty thanks for their kindergarten guidance months earlier. Micheline had made it into the desired Inwood school for September.

"Superb," Esau said as they FaceTimed. "Congrats on both counts!"

Dayita quickly texted a resting Susanna as the newborn slept. With Esau, Dayita was in her backyard near toddler Sandra busy in a new *Little Tikes* plastic house he had assembled the day before.

*From my 'rents of course,* Dayita typed. She sent Susanna a video of the scene. Much opening and closing of red window shutters and half door. *How do you feel?*

*Sore but sublime. My mom cried at naming Carl for my granddad.*

*Would like happy tears here for Xmas or New Year's.*

*Trying?*

*Just started.*

*Fingers crossed! Not legs!*

*Ha ha. You, nap now while you can!*

Later that day as Susanna nursed Carl, James looked in on Micheline playing in her room. On the floor along her bed's perimeter, she had lined up dolls, stuffed animals, and toys (several train cars and a crane with moving parts). That night, he described the scene to Susanna.

"She was naming or renaming them. Super serious."

"Don't boys do that? Girls name things. It's why I once argued with my mother about Adam getting all the credit for all the naming, *Genesis* 2:20. It had to have been Lilith or Eve."

"Well, she's over the moon now about Carl Cooper."

"You know the catechism she taught me: 'My mother's father was born in Arkansas in 1922, drafted at nineteen in 1941, promoted from private to PFC to Sarge, radio operator in the – always emphasized, *Pacific Theater*, *smart like you,* and his genes mixed with 'your father who read/spoke Latin & Greek.'"

In a nightgown, Micheline appeared in their bedroom doorway. She walked into the room and peered at the infant asleep in the co-sleeper attached to her mother's side of the bed.

"Why doesn't my birth certificate show a middle name?" she whispered.

"It's okay. He sleeps through quiet talking," Susanna said.

James answered, "We didn't think you'd need one. Micheline has three syllables already. Same as Carl-Coo-per," he pronounced. "A lotta letters to spell in Micheline Beekmans.*"

"That's *easy,*" the five-year old protested. "I want *Sooz.* That's what you call Mommy. Micheline S-O-O-Z Beekmans."

"That will work great if you become a lawyer," James approved. "Micheline s-u-e-s people. Files law*suits.*"

"Do I hafta wear a suit?" Micheline said.

"No," Susanna said.

James put Micheline back to bed, then returned to his own.

"Relieved she didn't insist on *Duckett?*" James teased.

"After all the limericks I've suffered? We'll make her a mock certificate for Christmas, frame it for over her desk," Susanna said. "She can choose if it still matters to her when she's eighteen or twenty-one."

"You've got it all figured out," James said. "As usual."

Vera phoned Pidge and Pearl after Drew received their ***Blue Monkeys*** manuscript. They could hear her exclamation points.

"Drew told me not to, but I had to tell you! We're thrilled!"

Pidge wanted to alert Pearl (in on speakerphone) to Vera's emphasis on the pronoun "we" which referred to her palm pressed to swelling pregnancy. But Facetime was on. Pidge was careful not to roll her eyes.

"How are you feeling?" Pearl asked.

Vera pointed her phone at her abdomen. "Fine, but I wish we could get vax'd!"

"Baby shower?" Pidge said.

"End of August! At Serendipity's! We should all be vax'd by then! She's due in September!"

"A girl?" they said together.

"Ultrasound says YES!"

*HITTITE QUEEN* had resumed shooting in November. The writers needed to modify Alan's character. The alteration was the result not only of the long arc to increase his voiceover commentary, moving the Prime Minister to Assyria out of the palace/competition with the show's star, but also to adapt to an obvious change in the actor. No more on set laughter from his genial impressions. Though Alan had gained back weight lost to illness, the sharp angles of his face had not softened. The look in his pale eyes was keener, the timbre of his voice harsh. His character had changed from conciliator to commander.

Production costs increased by orange-vested 'Covid workers', extra cleaning companies, blasting air filters, routine testing, and other safety protocols also affected costume changes, fewer extras and locations. The handsome Prime Minister stripped less and frowned more. In an early episode set at the Hittite palace in Hattusa, writers inspired by Alan's new attitude twisted the plot: the Prime Minister used a would-be assassin's own knife like a dart for a bull's-eye to his attacker's throat. The audience loved it. Directors also noted that keeping Alan from intimate contact suited the actor just fine.

One opined, "No more kissing, ass or otherwise."

Never to be outdone, the diva playing Puduhepa demanded a name change for the Hittite Queen. Early on, Pidge and Pearl had never reacted to her historical Nesite name, but current reports of the Latin meaning of *pudenda* as *shame* had reached the famous actress, and she became more vocal/visible than ever on social media and talk shows, "denouncing and renouncing any invocation of horrifying misogyny."

In lobby conversation, Pidge had assured Alan, "The term derived from the Latin verb *pudere*: *to be ashamed.* The Latin term for the vulva, including the inner and outer labia, the clitoris and the pubic mound, was *pudendum*. Translation: the part to be ashamed of. There's no equivalent word for male genitals."

Pearl added, "'In the beginning,' sexual shame knew neither gender nor species. First-century Roman writers used *pudendum* to mean the genitals of men, women and animals. But it stuck on women."

Pidge said, "In the 16th century, the word appeared in an atlas by Andreas Vesalius, the Flemish father of modern anatomy. A human uterus was drawn as a distorted penis; women were defective men. *Pudendum* became a synonym for vulva. Today, the word still appears in almost every medical textbook."

Pearl asked, "What name does she want instead of Puduhepa?"

"Now that it's win-win publicity, Her Highness wants no change at all," Alan said. "It upsets feminists and misogynists alike. Everyone can defend or insult 'Queen *Poo* or *Pud*.' She's getting more attention than even her agent can buy."

"Anyway, the Hittites spoke Nesite. Not Latin at all," Pidge concluded.

A masked Azul opened the glass door for the neighbors as they parted ways.

Though long, the walk to the supermarket in May was pleasant. The flowering pear trees on the avenue median were in bright new leaf. As they headed for the store's green awning a dozen blocks south, Pidge and Pearl relaxed into familiar conversational rhythms that required no explanation between them. Thoughts of **Blue Monkeys** related to Alan's Hittite talk.

Rolling their two folded shopping carts like luggage, they walked along Broadway. Nearby, a uniformed nanny pushed a stroller whose occupant was playing with a toy snake he loudly called *Hissy*. He shook it at the professors. His nanny took it away, and the toddler yowled, adding to the street noise.

Pearl nodded, "His snake's not Hissy, she's Pasikennae's *Asasarame*, Hittite's goddess

*Ishassara*, Khmer's *Apsara*, Canaanite *Asherah*."

Joining her game, Pidge added, "The Hittites also had bull worship, leaping. Pasikennae's everywhere."

"Like the song, '*They got around, round, round,*'" Pearl said as they entered the market.

Pidge was happy. "The Beach Boys! Boy, are we old!"

They didn't talk as they shopped. Pearl was thinking about the offer to join a Shoshone Language Project in Idaho. Not that Esa was urging her to move West as Pidge's daughter was. But coming out of the blue after they'd sent **Blue Monkeys** off to Drew with startling results, the contract via Vera, unheard-of-expedited publication schedule for *this* holiday season? If they can make a vaccine in one year, maybe they can publish a book for Christmas? … maybe she shouldn't be so quick to dismiss the idea of moving. Escapes went in many directions. What was she? A New Yorker … a Wind River Shoshone? False dichotomy or whatever *otomy* was correct for many more than two. Was *identity* – a popular obsession – still a question relevant to a septuagenarian?

"Good," Pearl heard Pidge. "They've got the fat free *and* whole *leche* this week."

Pearl held up packaged sliced Swiss cheese like a trophy.

Why the Spanish word for milk had popped out of her mouth, Pidge couldn't imagine. *Sin grasa y entera.* This was happening more and more, words and/or memories appearing like popups on her mind's screen. Images within images. A Zoom conference with overlapping voices. *Mute, people, please mute!* Yes, she was shopping – there was the whole wheat bread – but in her head, her parents were retelling the story of how a Black Puerto Rican met a New York Jew just before WWII. After, they returned to civilian life. She was born in 1946. They taught. *Mami* at Brearley ("which was how *you* went there and *de lujo* Vassar '68 after, *Mija*") and

Daddy at City College they call CUNY now. Born into rent control that Nina wants you to give up.

"*Loca*," Pidge said aloud.

"Crazy? Who? What?" Pearl stopped at marinated artichoke hearts.

On the walk home, they crossed West End Avenue heading to Riverside Drive. After the wide, busy intersection at 79th Street, it was green tree-lined, park views *all the way home* that reminded them both of tweaking baby toes.

Pearl looked toward the tree-obscured Hudson River. She said, "Maybe Pasikennae was content on the Orkney shore."

Pidge followed her line of sight and thinking. "Before the nineteenth century, before photography, art and memory were rare witnesses to the past."

"And without constant visual reminders, forgotten? Pasikennae never needed a prayer to say *Thy will be done*. It was a given that anything, everything that was, was HER will."

"So," Pidge said slowly, "Pasikennae's life in the Orkneys was more of HER Manifestation. Earlier lives as bull vaulter, sea captain, wife and mother, were Matryoshka nesting dolls inside/of HER. Nothing, no one, lost, all things dying but living in HER."

"Pasikennae may have forgotten her earlier lives, but she lived in HER perpetual Now."

"Didn't we write that at the end of *Blue Monkeys*?"

"Yes. In other words."

"In other words, we're repeating what we already knew."

"But forgot we knew," Pearl said.

A traffic light turned green.

"People remember where they are *from*," James agreed.

This was outdoor conversation with Susanna in May at his parents' home in the Bronx. They were seated on the small backdoor deck where seventeen years earlier he'd first kissed Marwa. Lab gossip – Marwa was expecting a baby in November. Now he and his wife overlooked the patch of ground and driveway, part of a common space of garages and urban gardens behind the attached homes. His mother was leading Micheline up and down her mini-farm's rows of new planting, explaining the stakes, identifying what would grow. His father was indoors taking an after-lunch nap in the same room with his new grandson.

"No need for a baby monitor," his father said. "CC wakes up, I wake up!"

It was a Saturday off for James. Susanna was on maternity leave from the hospital. The night before, while James slept and Susanna was nursing Carl Cooper, she'd watched a documentary about Neolithic sites in Turkey.

"Isn't that where Alan's *HITTITE QUEEN* is set?"

"They come much later," Susanna said. "This is *proto*-Hittite." Squinting behind sunglasses, she went on. "Catal Huyuk is the earliest known city on this planet. There was a house with a wall painting that might be a map, the community's memory of where they had come from, older Asikli Huyuk."

"Oh," James said, "the place names sound like gargling. What's that to Gobekli Tepe, then?"

"Gobekli Tepe is *thousands* of years before the Huyuks!"

"So hunter-gatherers built huge carved stone pillars, and it took millennia to build cities?"

"Memory is a Lost & Found."

"Eighty-six billion brain cells can only do so much with the rise and fall of civilizations."

"Where do *you* come from?" Susanna said. She reached over in the warm sunshine, and stroked his dark forearm. "You won't watch *Finding Your Roots* with me."

"You know as much as I've been told," James protested. "Were we part of the first 1619 haul of slaves from west Africa? Four hundred years of European … interbreeding? I don't see the point. Beekman Street, Manhattan, is Point A for me. Add the s, drop the apostrophe."

"You won't do a genetic test for origin? We tested for everything else."

James shrugged. "Busman's holiday for me. You wanna do some brain surgery at home?"

She poked his arm. "You've got a point."

He caught her hand and held it. Micheline ran up the stairs and held out a pink hyacinth blossom pinched by his mother from a toppling flower cluster. The child held it under his nose. He obediently breathed in. Hyacinth. Strong scent.

Micheline commanded, "Nana said your old microscope's inside!"

Susanna said. "Don't wake the baby."

Standing, James saluted them both.


A later weekend in May, when the rental lease on the Orient property was up, David arranged for a luxury SUV to take them all out to the end of northern Long Island. Mercedes sat in front chattering in Spanish with the driver, a relative of doorman Azul. David sat in one row beside Arno. Dylan was in the next row beside Alan. This allowed for plenty of room plus the boys' uncompetitive views of whatever video or game each chose to watch/play on rear seat monitor screens.

When they arrived, Mercedes began setting up a picnic on kitchen counter and table. David immediately took to the shiny black *Clavinova* under the bare wall intended for Alan's family portraits. The digital grand piano filled the high and wide space with Chopin. Quickly booed by the boys, David amiably switched to a TV theme song they approved. Alan showed the twins their rooms, but they ran outdoors to find "the barn," which, lacking animals, disappointed them.

But they found an old Japanese maple with weeping arms they could climb and began hanging like monkeys from branches. David followed them outside and wandered into the barn. Alan watched the boys in the tree.

Lunch was a familiar Zabar's feast.

After, Arno didn't want to go back to the studio in the barn because he didn't like "doing art with Dylan anymore. He splashes paint all over. He breaks all the crayons. He presses on them too hard and flattens the points. He outlines everything in black. He uses up the black crayons too fast."

"Thank you!" Dylan bowed with an arm flourish.

"We'll stay here," David played Solomon.

Dylan ran to Mercedes and took her hand. "*Tú vienes con nosotros!*"

Taking supplies they had brought from the City, Dylan, Mercedes, and Alan headed for the barn. Honeysuckle was already starting to bloom. Alan warned Dylan about bees. Mercedes put bowls of crayons on the floor.

"We can use paint tomorrow," Alan promised.

Dylan set to work immediately. Mercedes wandered outdoors down to the water. Alan sat at one of the high stools beside the table. The cleanup crew hadn't left a spot of pale green paint anywhere he could see. Pangs of memory reminded him of pain nursed with mixed feelings: Anguish. Arousal. Humiliation. Fear. Survivor's mingled Shame and Pride. This was an exorcism without incense. Finally, he thought, what am I doing but Actor 101, mining for future roles. 'Suffer *usefully*.' He laughed at himself loudly enough for Dylan to look up from drawing.

Gladly, Alan shifted attention to his son and Mercedes returning with sun-reddened, light brown cheeks. A rich color. Yellow ochre and oxide red? Being there made him want to mix paints.

She was breathing in a honeysuckle blossom she'd picked. She knelt at Dylan's side and let him sniff it while she admired his picture.

"*¿Por qué es el cielo verde pálido?*"

The child had drawn a good copy of the blue monkeys fresco facsimile on the wall in the twins' Manhattan bedroom. But here he had drawn three monkeys.

"The monkeys are blue. The sky can be pale green," Dylan explained. "I like it better when it's not blue. *Nuevo color de la hoja.*"

"*Si,* new leaf color," Mercedes said.

Alan nodded. Benjamin Moore *Scenic View*. He kept the wince out of his voice. "I like the pale green, too," Alan said.

Dylan beamed. He held up the crayon. He read the label, "It's *Sea Green*. The monkeys are just regular blue like you get in the box of only eight, but I outline 'em in black-black-black! Like Roo-oh."

"I do love me my Rouault," Alan drawled.

Dylan stood with his picture and danced around the open space.

"*Necesitamos monos azules en la <u>nueva</u> casa,*" he said. "We can put the picture in our new bedroom. In a special frame."

"But three monkeys? *Quién es el tercer mono azul con pelo largo y rizado?* Mercedes asked.

"*Ella es Micheline, por supuesto.*"

"Of course," Mercedes said, "Micheline is the third monkey. *Pero solo había dos monos azules de verdad"*

"*Los monos azules no son reales.* Blue monkeys aren't real. *De verdad es mayor que eso.* For real is bigger than that. '*La imaginación sigue sus propias reglas.*'"

Alan heard his echo. "'Imagination follows its own rules,' *mijo. Hablado como un verdadero artista.*"

Mercedes closed her eyes. Shaking her head, she stood up, blinking. Slowly, she said, "*Senor, hablas espagnol. Suenas exactamente como yo.*"

"You do sound exactly like her!"

But his nanny angered. Dylan had to swallow the laugh at his father's perfect imitation. "*Nunca supe que hablaba español,*" she said and then acidly translated, "I never knew you spoke Spanish."

"I grew up in Texas," Alan apologized.

Mercedes calmed herself. "Also Senor David knows?"

"Little escapes David unless he lets it go."

Returning to the house, Alan, Dylan, and Mercedes found David and Arno at the cleared table, playing '*solving for x.*' Arno thought it was a game his father created for him. It was Arno's turn, and he believed he'd stumped his partner with $7 + x = 30$ because thirty was a pretty high number. He and Dylan could count to twenty in Spanish. Mercedes had them practice it on their fingers and toes. *Dedos y de los pies.* In English, Arno could count to nearly a hundred.

"I know there's a trick," David said. "How do you do it?"

Arno looked at the equation as if for the first time. How *did* he do it? $7 + x = 10$ was easy because he just knew that three fingers and seven toes added up to ten.

David waited, looking unsure.

Arno punched his father's arm. "You know how."

"Do you?"

"I think you have to take away seven from both sides. Then *x* equals," Arno paused, "7 from 30. That's 23."

"How do you know?" David prompted.

Arno frowned. "I just *do*."

Alan patted Arno's head. "Daddy is just being Daddy," he said. "And you're right. It's twenty-three. *Skidoo*! Look at Dylan's new picture for your new bedroom. We can mount it and build a frame."

After Mercedes put the twins to bed, David sipped port and Alan amaretto. It was still cool enough at night in May to have a fire snapping in the fireplace. Alan looked at the tall space above it, thinking now 'no' to five portraits, 'yes' to just one giant canvas – fresco? an enlargement of De'Lynn's Madonna & Child in the Manhattan studio. He wanted them here. The image would be so large, the effect would abstract its parts.

David was musing that he couldn't hear but could smell the ocean mixed with burning wood. And honeysuckle? He thought of master perfumers' noses. They were called a *nez* and could tell maybe 200 essential oils from 1500 synthetic sources. He took in a deep breath then breathed out aloud, "We should invite the Duckett-Beekmans and Persaud-Kimanis out here sometime."

Lost in divine icon image, "Nice idea," Alan agreed.

By the end of the following weekend, Memorial Day, Marwa's father had finished *Opus Inshallah*. It would debut at Julliard in November.

## *Chapter 25  June*

By mid-June, *Perseverance* on Mars had been successfully roving the red planet for 116 *sols*, nearly three months of Earth days. The American West suffered a heatwave, widespread drought, and more large wildfires than any year since 2011, awaiting the peak months of July and August. The President signed a bill creating *Juneteenth* the first new federal holiday since 1983's Martin Luther King Jr. Day.  One of three major vaccine-makers reported first quarter sales at three and a half billion dollars. Twelve to fifteen-year-olds could get their shots. Vaccinations continued apace in places uninfected by misinformation and malice. Though the national death toll from Covid-19 topped 600,000, the daily number was down to 342 from a peak of 3,136 in January, and the general mood mirrored the summer's brighter promise.

"Sues, 'outdoors' is a destination, not a death threat," James said. "We'll wear masks."

This was intended to encourage Susanna to help him ready the baby and Micheline for a walk in Inwood Hill Park. She was anxious about returning to work fulltime soon. She was in no mood.

He tried another angle, rattling on about a Pittsburgh-Paris breakthrough in gene research that looked promising for sight restoration. "They turn ganglion cells into new photoreceptors. They take proteins from algae to make any nerve cell sensitive to light."

Momentarily piqued by this information, Susanna looked up from the JAMA issue she was studying about a plague-related swab testing for sinus and pituitary surgery.

"I can't, now," she said. "You go."

James eyed an eager Micheline outfitted in new sneakers, headband, and plastic sunglasses, plus three-month old Carl Cooper, pacifier-sucking, sleeping in his stroller. How long would that last? James had toys, onesies, and disposables in the baby go-bag along with a precious bottle of breast milk inside a cool pack. Susanna didn't even put him through the check list, so he knew she was immovable. He led the way to the elevator.

Outdoors, Micheline looked up and around, listening and scanning.

"No cicadas," she reported.

"Looks like the seventeen-year cycle is a big dud up here. Maryland, DC, and south Jersey, that's another story," James said.

"DC is where the President is. We have a LEGO White House at Rockefeller school. The one with the big dome is…?"

"*Dome* is a good word …The Capitol Building," James supplied.

They continued walking toward the park. Micheline was quiet.

Then, "People climbed the walls like cicadas," Micheline said. "Not good."

"Who said?"

Micheline shrugged. "When?"

"Back in January. Before the twins' birthday."

"But then the President moved into the White House."

"Right."

"Good."

"Can we find swings?" she asked.

"We can try,"

"I like the bridges in the park."

"So do I," James said.


Nina sent her mother a link to a condo for sale on Whidbey Island not far from her house and close to the island's hospital. Four attached units of different colors, pale green, brown, red, and blue were part of several similar others in a Coupeville development overlooking a cove in Puget Sound.

"It has the look and feel of Mystic, CT," Pidge said.

"With California Gold Rush," Pearl agreed, "and *High Noon* thrown in."

The condo was sunny and new, much brighter than their Manhattan apartment. Granitetopped counters in kitchen and bathrooms, stainless steel appliances. A wall switch for a gas fireplace. More space and windows than they were accustomed to.

"So far away," Pidge said.

"It's relative. Nina is your relative. Charlotte and Clarissa. *Char* and *Clar*."

Masked, Pidge and Pearl walked back from a lunch date in an actual restaurant, not even sitting outdoors. They had described the island north of Seattle to two younger colleagues they hadn't seen in person in months. The wine they'd enjoyed at lunch lubricated the conversation then and now. Maybe take their advice?

Pidge said. "We do need to see it 'for real.'"

"Today, lunch indoors. Tomorrow, inside a jet cross-country?"

"We could stop at Esa's in Wyoming on the way back. You could see your grandboy Pinaquanah. *Pinaq* Pie-Knock? I can't keep up with all the nicknames! We could go to your Montana family, too. Is their entrance to Yellowstone Park open now? Where is that, Montana? Is that near Jackson Hole? Is Esa anywhere near them?"

Pearl humphed. "Esa's Riverton, Wyoming, is five plus hours away from Gardiner, Montana, north entrance to Yellowstone. Out west, nothing's what you mean by 'near'-- it's miles and miles of miles and miles."

At the building's front door, Azul enjoyed their tipsy greetings.

Pidge tapped her head. "Time for a nap," she grinned.

They crossed the lobby as the elevator welcomed.

"Open, *Sesame*," Pearl pointed.

"Sez-a-*me*!" Pidge echoed.

In the elevator, they both sobered.

"Things are moving so fast," Pearl said. "Contract signed. MONKEYS in production. Drew and Vera must've had everything in place before we sent the ms. She convinced her senior editor it was his idea to include the illustrations."

"They saw 'dailies.' Alan calls it that. How pregnant is she now?"

"Six months? She wants the book published 'before she publishes baby.' Crazy… We could do it. Get on a plane. Buy a condo."

"We could move. Pasikennae did," Pidge said.

The elevator arrived at their floor.

Together, they whispered, *"Open, Sesame."*


Nina and Chad picked them up at SEA International. Snow-capped Mount Rainier competed well with the New York City skyline they'd left behind. Pidge managed not to make the comparison aloud.

"Where's Mt. St. Helens?" she asked.

"About a hundred miles south," Chad answered from the driver's seat. "There are five active volcanoes in Washington."

"The twins would've told you their names," Nina turned around from shotgun, 'but we thought we'd try not to make your arrival overwhelming. The drive, the ferry, at least an hour and a half in the car each way, with eleven-year-olds! They're at a mostly outdoor playdate with their pod classmates. The hybrid school year has ended."

Chad Satriano was fair-haired; the twins were towheads. His parents, Pidge remembered, were (father) northern Italian/Alps, Mom a California girl. Pidge touched her tongue over her new crown. Reassuring. Since their vaccinations, she and Pearl had made up all their medical and dental appointments that Covid had cancelled. Pearl pushed new glasses up the bridge of her nose. Pidge smiled at the similar nervous gesture. Cataracts likely in her own future, ophthalmologist had predicted. Bone density, so far, so good. She and Pearl weren't Swiss cheese yet. All that walking on the sidewalks of New York. '*East Side, West Side, all around the town,*' Pidge said *No*! to the song in her head. Had Pasikennae felt homesick?

Nina's new home was a surprise. Of course, there had been photos and videos, but in person, Pidge pressed her lower lip *Wow*. Nina watched her mother take in the hill view of open water and snow-capped mountains, first from outdoors (rhododendrons, flowering trees, wisteria vines, pines, rooftops of houses below), then even more expansive from the second-floor bedrooms and second family room windows. Pidge looked at Pearl taking in the view. She appeared calm. As if all of it were hers. She belonged.

They bought the condo. For Pidge, a November emigration west. For Pearl, homecoming? Before they'd left New York, they arranged for Pidge to stay with Nina while Pearl flew directly to the RIW airport in Wyoming. Esa wouldn't hear of her driving alone from Riverton to and from Montana. He would take accumulated days and his wife, Sally (nee Ironeyes), a fifth-grade teacher in Pinaq's elementary school, had begun summer vacation. Pidge's and Pearl's flights would return to JFK on the same day, departing separately from Washington and Wyoming.

Anyway, Pearl was glad to travel this leg of the trip alone. She anticipated contrasts between geography, natural and familial. On Whidbey Island, Nina was a daughter with daughters. In Wyoming, Esa was a son with a son. Nina and her husband worked on lucrative, futuristic plans while Esa worked for a government that historically worked against those he tried to protect. Nina welcomed her mother. Esa had for so long built a wall between them – admittedly with masonry grouted on her side – that Pearl believed there was no going home again to what she'd escaped.

While she waited for Esa to pick her up at the small airport, she looked at the hunter's world of taxidermized heads and whole bodies arrayed along the terminal's walls: moose, black and grizzly bear, elk, mountain goat, Big Horn sheep, mountain lion. In display cases, goose, pheasant, turkey, crane, plus a replica of a dinosaur leg, knives and compasses. The sign: *Welcome to the Rendezvous City!* Pearl thought about the past two decades. There had been occasional vacation visits. Pidge and she had stayed in Jackson Hole those times, nearly three hours away from Esa in Riverton and his half hour commute to Fort Washakie.

As Pinaq had grown bigger, Esa and Sally moved to a high-ranch like so many built on Long Island in New York in the 1960's. Detective Donnelly would have felt right at home except for the purple mountain majestic views. Three bedrooms, two baths, living room, dining room and kitchen on one floor, a finished playroom with half bath below. They had a big backyard and a collie-shepherd rescue named Jack.

Pearl missed Ginger.

In those past decades, she and Pidge had also made trips via Jackson Hole-run tours to Montana, to the Gardiner Geyser General Store at the northern entrance to Yellowstone. It wasn't as if Pearl's brother and nephew had welcomed them as anything more than tourists. Pearl didn't know if her nephew even knew her story. Her brother once said he didn't remember his childhood at all, that she made it all up. She wished she hadn't snapped, "If I had, you would've been better!"

If he needed a cost-free, infinite commodity to sell for a profit, his self-delusion was available. Her brother was a Shoshone in a red MAGA hat. That oxymoron, drop the *oxy*. But here was Esa … walking across the airport terminal, holding eight-year-old Pinaq's hand. How handsome and tall, like her father - and his own -- Esa was. He had Pearl's Shoshone eyes and his Italian-American father's wavy hair. Wide shoulders, muscled body. Intelligence, charm. That ease. Pearl remembered the attraction -- now it worked well for Esa as a bridge between tribes and federal government. Esa's private motto? "More against pipelines than for peace pipes." With a laugh that invited friendship.

In facemasks, the trio greeted without embracing. Pinaq accepted the gift Pearl had brought. The boy had been clearly instructed not to open it until they got home. Pearl held out a bouquet of flowers she'd bought for Sally. Esa nodded at Pearl to hold them as he carried her luggage to the car. At least the next day, Sally was in the SUV when they drove north to Gardiner. They stopped after two hours less than midway in Moran, Wyoming, and stayed that late afternoon/ overnight at a log cabin-y resort called *Teepee* where Pinaq wilded the playground and fought to stay in the pool.

The following noontime, by the end of another longer morning drive to Montana, Pearl endured the visit with her unmasked brother and nephew at their busy Geyser General Store. "We got killed by Covid last year," her brother said.

"Not literally," Pearl mumbled behind her mask.

"But last month," her brother raised his voice so shoppers noticed, and he grinned at them, opening his arms, palms up, "was better than 2019!"

After an obligatory but limited stop in Yellowstone (there were closures at some sites), they spent an overnight in a Gardiner tourist hotel. Entering the lobby, Esa followed his mother's line of sight. He spoke to her *sotto voce.*

"People either wear masks or don't have a prob w'em. It's not New York City."

Pearl took his remark with the grains of salt she sprinkled on supper in the hotel's restaurant. Anyone could read the unobscured faces of the unmasked. Unfriendly. Problematical in many ways. Though the Yellowstone trip had evoked more than mere nostalgia – Proust had his cookies, Pearl felt visceral shock at the rare sight and sound, omen-like, of trumpeter swans – those enormous wings! – and the smell of childhood's egg stink from mists above bubbling thermal pools – Pearl had had more than enough. So had her son and family. Pinaq just wanted to return to the *Teepee* swimming pool.

On the journey back to Moran and Riverton, Esa talked about "high transmission rates in Montana and Wyoming. Wyoming offers free at-home testing at no cost. No nasal swab, either. The sample collection process is under the supervision of a Vault healthcare provider through an online, video-based telehealth visit."

Pearl did not mention the obvious: Wyoming's numbers were as bad as Florida's. And online access wasn't assured. She worried silently about Pinaq, too young for vaccination. Sally had welcomed Pearl's arrival bouquet. Her daughter-in-law was attentive to her mother-in-law. For the return trip, as "a treat," she put Pinaq in the front seat with Esa and sat beside Pearl, often putting her palm over Pearl's hand. Sally's mother, younger than Pearl by more than a decade, had died in March from the virus. Back home again in Riverton, when Pinaq was out of hearing, Sally had again thanked Pearl for the visit.

She said, "I want Pinaq to know his only grandmother now."

Pearl admired Sally. She was playing a role in Esa's stead, showing him how. The trust between her son and his wife impressed Pearl. Affection came naturally to Sally. She mellowed Esa – and Pearl. Some people were like that, 'balm in Gilead.' Pearl felt a familiar pang – she'd been more bomb than balm. She looked like Popeye's girlfriend, a Shoshone Olive Oil. She was all flint striking sparks. Sally was clear water smooth over stone. She was plump and calm, the colors of autumn, young in the ingenuous way of teachers of the young. Sally knew how to play. *Ha*, Pearl thought, Sally was like Pidge without New York angst!

That night, Pearl showed Pinaq where he lived on the standing globe in his bedroom, and, spinning the planet, where the Aegean was. She pointed to Crete and generally the distance to Pylos.

"It's like the trip from here to where I'm moving, from Riverton to Seattle."

Then she told him about bull leapers and blue monkeys and recited an improvised revision of one of Pidge's children's stories.

"*Pinaqus watched as great ships from Knossos entered the harbor at Pylos. He knew his friend* – what's the name of a girl you know?" Pearl asked.

"Adele," he said.

"*– Adeliae was on one of the great ships. Pinaqus knew that Adeliae was learning how to jump through the horns of a calf. He had been practicing jumping over his dog.*"

Sally was standing in the doorway. She laughed quietly.

"That's gonna be trouble," she said.

Later that week, Esa drove his mother back to the airport. Sally stayed home minding Pinaq's playdate with friends, dissuading them from dog-vaulting. She got them to create their own ("rounded!") horns out of Play-Doh and cardboard and to come up with their own name for 'leapfrog.' *Jump You* won.

Masked farewell at the airport terminal, mother and son embraced.

"I'm so proud of you, Counselor," Pearl said.

"I'm proud of you, too, Professor."

"Esa."

"Mom."

At nearly the same time, Pidge was on a jet also heading back to JFK from Seattle, eyes closed, her mask in place. She reached up to close the vent blowing cooled, recycling cabin air onto her head. The plan was – move in November. Pidge had lived in one apartment – home – for seventy-five years. She wondered how the plane could lift the weight pressing on her. Enormities. Instead of this one, she concentrated on listing others. Lists usually calmed her. Nina now uppermost in her mind. Her husband Chad had had so many questions.

"Why Linear A? What drew you and Pearl to it? Your mother from Puerto Rico to New York City? Where was your father from?"

Nina tried to temper his tenacity, but the twins, nearing their twelfth birthday, amplified Chad's curiosity. Together, they all celebrated the upcoming move.

"You'll be here for Christmas!" Char and Clar said in blond unison.

Now, dozing on the jet, Pidge heard some answers. Her mother and father had been brought together by war, no more making a choice than Pasikennae had, vaulting through the horns of a bull. Gibraltar those same horns, the word/image of passage to eternity that SHE carried Pasikennae through how many times? Why Linear A? Because like the mountain peak, it was there. At first, neither Pidge nor Pearl knew the other was climbing, but eventually through competing (with men), they had realized cooperation would suit them both and the quest better. Pearl had her own Enormities, the native Diaspora of stolen land and lore. *Diaspora*.

Where was her father from? Obedience to the harsh order given to his tribe. The original application of the word. The Septuagint in Deuteronomy 28:25 was the echo of God's dire warning in Exodus 34:10, *"for it is a terrible thing that I will do with thee.* The Hebrew word *galuth* "exile." As in, from Palestine. Greek *diaspora* from *diaspeirein* "to scatter about, disperse," from *dia* "about, across" plus *speirein* "to scatter" like seeds. An earlier word in English was late 14th century Latinate *dispersion*. Related: *Diasporic*. *Spore* (noun) "the reproductive body in flowerless plants corresponding to the seeds of flowering ones. Modern Latin *spora*, from Greek related to *sporos* "a sowing," from Proto-Indo-European *spor-*, variant of root *sper-* "to spread, sow." (also *sparse*).

Pidge slept. In her dream, Pasikennae was the miniature icon of homelessness revealed at the last, safely nested in the center of a divine Matroska doll.

June had begun with the move of pregnant Marwa and her father with John and his daughter Beckett to the expanded apartment on the fourth floor. They called the place *The Merger*, name-changed from its previous morbid labels. The month ended with a unanimous vote to move the Theodore Roosevelt statue on horseback flanked by Black and Indigenous humiliation in front of The American Museum of Natural History to a yet-to-be-chosen institution dedicated to the Rough Rider. Debate about where the plague had started – in Chinese animal markets or research in laboratories, benign or malevolent – continued. Also, unmasked crowds that had partied and rallied during the Springtime honeymoon of lowering Covid case numbers caused rising graphs, more deaths, and dread.

Alan's time was divided unequally among work, family, and art. Did he even have any friends anymore? Of his own, he meant. He'd cleaned up brushes and paints. Now showered and dressed, he had about an hour to get to the *HITTITE* set in Queens, car waiting outside. Did he know the name of the production assistant at the wheel? He was another actor from Texas, Alan remembered. Smart guy, trying to impress him. He'd flattered, *"HITTITE's not Merchant-Ivory or PBS, it's the WEST WING in ancient Turkey."* Alan now sent a text inviting – yes, Jeff – upstairs for a bathroom break. P.A.'s were overworked and underpaid. Don't let him get the wrong idea, though.

Alan eyed the breakfast banana he had yet to peel. What might it taste like on this early July morning? Over the smell of floors and walls long steeped in paint, linseed oil, turpentine? He was alone in the Manhattan studio. He'd spent the night working on the abstracted De'Lynn Madonna. Slept on the now closed sofa-bed. Alan was pleased with his solution to moving the artwork in the future. Practicality had inspired an arguable aesthetic decision. Instead of one huge, mural-like canvas, he was doing the portrait in parts. Fragmenting Her and then putting Her together over the high fireplace wall on Long Island. He liked the idea of moving Her around in parts, reflecting seasons, perhaps. Moods. Now. To the banana at hand. Would it taste like soap again? Since the plague, fruits sometimes changed their flavors. Fortunately, neither David nor the boys did. David always smelled like David (walnuts or sand paper), Arno (sugar cookies), and Dylan (raisin bread). He peeled and breathed in. Ripe banana for real – now evoked monkeys -- blue monkeys! The P.A. buzzed. Alan buzzed back and put on his masks.


It had been crazy for Marwa and John incorporating Anam Al-Halimi's household into their already complex move two-floors down to *The Merger*. They hadn't even noticed the Fourth of July fireworks downtown, but by the mid-month morning when *The Running of the Goats* returned – after its plague year hiatus – the Al-Halimi/Donnelly family was part of its welcoming crowd. Masks on most children, some adults, on all of *The Mergers*. It was too long a walk uptown to 120th Street for Marwa's father or almost-eleven-year-old Beckett. Marwa denied her pregnancy was another excuse but allowed John's protective reaction. She decided it was biological, not cultural.

Another dictate was no more than three to a cab, so Azul waved down two taxis to take them to the run's start. Twenty-four weed-grazing goats were released into a fenced enclosure on a steep hill to eat invasive species in Riverside Park. Five of them would stay until the end of August. Beckett was excited to vote online for her favorite. Along the way in the park, the family stopped at live music but not for masked-politicians giving speeches. Free goat-embroidered fanny packs were handed out to Marwa and Beckett as they followed the herds of bleaters and noisy people.

"*Skittles* is in the lead," Beckett said, "but Number 21, *Chalupa* looks good to me." She pointed at a big, white-bodied goat with a white-striped nose on a hornless brown head. "Is that a he, she, or they?"

John took a photo and searched. "*Chalupa* means a kind of shallow-water boat. *Scallop* in English. Says horns don't necessarily reveal gender in goats. Uses *he*. Could be a *wether*. Don't ask. *Chalupa* looks what they call *polled*. Horns removed."

"Ouch," Beckett said, reaching for the phone. "I need to *observe*. I have to make a video for a science assignment over summer vacation."

She quickly found, "The goats will eat *porcelain berry, English ivy, mugwort, multiflora rose and poison ivy*. What's *porcelain* berry? This'll work great!"

Marwa approved, "Flora *and* fauna." The goats began grazing. "I had no idea the park had so much poison ivy," she said.

John observed her move her palm protectively over her small baby bump.

In the park, '*Jiddo*' bought Beckett "a celebratory goat tee shirt, an 'early birthday gift.'" Avoiding food carts for lunch, no argument, John used Marwa's phone to get them a UberXL back to the apartment. The driver found the quartet sitting tucked together on a Riverside Drive park bench. Much later, when the votes were counted, it turned out that *Chalupa* had won.     A week after, Marwa commiserated with Pidge and Pearl about the rigors of moving and described what they'd missed at *The Running of the Goats*. She had gotten on the elevator on the fourth floor as they were descending from the ninth.

"We're going to miss *you*," Marwa said. "Rome's the Eternal City, but New York never stays the same. It's all excavations and scaffolding awaiting disorienting reveals. John says, '*A veritable Belasco*,' which is, I believe, a reference to THE GREAT GATSBY but I forget why." She saw Pidge eyeing her abdomen. "Fifth month," Marwa patted. "Size of a banana, I'm told.

Doesn't feel like it."

Pidge said, "First time I felt Nina, I didn't know – woke me up in the middle of the night. What had I swallowed? A butterfly? A minnow? Then I realized – what joy!"

They both turned to Pearl.

"I remember a distinct thud," she complied. "Something with small bones. More slippery salamander than fish. My mother had a hideous expression for the first sensation of life. I refuse to recall it."

Startled by such uncharacteristic revelations from Pearl – she'd never spoken of either pregnancy -- Pidge blurted, "Pearl's received an invitation to join a Shoshone Language Project at Idaho State U. in Pocatello, Idaho. It won't be necessary for her to be on campus any more than she had to be here at Columbia, Zooming. She can stay with her son for rare occasions. Pocatello is over five hours from Esa, but there's a direct flight from Seattle to Riverton, Wyoming, and he'd likely do the drive, breaking it up into a couple of days."

"There's also a flight from Seattle straight to Pocatello," Pearl said, "plus faculty housing."

The elevator opened to the lobby flooded with bright morning sunlight through the wide entry and bay window. Azul held the door for them, and they soon parted company.

In the heat, Marwa walked to the crosstown bus stop to the beat of her sandals on the sidewalk, 'Poc-a-tell-o, I-dah-ho.' Where was that? *'Eid-al-A-dha'* added itself to the rhythm. 'Poc-a-tell-o, I-dah-ho, *Eid-al-A-dha.*' What was that?

She and her father had just again blasphemously ignored a major Muslim holiday – the one scapegoating Ismail's cut throat, her mother's delicious lamb cubes, and *fatta*, rice toasted with tomato sauce and bread chips. With these memories rose the bile of 9/11 (high school) and her pilgrimage to Mecca (college), both catastrophes. You could take the girl out of Islam, but you couldn't take the guilt out of the girl. Marwa sat on the bus with crossed arms resting on her pregnancy. *You won't carry that.*

Pidge and Pearl were silent their whole slow, hot walk to Zabar's.

Pidge's thoughts about Pearl's secretiveness led to her parents'. Were they spies in WWII? Don't ask! What she'd been told was contradictory. They met working on code-breaking? Where? Her mother was born in Puerto Rico during the 1918 flu pandemic. She survived diphtheria as a child. 'They had to burn all my bedroom furniture and clothes.' In 1940, when Mom was a senior at UPR, a Classics major, fluent in English, Spanish of course, French and Italian, she took a math class with Pidge's father, a visiting professor from NYC. He was twentyseven. So she'd met him there. The university's *Torre* was new then, dedicated in October, 1939, the month after the Nazi invasion of Poland. That Auden poem – John Donnelly would know it. *We must love one another or die.* Auden couldn't decide on the ending. *Or/and?*

Pidge thought of Pearl's silence about origins on the Wyoming Wind River Reservation. How had *Mami* felt about leaving Puerto Rico, never returning, not even for a vacation? Her parents didn't marry till the war's end in 1945, the year before she was born and named *Paloma. Shapiro.* Her father was a lapsed Jew, also estranged from his family. Pidge knew so little about her own past. So many lapses in so many lives! The July heat made her sigh. Zabar's was still a block away.

Pearl had disconnected from the elevator conversation. She was thinking in Shoshoni of this summer (*egi da'za*) and next (*egi da'zan gimaginde*), how different life on the Pacific coast would be. How hot this early morning (*beaichehku*) already was, what bread (*degumahanipe*) Zabar's would tempt them with today (*egi dabai'yi*). How pleasant, almost liquid (her bare feet in a cool stream) it was to think in Shoshoni (*sosoni'daigwape-ha*) something to look forward to. She smiled.

"Good thoughts?" Pidge asked as they entered the busy store. Breathing in the delicious aromas through her mask, she sighed this time with pleasure.

It took Pearl a reluctant moment to return to English. "*TsaaN, getaaN. Haa.* Good, very. Yes."


That hot July morning in the precinct, Detective Donnelly had no Auden on his mind. The day before, he'd dropped by the Duane Reade where Ellen Grenley worked, only to find out she'd been fired, and no one knew where she or a possible safety deposit might be. Also yesterday, Malcolm Ackerman's ringtone had sung *Mack the Knife* to him, his message demanding news about the Luster case. John didn't like coincidences. He didn't like starting another day feeling uneasy. Technique: as he rearranged objects around his desk, ditto thoughts.

Beckett and Marwa talking the night before. All right, he'd eavesdropped. Marwa was answering Beckett's questions about her synesthesia. The two were sitting on the bedroom floor at either end of the pulled-out trundle bed, stretching a fitted sheet over the corners of its mattress. Beckett hoped for a sleepover party with a private school friend whose parents had a pied a terre in the City.

Marwa said, "Your upcoming birthday is a prime number, eleven. It's the fifth prime, like how many fingers you have on one hand. I always see the primes in the red-brown range. Eleven was Crayola's *Burnt Siena*, a favorite. It's the color of your hair. From now on, it'll be *Beckett's Birthday.*"

Then, Beckett surprised him as much as she did Marwa.

"When I was little," she said, "I thought five was 'a celebration' and two was an 'office worker', so I said that 5 + 2 = an office party. Which was tan."

"How little?" Marwa asked, interested.

But Beckett wasn't. "Maybe I've got what you've got."

Marwa teased, "That's weird."

"You're weird. Are you and Daddy engaged?"

The way his daughter asked encouraged the detective. He and Marwa could get married at City Hall in October before the baby arrived. She'd already named *A. Donnelly Al-Halimi.* A for Anam, but they'd call him Donnelly. Never Don. Marwa was emphatic. Also about prime numbers. He remembered her dream. And their conversation the night Donnelly had likely been conceived.

"The most beloved method for producing a list of prime numbers is called the sieve of Eratosthenes."

"Beloved?"

"The method results in a list of <u>prime numbers up to 100</u> in colored boxes my synesthesia saw as a kaleidoscope. Two is the only prime number that is even and the rest of the primes are odd."

John had asked, "Why is one not a Prime Number?"

Marwa whispered, "A <u>prime</u> must have two positive factors. One has only one divisor, itself."

"But two can make three."


Susanna and James were in the car driving back to northern Manhattan from a day trip upstate to Cold Spring to visit Dayita and Esau. Their toddler Sandra would be two in August. In the Duckett-Beekmans infant (back-) and child (front-)facing car seats, Micheline entertained four-month-old Carl Cooper.

"But mostly, I just keep his binky *en su boca,*" Micheline reported as she tucked it between CC's lips.

Since James had done the to-drive, Susanna was doing the slightly over an hour fro-. He occasionally roused from his thoughts. Aside from childcare, much of the day had focused on the consortium of ninety-nine scientists – James among them – whose six papers had just been published to fanfare: they had deciphered the entire human genome.

When Dayita asked, James answered, "The human genome contains 19,969 protein-coding genes. We found more than two million new places in the genome where people differ."

Esau mused, "Is that more or less complex than the professors' deciphering of Linear A?"

"Yes," Susanna laughed.

It had been a doubly warm reunion outdoors. The car's air conditioning was welcome after the day spent in July's heat. It bothered their hosts much less than it did Susanna and James. But in the Persaud/ Kimani's yard, the leaf-trees had shaded and the pines scented more than in the Inwood Hill Park. James must had dozed. He wakened to increased traffic as the GPS voice directed Susanna to an exit. He waited for her to complete a turn.

Then he said, "I was dreaming – drum roll, please, was it the Muppets ripping off Mel Brooks," James intoned, "*PIGS IN SPACE'* – now *BILLIONAIRES IN SPAAAA --SSSS* -- unholy trinity of Branson and Bezos in July, Elon Musk for the Ides of September."

He must've awakened the baby. James paused as CC cried in the back seat and Micheline fumbled for his pacifier.

James resumed in a quieter tone, "You can't make this stuff up -- taking off first on July 11th from Spaceport America in *Truth or Consequences, New Mexico* – Branson's *Eve* delivered *Unity* beyond the border where outer space begins, then Bezos's Blue Origin *New Shepard* on July 20th."

"I think Bezos wins phallic image." Susanna said. "His penis rocket."

"Branson was first, but no erection." James agreed. "A shepherd chasing a virgin. Toto, I don't think we're in Arcadia anymore."

"What's an erection?" Micheline asked from her front-facing backseat.

"We're almost home," Susanna answered.

*Infrastructure* had become the word of the day. June had seen the catastrophic collapse of a condo building north of Miami, ninety-eight dead. In Manhattan in July, two sinkholes had opened on the East Side and West Side, and all around the town, as the songs went, the earth seemed to move under feet -- and vehicles. The Sunday it happened, Pidge and Pearl had slowly walked up to see the damage on Riverside Drive at 97th Street. By the time they got there, the two nearly-swallowed cars had been removed, but M5 buses were cancelled in both directions between 110th and West 72nd Street. They had to walk several blocks to find a cab to take them back to the 80's.

Just several days later, a twenty-foot hole opened up at 89th Street and York Avenue during Thursday morning traffic. Pidge looked up from her phone and breakfast. She raised the small screen to Pearl.

Pidge said, "I lack ambition to see what happened. I just hope James Beekmans isn't caught in that with Micheline."

Pearl looked up from the morning newspaper. She had already been working on the crossword.

"*Tetragrammaton*, is that splendid or what? Another *r-a* containing word! Five so far. I'm looking for Egyptian god *Ra* and more solar words for summer heat."

"Pearl, another *sinkhole*. On York Avenue. Now."

"Either the sky -- or ground -- is always falling somewhere, Chicken Little." Pearl frowned at the puzzle, then, "Do you remember, what was it, an Op Ed –"

"– Guest essay, if you please –"

"Okay, *Guest Essay*, the four-Hebrew-letter name of God, the Tetragrammaton, *YHWH*, was probably not pronounced *Jehovah* or *Yahweh*. The Israelite priests would have read the letters in reverse as *Hu/Hi*. So the hidden name was Hebrew for "*He/She*."

Pidge was remembering. She searched on her phone and found, "You're right, five years ago, it was still called *Op Ed –*." She read aloud, "'Counter to everything we grew up believing, the God of Israel — the God of the three monotheistic, Abrahamic religions to which fully half the people on the planet today belong — was understood by its earliest worshipers to be a dual-gendered deity.'"

Pearl leaned toward Pidge's phone to read the title. "*Is God Transgender?*"
What's the Shoshone answer?"
"Trans-*species*? Wolf and Coyote?"


Masked in the elevator, another encounter occurred, this time as Alan descended from the ninth floor, and Detective Donnelly got on at the fourth. He wished he'd taken the stairs, but it was a hot midday.

"How's it going," Alan said politely.
"We're always running out of something."
Like conversation, John thought. Their few details about high school and college sports had been shared long ago. The actor was high school football; both played first base in college; no need to repeat. Both were familiar enough not to have guards up; Alan was always more defensive than flirtatious, and John was no one's mark.

"Strange living where --?" Alan asked.
A reasonable question, John nodded but said, "No. Not even at first, I was surprised, to be honest. Too busy, and thankfully, I'm the only one with the red memory." He shrugged.

"Occupational hazard."

Alan saw the barn studio, the green memory. "You don't forget?"

John was piqued, but the elevator door was opening.

"It's there, but not there, like all ghosts," he said.

Separating, they crossed the lobby to the front door. Azul opened it for them, letting in a wave of hot air. Alan walked outside seeing not ghosts but a painted plastic overlay of an image that revealed and covered what the artist required.

*Chapter 27  August*

By August, the global plague cases passed the 200 million mark, more than 614,000 fatalities in the US. More patients were hospitalized than at any point since February. Daily caseloads increased tenfold since late June, and death reports, lagging behind case data, had doubled. The FDA also received reports of hospitalizations resulting from self-medication with *ivermectin*, a drug intended to treat parasites in horses. David became a (free) source in the building for home testing kits and N95 masks for adults and children. Arno and Dylan considered themselves "poster twins" for masking; they phoned Micheline "to make sure you have plenty."

"My mother is a *brain* surgeon," Micheline said on Susanna's phone. "She has PPE from the hospital. It means *Personal Protective Equipment*."

"We know!" the boys said in unison.

Susanna frowned.

"But thank you," Micheline added.

Susanna nodded.

"Do you have polar bears *in In*wood? Dylan teased.

"We're not that far north," Micheline said. "You don't have to cross a bridge."

"We go over the Triborough Bridge to Long Island. We're going again this month to see the Perseids," Arno said. "Named for the constellation Perseus. He cut off Medusa's head."

"I know," Micheline said. "She turned men into stone with just a *look*."

"Maybe next year, maybe you'll come along."

"We've all gotta get vax'd. But maybe not the baby."

Arno and Dylan were not interested in babies. They handed the phone back to Mercedes.

Marwa's father, Anam, met with his visiting nurse, while in The Merger living room, the rest of the quartet was again watching Beckett's favorite moments from the Tokyo Summer

Olympics a week earlier. The eleven-year-old had been spending a lot of time with Pidge and

Pearl back and forth in their apartment on the ninth floor, often accompanied by her "almost

step-Jiddo." When the older women came down to the fourth floor, Anam played requests on his

new upright e-piano – David's apartment-sized *Clavinova* recommendation -- backing an

Lshaped couch. Behind Anam was a wide window looking through branches of healthy trees

lining the street. A rainy summer. Anam, Pidge, and/or Pearl had been taking Beckett to classes

at a gymnastics studio overlooking Pier 1 on the Hudson and its café on West 70th Street, nine

blocks south of the closed café they missed. This new one had green umbrellas instead of blue.

Now watching TV, Beckett was again mesmerized by the young Olympian women's vaulting.

Imitating, she pointed at the screen with both arms and had to be discouraged from doing

cartwheels in the living room.

"The professors said Captain Pasikennae vaulted over bull*s*! Starting even when she was my

age! Over *bulls*! It's where the cow jumping over the moon comes from."

Marwa saw her father walking his nurse to the door. Then Anam walked into the living room,

saw what was again on the widescreen and reassured his daughter.

"My bill of health is all paid," he whispered to Marwa.

Beckett heard him and looked up from the floor where she was balancing on her tailbone,

stretching her legs and pointing her toes into a raised V.

"Jiddo, what's older," she asked, "Muslim or Minoan? Professor Pidge says *Pasiphaean*, but

Mom says" – imitating her mother's voice – 'that's feminist. *Which isn't a bad thing, Beckett*, but

it's a looonngg story.'"

She rolled her eyes.

"You could be an actress," Anam said.

John moved so her father could sit beside Marwa, who had her legs up on the chaise side of

the couch. The detective was thinking about the recent discovery of the Luster safety deposit

box. It contained a memory stick w/info verifying and amplifying the previously obtained cell

phone data.

"So the short answer is Minoan," Anam answered. "Captain Pasikennae is about 3600 years

ago. Islam about 1400 years."

Beckett reached for a handful of popcorn from the bowl on the coffee table.

"2200."

"You could be a banker," Anam said.

"My Donnelly *jiddo* taught physics," Beckett said. "You need math. He tutors now."

"Closing ceremonies of the Olympics tonight," John said. "Have you kept a tally?"

Beckett's mouth bulging with popcorn, she garbled, "U.S. overall medals, 113, China next,

88. Russia, third, 71. U.S. gold, 39, China 38, Russia 20."

"You'll choke." John handed Beckett a juice box.

"It's the Islamic New Year tonight," Marwa realized. "The *Hijri* marks the start of the

Muslim lunar calendar. It's approximately eleven days shorter than the solar, Gregorian calendar.

The Jewish calendar is also lunar."

Anam's mouth gaped. John handed him a juice box.

This time when Beckett spoke, she looked at her father and pointed at her empty mouth.

"Jiddo and I saw the end of the ending this morning before you two woke up. They put out the

Olympic flame." She looked at Anam. "*Extinguished.*"

Anam smiled and nodded.

Basking, Beckett said, "The next time they'll light it will be in Paris in 2024." She paused.

"Wow. I'll be four*teen*!"

John added, "The baby will be three."

Marwa's hands were folded, spread on her swollen middle. She kept to herself the other memories that August had roused. Hiroshima. Nagasaki. She unfolded her hands to reach up and touch the gold hoops in her earlobes. Impulsively getting her own ears pierced on that scorching hot day at *Adonis Piercing & Tattoo* on Canal Street, where Judy Yamaguchi had made an appointment to have a boat tattooed on her right shoulder. Afterwards, they acted like tourists and boarded a tugboat at the South Street Seaport. Pre-her first time. Pree's letter. She folded her hands again. Marwa glanced at John who seemed to be reading her thoughts. Her father moved; John sat beside her again. Abreaction in Dr. Rawi's office. Condi Rice ignoring the August 6th memo warning. That daughter's witness outcry at the 9/11 hearings. *Shame!* Marwa must've made a sound. John took one of her hands and held it. She put them together on her belly so he could feel the lively foot or elbow.

To include her father, Marwa explained, "It's pointy! We sleep like spoons so when this one wakes me, he wakes John, too."

Anam said, "Your mother said that, 'sleep like spoons.' I remember when she carried you. You kicked so much more than Sharif or Joey."

John felt good and laughed. Marwa gently elbowed him.


The *HITTITE QUEEN* shooting schedule allowed Alan a few days off so they drove out to Orient again, mid-week, hoping to see the Perseid shower. For the kids, it would be like trying to stay up for New Year's Eve because they were looking for what Arno had read about.

"*Earthgrazers* are before midnight. We gotta look northeast," he displayed his new, large compass. "That's to the left of where the sun rises," Arno gestured in the middle seat, which allowed him to swipe at Dylan, who blocked, then caught his brother's hand and squeezed it. Mercedes scolded them in rapid Spanish.

Dylan said he intended to make a painting of the event. "A dark blue almost black sky with meteors and a full moon over the water, reflecting."

Arno snorted. "You can't put a moon. There's no moon this year. That's why you can see the meteors."

Alan squelched the latest conflict. "Indanthrone or Ultramarine blues are good for that. I can show you how to mix them."

Adirondack chaises were already on the slate patio at the back of the house. While Mercedes started the barbecue and the boys got in the way outdoors, David and Alan carried the lawn furniture onto the grass, facing the water. After supper, they all reclined and listened to Arno's directions – he had warned against binoculars or telescope. Arno spread both arms wide.

"You've gotta take in as much of the whole sky as you can and look straight up, not at the Perseus constellation. That's where they come from, but the meteors are really just sixty miles above Earth."

The five-and-a-half-year-old pointed above his head to the night sky with one bare arm. It was still hot out. Citronella torches blew lemony smoke across the observers, making Arno cough and mostly keeping mosquitoes away.

But it was overcast and the clouds never broke. The twins fell asleep on the chaises before ten p.m. when the meteor shower was supposed to begin. Mercedes was grateful for an early night, and the fathers carried the twins to bed. It was too hot for a fire in the fireplace, not enough to alter the mood and turn on AC. David played the piano, gentle Chopin, not the pounding Liszt he'd kept practicing.

Alan sketched, facing the fireplace wall, mind racing hand with images of his fragmented Madonna. All the screened doors and windows were open. Scents of ocean and citronella were swirled through ducts and vents by attic fans that hummed, accompanying pianissimo music and the sounds of Alan's pencil on paper. He wasn't thinking in words but somehow saw and heard *exorcism* echoing *orgasm*. Blinking, he wondered was that like synesthesia? David began the chords of a familiar prelude in a minor key. Alan's left hand tugged him back to Her.

*Serendipity III* was a boutique restaurant in the East 60's known for costly desserts. Pidge had assured a disappointed Vera it was lucky it didn't do private parties anymore. In the taxi over from the West Side to a different according-to-Vera "destination restaurant" in the Burgos neighborhood, Pidge elaborated for Pearl.

"It was a total tourist magnet that Brearley girls loved to disdain when they schlepped twenty blocks-plus south after school for burgers and *Frrrozen Hot Chocolate*, if they had that then."

"Half a century ago-plus, you weren't a fan?" Pearl asked.

"Didn't have their money to burn. *My* Daddy was a City College prof. Mom was our language teacher. I was in-with-the-out-crowd," Pidge sang.

"That should be an anthem."

"Dobie Gray would have to sue me."

Finding the singer-songwriter's photo on her phone, Pearl said, "He died in 2011."

Hurricane Ida had just made destructive landfall in Louisiana on the sixteenth anniversary of Hurricane Katrina. Already saturated by Tropical Storm Henri's effects, New York also had its rainiest August 21st on record – 4.45 inches – the next day broke the record again. July had been wet, but this August was wetter – nearly two feet of rain, two months' worth, had fallen in a day and a half.

"If it had been snow," Vera said, welcoming guests to a dining room with an East River view, "it would've been nearly nine feet of it!"

The women agreed that snow was "a cool idea in August," how lucky they were to have this cloudless day, and most of all, that they were all masked, vax'd, and *could* get together indoors. But kisses or hugs were replaced by fist bumps.

A colleague of Vera's from the publishing house had just returned from Europe.

She said, "It was 119.8 degrees in Syracuse, Sicily. Wildfires in Greece, just like California."

"Well, you look cool as a cucumber today," Vera complimented, "while I am a watermelon!"

Vera was enormous. The women avoided comparisons, but Vera anticipated them, displaying her transformed body profile, her hands running over her enlarged breasts and pregnant belly.

"I look like the capital letter *B*."

"You'll be hearing that a lot soon," said another colleague who phone-found *Sesame Street*'s Count introducing orange-haired Muppets singing "Letter B" to the Beatles' *Let It Be* melody. The cluster laughed and briefly became a singalong recorded on another's phone.

Nearly everyone invited was present and mingling in the new plague-distanced way, including Vera's widowed mother and her aunt with daughters and other cousins from uncles in Queens. Speaking among themselves in Mandarin, they envied the extravagance of a party room in a famous Manhattan restaurant with a river view.

For a trio of non-Asian thirty-somethings who'd just joined Vera's family, her aunt translated a long, snarky remark contrasting Vera's youth with Drew's age and money into unbelievably fewer words as, "What a lucky baby!"

As two of the women drifted away, Vera's aunt said to the one remaining, as if asked, "We took the 7 IRT subway from Flushing into Grand Central and a cab from in front of the 42nd Street Library where we know the exit."

"I'm from Indiana," she said. "Flushing? Isn't that in the outerboro where *The Nanny* came from? Fran Fine with her hammy Jewish accent?"

One Chinese cousin laughed. "Jewish ham?"

Another added, "Now Flushing is a Chinatown."

Overhearing as they walked by, David commented to Drew, "In the seventeenth century, Peter Stuyvesant-time, the Dutch named it *Vlissingen* after the town in the Netherlands. The English, also there in north Queens, shortened it to *Vlissing* -- called it *Flushing*. <u>Samuel Pepys</u> referred to *Flushing* in his diaries. Flushing in Queens has the highest population of Chinese Americans in the metro area, and the metro area has at least twelve Chinatowns, the largest ethnic Chinese population outside Asia."

"You don't say," Drew joked, "I wish."

They were the only men at the shower except for the waiters. Alan had bowed out not only because he was scheduled on the set in Queens but also because Drew made it clear it was to be Vera's show, not inevitably his.

Drew had said, "You don't put catnip in a roomful of cats."

David had translated the compliment to Alan. Drew's mother "Super-Couth Ruth" and sister Andrea had flown down from Maine and were staying in the Burgos Park Avenue apartment. Pidge and Pearl stood beside Susanna Duckett as she asked Marwa when she was due.

"November," Marwa said.

"We're a population explosion," the doctor said, "dreading loss of choice for our next gen."

"How old is --?"

"Carl Cooper is five months. Micheline starts kindergarten next month."

Marwa glanced out the sliding glass window doors at the East River. "We have a closer view of the 59th Street Bridge from the new Rockefeller dining room."

"You'll love the Rocky nursery and daycare," Susanna assured.

"Too bad Dayita couldn't be here today," Pidge said. "You stay in touch?"

Dr. Dayita Persaud was the sole absentee, her hospital schedule ruling out the trip from upstate Cold Spring.

"Yes," Susanna said, pointing to a light wood-paneled wall where one unset table was covered in packages and balloons. "She sent me the gift to deliver for her. I guess 'delivery' is the word of the day."

But Susanna didn't add that it had arrived with a private note. She had read between its lines that Dayita couldn't cope with a baby shower. So she wasn't pregnant yet.

The restaurant's décor was a lively topic of conversation. Though lacking Serendipity's Tiffany chandeliers and neon-unicorned *Mobil*-logo Pegasus that Vera bitterly missed (to many guests' reassurances), the replacement venue's river-facing sliding window-walls of polarized glass were half open, partially filtering the glitter of August afternoon light on the water. The ceiling was a modernized version of old New York white tin tiles, and the floors a highly-urethaned dark wood, reflecting like mirrors. White-clothed round tables were set with variegated crystal, silverware. Unmatched porcelain dishes were centered by floral arrangements of similarly Fauve-saturated colors.

Drew and David overheard Vera saying, "They told me strong color would be perfect for the shower."

The men exchanged a look.

Drew said, "News to me. I didn't know she could be told anything. Whatever Vera wants…"

"Well, you wanted her, and she also wanted **Blue Monkeys** to be published before the baby arrived."

"Breakthrough compromise – it'll be out for this holiday season. After Thanksgiving. Even the gods must demur to Time. *Chronos*, right?"

David wanted to detail the birth of Zeus on Crete and his Mother Rhea's plot to trick the filicidal Father Chronos, but Drew recognized the look in his friend's eye and stopped him with a raised palm.

"You're allowed just one detail."

David laughed. "The milk of a goat named Amalthea kept Zeus alive."

Drew patted his shoulder. "You deserve a drink. You can order what you like, but *I'm* told I'm 'on the Vera wagon.' She wants me alive to raise the *gōngzhǔ*."

"You sound happy to be hen-pecked."

David laughed, and on a paper napkin, he penned two Chinese characters: 公主 "Write or pronounce it wrong, and it's a card game like Hearts. I don't even try to say it out loud."

"Princess," David translated. "Also, *wáng fēi*. Get that one wrong, and you're literally 'wasting your breath.' Trying in vain."

"Apparently, I was," Drew patted David's shoulder again.


August ended. On its next to last day, the U.S. pulled out of a generation of war in Afghanistan.

"'Tonight's withdrawal signifies both the end of the military component of the evacuation, but also the end of the nearly twenty-year mission that began in Afghanistan shortly after September 11, 2001,' said the head of U.S. Central Command in Tampa, Florida. 'The last C-17 lifted off from Kabul airport this afternoon at 3:29 p.m. East Coast Time, and the last manned aircraft is now clearing airspace above Afghanistan,' he said, which was one minute before midnight in Kabul."

Five of the goats eating poison ivy in Riverside Park, including Beckett's winner *Chalupa*, also returned home to Green Goats Farm in Rhinebeck, NY.

"That's north of Cold Spring *and* Poughkeepsie," Pidge told Pearl. "When I was in college, we had to take written tests every year on college rules – we sat on the floor outside our rooms in the halls of our dorms – one question on the test was how far 'young ladies' were allowed off campus. Maybe Rhinebeck was our northern border? I remember someplace called Wappingers Falls. Were you tested on rules at U. Montana?"

"I was Shoshone. I broke the ruler."

*Chapter 28  September (Waiting)*

Eighty-two years before, the Nazis had invaded Poland on September first, beginning World War II. Detective Donnelly walked toward the precinct on the anniversary morning that reliably returned lines of the Auden poem. He was thinking about Ellen Grenley and the new safety deposit box she had opened in a neighborhood bank. He walked to the rhythm of the words. *Lost in a haunted wood, / Children afraid of the night/ Who have never been happy or good.* Was it "haunted" or "hunted"? Because he certainly was hunting Grenley. Enough to arrest but not convict. Yet. The 20th Precinct came into view.  He saw the entry mural's bronze hieroglyphics. *There is no such thing as the State/ And no one exists alone;/ Hunger allows no choice/ To the citizen or the police;/ We must love one another or die.* Or *and.* Definitely *and.* Detective Donnelly was waiting – and waiting -- for the appropriate court to be persuaded that there was a reasonable cause to suspect the Grenley safety deposit box hid something illegal, a weapon, drugs, stolen property – whatever. And where was Grenley? Neither vaccine nor hospitalization record, disappeared?

That night, the end of Hurricane Ida flooded the New York subways. Dr. Susanna Duckett's uptown hospital buzzed with talk about its network member, Mount Sinai West, formerly Roosevelt Hospital, a few blocks south of Lincoln Center, where the OR and X-ray areas were inundated. Nurses trying to return to New Jersey got stuck midway and couldn't get home or back to work. In the midst of plague, "What next, frogs will fall from the sky?!" Flash flooding turned platforms and stairwells "into waterfalls. The century-old subway system stopped like a heartbeat."

Two weeks after the flooding downtown receded, on the upper East Side, Vera's water broke early in the morning of the autumnal equinox, Wednesday, September 22nd – possibly as Dayita and Esau conceived Sandra's sister who would be born in early June, 2022. The Burgos baby was named for Vera's family surname, Mifeng, pronounced *Mee-fun*.

"It means a bee," Drew phoned David with the news. "I'm calling her Muffin, but I bet at Willard or Walker's, she'll become Muffy – or Stinger!"

Alan had been meeting with his THE FIRST END OF THE WORLD Scots dialect coach for nearly a month. He'd had to move from easy mimicry of famous Scottish actors into the grind of character. The *HITTITE QUEEN* diva finally learned she hadn't been cast for the movie, which made for icy filming in the Queens studio. While a relief from hot September weather, the chill was a motive along with rising plague numbers to get out of town while the going was possible. Travel to/in/around Crete was going to be tough enough in mid-September. Alan waited for his character on *QUEEN* to go into a coma and for departure to begin.


Marwa was also awaiting endings (an experiment, gestation) and beginnings (labor, birth). Earlier in the month, when the Jewish holiday absented some grad assistants, she had thought about religious lunar calendars and days that began with sunset instead of secular dawn. She wondered about the eons of clockless time. Measurement was innate in the amount of *relaxin* softening the ligaments stretching her pelvic girdle. The twentieth anniversary of 9/11 approached.

John was at work. She was in the kitchen looking out the open window. Beckett was at school, Marwa's father at the piano in the living room. An image of the window in James

Beekmans's dorm room – 2004 -- opened behind her eyes with a late April scent memory of wet breeze bringing lilacs into his room like a bouquet. He had sat at a blue plastic desk chair, and she sat cross-legged on his neatly made bed. He stood and walked to the window, his back to her.

She had told him, "When those planes hit the Twin Towers, for me, they crashed into *arkan al-Islam*, the Five Pillars of Islam, and when the Towers fell, those Pillars fell. I was on the Hudson in a Fire Department boat, holding Joey's hand. They were evacuating children from the City. The Towers fell. Black clouds, many shades of white and gray. I didn't know Pree was inside one of the planes. Inside those clouds."

James Beekmans said, "I had two classes that Tuesday. Sirens all day, but no jets overhead. We could see the billows of black smoke rising all the way up here. 'Pillars of cloud by day, fire by night,' someone said. I just started walking, west, off campus when we heard. It's not an easy walk to the Hudson. Girls always worry about rape, but if you're Black, you worry about everything. 'You're a neighborhood of one,' my uncle told me. When I saw those blurry videos of Atta and the rest of them boarding the planes, you know what I thought? I thought how easy it had been for them to pass through security because they didn't have Black faces, how any of *us* are routinely stopped anywhere, even by Black screeners at airports, cops, wherever. That day, no one stopped me. I got all the way to the river, well, this side of the train tracks. Nothing was running. Everything stopped. Except the sirens. I had to sit down on a curb. I saw other people did that, like our batteries had run out. Drained by all the *hurt* done in this world, from monster microorganisms I looked at under a microscope -- to us."

"*Lex Talionis,*" she had agreed.

"Law of Tooth and Claw."

James Beekmans then turned. Against the window's white background, momentarily she saw the black silhouette of a gentle giant.

"Y'know, when you first started going out with me and told me about your synesthesia color blindness, I thought maybe that was it, that was why, because you couldn't see what color I really am."

"Oh, James Beekmans," she said rising to her knees on the bed and reaching out for him. In the present, Marwa shut her eyes and shook her head. This hormone-flooded body routinely cycled to ridiculous lust.


Pidge and Pearl had easily gotten their annual shots for flu. Like John Donnelly, they were also waiting for approval – but for a third vaccination. September was winding down before both the Food and Drug Administration and the Centers for Disease Control and Prevention authorized COVID-19 boosters, only Pfizer vaccine, not Moderna yet. They'd both gotten the Pfizer in late January thanks to Susanna.

"Our lives have devolved into packing ourselves into boxes or letting go," Pidge said. She was at the table, writing labels and checking off a list.

"It's existential," Pearl agreed.

"We'll be packed into a box before long anyway."

"I intend to go up in smoke though I'd rather limit my carbon footprint planted under a tree."

"We'll have to tell Columbia Medical School to remove us from the donor list," Pidge said, "and see what works in Seattle."

"I already found us three there, similar sign-ups and witnessing."

"Andi called me from the Brooklyn Museum," Pidge held up her palm as if holding a phone, "to prove she was there. In a mask, surrounded by masked others. Asking – making sure -- we were taking the *Elk Hide* canvas to Whidbey Island. 'It will go over our gas fireplace mantel,' I told her. When I whined about the move, she said – she scolded me, '*Life* is a dissolving smoke ring. A contrail. Cosmos to chaos.'"

Pearl stood up from her position bent over a box of books.

"Artists. Metaphors. Science says we're the least, maybe four percent of all matter in the universe, dark matter twenty-three percent, dark energy *seventy-three* percent driving force causing the universe's accelerating expansion rate."

Pidge said, "Life *is* rare. Sing that *September Song*!"

"Well, we can dangle our rare toes in Broadway once more. We have tickets to a preview. *The Lehman Trilogy.*"

"Oh, you got them!"

"Brexit didn't block the import – your crush from the TV series is one of the Brit stars. The rise & fall of American financial history. So who won the Revolution, after all? And we'll get our fill of Broadway. It's over three hours. Two intermissions."

"We'll need catheters," Pidge worked on a smile.

"I know it's hard. You've only always lived right in this place."

Pidge swallowed. "I'm shamed by the grace of the truly displaced. Past and present."

Then Pidge held up a palm-sized Minoan memento, a blue-green bronze replica of the *Phaistos Disk*. Pearl nodded in approval. Pidge taped it in bubble wrap and placed it carefully in a box.

"But we traveled," she said.

"We danced," Pearl used Pidge's expression, then abruptly stopped.

Pidge waited.

Finally, Pearl said, "And Pasikennae? What did she pack for the Orkneys?"

Pidge put her elbows on the table, her hands pressed together, then spread them open, her palms bent back in echoed question.

Micheline had begun lottery-winning public kindergarten. It was neither Rockefeller Pre-K nor a nanny and twins in a big Upper West Side apartment with the blue monkeys fresco on the wall. Susanna dropped Micheline off at schoolmate Dominic's apartment in their building, the five-year-olds returning there at the end of the day, picked up by Marisol, the first grader's mother, who stayed home with Dominic's siblings, a three-year-old and infant. She was glad to earn the money Micheline added to her husband's income from a corner grocery he owned with a brother. James took Carl Cooper with him to Rockefeller's daycare.

"The teacher thought it was very funny that I knew *either or neither nor and but*," Micheline ran the words together in sing-song. "And the kids all thought I said *butt*, so she explained it."

"So you like Inwood kindergarten," Susanna said.

"We're Muscota, P.S. 314!" Micheline proudly corrected. "The public library is just across the street. And Dominic is in first grade so *el sabe todo*. *But* I speak Spanish fast. Mercedes's family is from Mexico, *butt,*" she giggled, "Dom's parents are *Dominicanos*. I said I was from the UWS and he said what country is that?"

"You're a real comedian," Susanna said.

Susanna had texted Dayita to thank her again for the help with Micheline's school placement. She'd read the fingers-crossed expectant news for June next year. The two doctors back-andforthed re the New York elderly who were lining up for boosters and the anticipated –

"November?" -- CDC approval of vaccination for five to ten-year-olds.

"Maybe," Dayita messaged, "the macabre roller coaster at hospitals can end."


On a masked line in the Duane Reade pharmacy on September's last day, Pidge and Pearl waited to get their shots They couldn't avoid overhearing a nearby conversation.

"The Arizona recount showed who not only won the country, but by 360 more votes than before!"

"Did you hear –? Of course, denied – told a crowd in Georgia that he won Arizona 'at a level you wouldn't *believe*!'"

"Of course, they did."

"Of course, I don't."

Pearl and Pidge nodded at each other. Then Pearl quietly invoked a sci fi novel by Fred Hoyle.

"*OCTOBER THE FIRST IS TOO LATE*," she emphasized *IS*.

"Everything does happen at the same time. Medieval one place, modern another. Oh, and the future, *upwhen* –"

"That's Asimov's *THE END OF ETERNITY*, which this feels just like," Pearl said, her sleeve already rolled up and ready for the booster's needle.

***Chapter 29  October***

February's October expectations for the Webb Telescope launch – Hallowe'en – were postponed. So its mission was delayed -- to learn about the 150 million to a billion years after time began and to see a different kind of light the older Hubble couldn't. Uptown in Inwood, James Beekmans was descending from the top floor, mentally joining photos of the Webb with images of Einstein's elevator thought experiment that led to his General Theory of Relativity. But James silently *hmphed*, Einstein's elevator had been *ascending*. An acquaintance from his Fordham Presidential Scholar days (when she was at Harvard) was one of the thousands of astrophysicists from many countries, states, and territories who had submitted proposals to be in the first round of Webb observations. She was at UCLA now, among the first chosen. She'd texted James, "The Webb will send back cosmic postcards in colors no human eye can see."

Detective John Donnelly was walking out of a different elevator to the lobby of the Upper West Side building. Azul opened the door at the entrance but avoided eye contact as John thanked him. October remained an antsy time in the building. This year was the second anniversary of the Luster murder.

Marwa had warned him, her hands on her swollen pregnancy. "People are looking at us so funny this month. Or looking away. Beckett guesses it's not the baby. It's the apartment. We have to tell her why."

John warmed to *we* but said, "Cold cases give people the chills. Hallowe'en doesn't help. Skeletons and severed limbs. The autumn stench of ginkgo trees adds to the ambience."

He hadn't said the word *blood* nor told Marwa the court finally allowed the opening of Grenley's safety deposit box. At last.

The Delta variant death toll for the plague had topped 700,000 in the U.S. There was optimism because numbers had been dropping since September.

"But we have the lowest vaccination rate, behind Uruguay, Cambodia, and Mongolia," Pearl said.

She and Pidge were eating a makeshift supper, standing in the kitchen as they put away food from the market.

Pidge carefully washed a sweet red pepper and dried it in paper towel. She removed the seeds and took a big bite, talking with her mouth full.

"'It was the best of times, it was the worst of times,'" Pidge quoted Dickens. "As always," she added.

Pearl grudgingly nodded. She was eating fresh rye bread. "Well, overlaying Columbus Day with Indigenous Day is good." She waved the heel of the fragrant loaf. "I can celebrate that."

"And Jefferson's gone from City Hall, just like Teddy R. fronting the Museum."

"Maybe history isn't the nightmare we're always trying to wake from -- so much as that frog in the well, three steps up, two steps down."

Pidge finished the pepper and offered another washed one to Pearl. Pidge glanced at the newspaper on the counter.

"I guess the new phrase is *supply chain*."

Pearl took one snappy bite from the pepper and put it down. "Supply chain *issues*. None of your favorite pasta this week."

"I stand corrected. I'd like to sit."

"We still have so much packing to do."

Pidge took a freshly brewed milky mug of tea to the round oak table in the living room. Pearl followed her. They both sat down, sipping quietly, taking in familiar street noises they realized they would not hear in the future.

"I guess," Pidge said finally, "we can make the journey if Odysseus made it back to Ithaca after twenty years…"

"It took twenty for America to leave Afghanistan…"

"Epic egos, then and now," Pidge sighed.

"I'm still partial to Medea and Themis."

Pidge laughed. "Vengeance *and* Law? I'll go with Pasikennae and HER."

Pearl took a long swallow of honeyed tea. Then she lifted her mug, toasting Pidge with their translation.

*"How sweet the drink. /How strong the song."*

The day before, they had taken a "last visit" to the Met Museum. Pearl headed for the Diker Art of Native America section whose coffee table book was already packed. She had walked around looking at familiar objects from cultures as disparate as the museum's far more enormous European collection. Pidge could never remember where what she was looking for was displayed. She liked "just happening upon it" around a corner – as always, it came as a shock – the Early Renaissance *Ecce Homo, Christ Crowned with Thorns*, whose face was the image of a Yalie she'd dated who'd committed suicide in an acid flashback in 1968. She said goodbye to him for the last time.


In Inwood, the quotidian for the Duckett-Beekmans followed the rhythmic tympany of work and home accompanied by gentle grandparental drum brushes in the Bronx, often interrupted by Carl Cooper on late night trumpet or loud snare drum solos. Micheline was at public school, and the twins were still at Calhoun, soon leaving for Crete. David had already arranged for distance learning, and he was glad when, one evening, Susanna helped Micheline text with Arno and Dylan.

Micheline messaged, "Muscota School is great!"

Arno replied, "Azul said he missed us, *el trio estelar*! We were the three stars in Orion's Belt."

Dylan wanted to send an image of the constellation. But Micheline was already on to a list of words she had learned.

"Do you know *solo, duo, TRIO, quartet?* Goes up to a hundred, but I like nine best. *Nonad.*"

"Gonad?" Arno texted.

Dylan collapsed laughing.

Micheline was not amused (though her mother was). "*Nonet* is less used because it's for music and atoms."

"Subatomic particles," Susanna corrected. "And for computers. A nonet is a byte of nine bits."

"I'm not texting that. They don't care. Computers bite?"

"Tell them what you like best about school."

Micheline texted, "After lunch we have quiet music time. We *try* to identi*fy* the instruments." Susanna was startled that Micheline knew how to italicize the teacher's rhyme.

Dylan interrupted. "We move soon. To HERAKLION. You can ski on Crete in the spring."

Arno took the phone from him and texted, "We're getting a tutor."

They did. Awaiting pre-production, before moving from the villa near Heraklion to the set at Akrotiri, Alan wrote an actual letter to Pidge. Around its margins were sketches he did for illustration. In New York, Pidge read the letter aloud to Pearl:

*Heraklion, Crete*
*October ending, 2021*

*Dear Pidge,*

*Glad to hear you were both boostered. We left my studio in a deserted Cast Iron district. Haunted sidewalks. Here for now, plenty of masks but most plague restrictions are lifted. How long can that last? Mercedes took the kids to the nearby beach. As usual, David has his hands full, dealing with reaction to his recent Times thing you probably saw about naming relations with China, bat origins of Covid, and bats in Tanzanian toilets. Yikes. David wants details of Pearl's Shoshone language work. He's acclimating the new nanny, who looks like a club chair [arrow to sketch]. Alice is a math major [David's description]: "from Kansas to Cambridge [MIT, not England] to Knossos, 'self-contained, like an egg,' from DAY OF THE LOCUST by Nathaniel West."*

*So far, Alice gets along fine with Mercedes. David says they're both workers, not Queen Bees. She minored in classical languages – you like? – and plans to visit local ancient sites with the boys. Arno should love measuring/math/architecture, and Dylan will soon be imitating the art. Our walls will be papered like Minoan murals of waves and fronds. Micheline texted the word 'octet' -- Dylan already illustrated with a copied Minoan octopus. They text now! Nannies, tutors, coming & going, the twins are having a wandering childhood. No moss on rolling stones. Hey, first time I get the meaning of 'Rolling Stones'! I got Keith Richards as Dorian Grey. My agent handles my Instagram/ TikTok platforms. No FB! I avoid it all except for personal phone and an actual letter. Privacy is hard to come by.*

*Which October did the boys get a Hallowe'en advent calendar book -- when I bought the Orient land? It all blurs. "Why do ghosts like to ride elevators? Because it lifts their spirits!" How long do you think before Mercedes wants to leave us? Now I can see the advantages of doing streaming TV series in NYC. Boys in school, David in his element, SoHo studio plus Orient available. Santa Monica still there, too. (We'd be on the same Coast!)*

*I go on ferries: Heraklion, Akroteri, Athens. Pre-production meetings with co-stars. P.A. Jeff still grumbling about a new union contract. Film leads are called 1, 2, etc. Since there are three of us, I'm 2, and we have other nicknames. 'Omni' is mine. I sketched 1, first as an orange [arrow] but she's more pomegranate [arrow] and granite because she's solid igneous [David tells me] to the core. We call her 'Pom' and she's scary great. 3, Jimmy, is Shriek [hear muti-gendered teen squeals]. His character is gay, but he's not. He's 26 playing 19, not a stretch. Super script. The plot is a troubled 1960's archeological dig [rights to Beatles & Stones music!] at Akroteri where I'm a yelloweyed [contact lenses] Scottish artist from Cambridge [England], Pom is the American dig director, and Shriek is one of the Athenian kids who mugged her – The Scot defended the director & lost a tooth she keeps in her pocket.*

*Background/title is THE FIRST END OF THE WORLD, the ancient volcanic Atlantis eruption. 3 follows both $ plus 2 from Athens to dig on Thera, crushes on the artist who becomes director's lover. Complications. She's a divorcee whose ex (another prof) left her for a student. 2 recognizes mugger, but 1 doesn't. 3 pursues, lures, seduces 2, but when they bed [big scene], 2 recognizes it's the kid's first time. It's an Agatha Christie sort of mystery. 2 is a hinge the plot turns on. Another is locals seeing ghosts of invading ancient Greeks -- interrupts the dig, allowing opportunity for 2's infidelity. Which feels like mica schist in my lungs. Won't tell you who kills who/why, but Dig Director is NOT going to be left twice. No spoiler – that doesn't guarantee she survives!*

*My hand is getting tired! Early hype for the movie: "Prepare to wear asbestos to this lust triangle!" David's reaction is that sounds "carcinogenic" and "has more dimensions than a triangle, wheels within wheels, should be called a 'star tetrahedron' –*

*[arrow to ⬧ ] aka the Merkabah, two tetrahedrons combined, interlaced, and balanced, Matter and Mind."*

*Pidge, I don't even. We are islands. Moving from one to another. You and Pearl, too, from Manhattan to Seattle-ish. Don't you love ferries?*

Φιλικά, Alan

"As long as it's not Charon crossing the Styx," Pearl said.

Pidge laughed. "He signed *filika* in actual Greek. Look," she showed Pearl the sketches. "Isn't his tired left hand a perfect lower half copy of the Escher lithograph?"

"A master of mimicry. Or forgery. I wonder if he'd do us a Phaistos Disk image to display with your replica from the museum they live near now. Who said, 'No man is an island.' Who said 'no man?'"

"No Man? Odysseus. Escaped the Cyclops," Pidge said.

"No, I mean … Hemingway, bells."

"*It tolls for thee?*"

"I hope not," Pearl said. She paused. "But worlds do end."

Pidge was re-reading Alan's letter. "Mica schist, huh," she said.

"Thereby hangs a tale," Pearl agreed.


Mack Ackerman left another ringtone message, indignantly anticipating a second anniversary of the Luster murder. This time, Detective Donnelly returned his call but only briefly, omitting details. He'd found the letter in Ellen Grenley's safety deposit box. It had been notarized on the anniversary of the Luster murder and was still in a USPS plastic sleeve with an official apology ("torn in transit"). So Grenley had snailed it to herself to doubly verify the date. So much method in her madness, John thought. It was typed in one block:

*To Whom It May Concern (ATT. Detective John Donnelly)*
*Would it have killed Laney to share ONE wall in our apartment paint it BLACK as I wanted? With shades of brown? also frame the print I made of Crosby's I REFUSE TO BE INVISIBLE so I guess it DID kill her but what I gave Laney your forensics will have to*

*identify ha ha so she would feel no pain but be alive so there was time for all the blood so I could move her around like a paintbrush. Those WHITE walls! she didn't weigh a whole lot. I am sorry I cant leave spaces in this letter because notaries have to black out spaces. About that Crosby print, that's another crime, in for a penny, a pound.*

2010. Ink, charcoal, acrylic and xeros transfer on paper, 10 ft. x 7 ft.
https://www.ronifeinstein.com/1341/njideka-akunyili-crosby-on-the-rise/ *I blacked it so notary won't have to nose in. (MY BLACK WALL!) I scanned it framed a copy. That is not why Laney would not put it on the wall. It was because she was leaving me we wouldn't be sharing a wall but she wouldn't admit it. I will take the same cocktail but different dosage so I can function and say where later. So you can find me. I didn't call a suicide hot line because I didn't want to burden the Ear or risk police sent so I also apologize but Justice needs to hear this. I went there to kill her but didn't know when but when she started TAKING OFF her wedding ring, that was it. Duane Reed FIRED me? my adoptive 'rents RETURNED me? Justice?! I broke the bottle of wine I brought to have edges for arteries. I AIMED her. Laney taught me 3 rules of court: pound on facts, on the law, or on the table. She missed one. I pounded on HER. If the court allows, I want our estate to go because we were not divorced so Laney's also to legal support of immigrants like her doorman's wronged relative Laney told me about that he was so mad at her but she wasn't involved. Where am I is what you're waiting for? Soup in a sleeping bag by the time you find me! Back in the day, we'd rent a car drive out to Orient Point to ferry to alphabet soup LGBTQIA mecca, Provincetown on the Cape. No cod, LOBSTAH! Laney said it stands for lesbian, gay, bisexual, trans, queer, intersex, asexual. Some call a big Black woman trans. Race trumps gender. Little white Jewish Laney think so I should of asked? I guess now she's Uptown and I'll be Down. Where am I? Drive around Point Road. Waiting for the ferry, I liked to get lost in the tall grasses for Laney to find me. You should find a shovel & a scythe. Good for autocorrect who can spell it? I'll cover sleeping bag w/they call it Indiangrass.*

Grenley signed the confession at the bottom of the page, just above the notary's stamp. After, in the left margin, she added her middle finger and thumb print in her own blood. Mouth slightly open, the detective's tongue moved slowly over his molars, up and down. John recognized his usually unconscious tic. Grenley's brand of crazy also explained that blood-caked wedding ring she'd forced back onto Luster's finger.

A Suffolk County team found her. It was a long, early morning drive out to the northern end of Long Island and a longer day of verifications that ended after a spectacular October sunset over the ocean. Indiangrass, native to the porous, sandy soil, tossed soft susurrus of seeds into salty air.

Mack Ackerman sent a metal-standing, heart-shaped arrangement of strong-smelling white lilies to "Detective John Donnelly, NYPD 20th Precinct." He waved away colleagues ribbing "Funeral or Derby-winner?"

*Chapter 30  November*

David had sublet the ninth-floor co-op, the Orient property, and Soho art studio. It could be inferred that Drew whispered in the ear of Alan's gallery rep about the four canvases making up the *De'Lynn Madonna*; they went to a designer who bought them to cover a penthouse statement wall (with the proviso that they were to appear in a future gallery show and *Architectural Digest* issue). Alan returned to the idea of family portraits over the Long Island fireplace, but by Thanksgiving, he was occupied in front of a camera and behind brown-rimmed yellow contact lenses as an artist sketching "archeological Atlantis" under the 1960's set at the Akrotiri site.

In October, Azul had welcomed the reunion of *el trio estelar* to the wedding reception luncheon for Marwa and John, held in the rooftop common space before the bubble top and heaters were in place. It had been a small, socially-distanced affair. The caterers wore masks. The guests wore jackets, scarves, and some gloves, but Marwa explained her open cardigan tunic, "I'm always 98.6. His exercise," she patted her near term pregnancy, "keeps me warm."

It had been as much a farewell as a reunion/reception. Pidge and Pearl answered questions about the new condo and islands around Seattle. Alan tried "to avoid spoilers" for THE FIRST END OF THE WORLD. Drew and Vera waved around phone photos of baby Mifeng. The *trio* was busy among themselves, at first reverting to age-inappropriate behavior. Micheline and Arno blamed Dylan who sulked until the three were seated, ate, and forgot. On the drive back to Inwood, Micheline read the sequel to her previous gift that Pidge created for her as she had for each of the six-year-old wedding guests. Drew requested copies of the three, which a puzzled Pidge promised to send him. Absorbed in her own ancient Aegean story, Micheline ignored her mother, who was driving.

Susanna said, "Did you notice Dayita wasn't drinking?"

James was following the phone GPS and the road. "What?"

"Dayita. No rum. She likes rum."

"Did she say?"

"No, but I can guess. When, then?"

James calculated. "June?"

"Good for weddings. Better for babies."


Pidge and Pearl had been New York City Hall witnesses of the Marwa/John October wedding. In November, the emeritae were Zoom subjects of author interviews for **Blue Monkeys** and joined the Zoom audience for the debut at Juilliard of Marwa's father's *Opus Inshallah*. The symphony climaxed in a celebratory chorale like Beethoven's Ninth. The 50th New York City marathon was run early in the month after its plague-year hiatus, and the news media also proclaimed the Macy's Thanksgiving Day parade "was back with all the trimmings" though missing from its start on the West Side were two of its avid annual fans, Pidge and Pearl. Preparing desserts in their new kitchen, they worked with the parade on TV in the background, starting as usual at nine a.m. and just as usual, Pidge tearing up when Santa's float arrived at noon in front of Macy's.

"How do they do that? It's three hours later here."

Pearl was removing pot holder gloves after setting down a fragrant apple pie. She stared at Pidge. "Really? The move fry your brain? Record/replay?"

"Oh," Pidge said. "They can put Time in a can. Like soup."

"New York City really isn't the *omphalos* of the cosmos."

A few hours later, traditional turkey dinner was ready to be served at Nina's house on Whidbey Island. By Thanksgiving, the nation's adults through five-to-ten-year-olds had been able to get vax'd and/or boostered.

"Even Pinaquanah in Wyoming," Pearl said.

"*Pie-knock* --?" Clarissa echoed.

"That's just what we call him," Pearl explained, repeating his whole name.

Pidge stopped nibbling bits of turkey off the waiting platter. She cleaned, then counted on her fingers, one hand, then two, "Micheline, Arno, Dylan, *Pinaquanah*, Beckett's eleven, you two are twelve now, Clar and Char…. But not the toddler-babies – Sandra is two, Carl Cooper eight months, Mifeng just three … and Marwa's newborn, Anam Donnelly Al-Halimi." She looked at the turkey and her fingers. "That's some mouthful."

"*Mee-fun*," Charlotte tried out.

"I guess Azul and *The Merger* are the only ones of us left in the building," Pidge said.

A serving bowl of cranberries in one hand, gravy boat in the other, Nina gave her mother a peck on the cheek, startling them both.

She said, "We're all snails, Mom. Carry home on our backs."

"I'd rather be a Chambered Nautilus."

"Okay, 'Build more stately mansions, O my soul.' Did you get to see -- Donnelly?"

"Just before we moved," Pidge said. "At the hospital, through a thick glass window. We were masked. Newborns not. 'Daddy' is *Abi* in Arabic. According to Marwa, baby is 'more compound than mixture.' Darker than *Abi*, paler than *Ummee*. Donnelly's got Marwa's big black eyes and wavy hair, but it's 'Irish red,' John said, his 'Mom's original color.'"

"Grandie, how old are you?" a twin asked.

"Clarissa Abes-Satriano!" Chad scolded.

Pearl said, "This kitchen is enormous but with all of us and Honey, it feels as crowded as Amsterdam Avenue – before Covid!"

'Honey' was the perpetually underfoot blond spaniel-Scottie mix Nina and Chad had 'inherited' from an elderly neighbor who had recently died. The young rescue dog had not taken to the move. Having sniffed and stayed near the professors during earlier move-in get-togethers, Honey was waiting at the door when Pidge and Pearl arrived.

"Ancient," Pidge finally answered as Honey licked her fingers.

"She's opinionated, like Ginger," Pearl spoke warmly. "Honey appreciates old bones."

"And turkey," Pidge said. "We have so much in common."

At the end of the evening, Nina sent Honey home with leftovers to the new condo, dog bed and all.


David was mildly surprised by the weather – Heraklion reminded him of Seattle. There had been snow overnight, but mostly it stayed around $50^0$, cloudy, rain. Crete's olive harvest was ongoing, but grapevines were in and *raki*-making was the talk – and drink -- at *tavernas*. David had been told that after the November rains, it would feel like Spring. His mind was wrapped around a deadline for an opinion piece for the *Times*. Alice, the tutor, was teaching the twins *'Twas the Night Before Christmas*. He could hear them reciting "sugarplums danced in their heads" and the predictably instantaneous question, "What's a sugarplum?"

In his own head, David questioned (1) if the Willard Hotel were the new Watergate (subpoenas, everyone?!), (2) how Jeff Bezos was coping with Elon Musk's newly reaffirmed travel hegemony to the Moon, and (3) what the successful infrastructure bill meant for the summer sinkholes on New York's East and West Sides. Start with the sinkholes.

Holding a picture he'd drawn, Dylan wandered into David's office.

"What's up, doc?" David asked in his best Bugs Bunny voice.

Dylan's frown reminded David how much better Alan's impressions were.

"Candles. Ms. Alice is all s-o-l-s-t-i-c-e and it's about light."

David admired the picture. "It looks like the President and wife on *Diwali*. They lit candles in the White House this month."

"I copied a photo. What's *Diwali*?"

"A Hindu – Indian – holiday."

"Like Chanukah?"

"And the Yule log."

"You'll?"

"Ask your tutor."

"You're busy."

"I am."

"I miss Da."

"So do I."

"Does it ever stop raining?" Dylan said. "Is it raining in New York?"

"We can find out."

Arno had followed his brother into the room.

"Did Ms. Alice lose you two?" David asked. "Where's Mercedes?"

"Went to the bathroom," Dylan explained.

"The little church," Arno said.

"And you two made a break for it."

Dylan added, "Mercedes met a man from Spain at church. He's a Spaniard."

"Rhymes with *lanyard*," Arno said. "Ms. Alice said she'll teach us how. And knots. It's math."

Dylan vied for attention. "He's from Barcelona. His name is Guillem Abello. He's a dentist."

"Abello is a nickname for a bee. In Barcelonian," Arno said,

"Catalan," David corrected. "No lisping in Barcelona, no Bartheloma."

Both boys stuck their tongues in position to "th" and cheerfully spat at each other.

The tutor appeared in the doorway, said nothing, gestured with her first finger.

David read the boys' faces and hands trying out their middle fingers and shook his head.

Alone again, David thought: honey/bees/sting.


Mercedes was at Saint John the Baptist Church in Heraklion, but Guillem was at work. The dentist's office was walking distance. Inside the church, it looked almost Protestant. It was smaller and less decorated than the one in the LA *barrio* where she grew up. And nothing like the big brick one that looked like cake layers in New York. The West Side church had so many aisles, so many pews, and a zillion stained-glass windows, even high up in the center of its big dome. Senor David said it was one of the best examples of Byzantine architecture in America. Mercedes thought 'Byzantine' meant complicated and difficult, like a maze.

The small church in Heraklion was a cab ride from the rented villa. Outside, it had four pink, round pillars. They held up three tiled arches. The church doors opened to a narrow, lighter pink and white space, only one line of pews on each side of a center aisle. A small lace-covered altar table was in front of an arched painting of St. John baptizing Christ. In Los Angeles, her Glendale church had a huge cross to the side of the altar. When she was little, the crucified Christ was bigger than she was. She had cried.

"It's awful!"

Her mother said, "*El temor.*"

"*El terror?*"

But now, Mercedes sat on the left side of the small church. She looked up at the gold painting of the Madonna and Child to the side of the simple altar. Here, the Madonna's eyes gave her awe, not terror. In his Barcelona Catalan, Guillem's name was the same as 'Guillermo' back in LA. So here was where *Santa Maria* wanted Mercedes to be! It had only been over a month, but Guillem called her *Carina* and *Querida* and had asked her if she could see a future for them.

"*¿Puedes ver nuestro futuro juntos?*"

Mercedes knelt to ask the same question. She was twenty-three. It was raining outside. The church door opened behind her. She turned. It was Guillem, closing a black umbrella. He was ten years older. His coat was open to his v-neck purple uniform top. He knelt to genuflect. Then, standing, he saw her and smiled. He walked to her pew and knelt again beside her. He wore a silver chain around his neck, and his eyes were blue.

Mercedes heard the words come out of her mouth as if someone else spoke them. She knew she would remember this moment for the rest of her life.

"*Podríamos tener un futuro juntos.*"

Guillem drove her back to the villa.

It wasn't clear when anyone would be able to travel back to the States after Senor Alan's film was done. 'Variants' were again closing borders. On the drive, Guillem pointed at mountains in the distance. One was where Zeus had been born in a cave, and the other, shaped like a man's head, was where Zeus was buried. Mercedes looked but didn't listen. She was picturing their wedding inside the little church and a reception on the beach Guillem had taken her to in golden October.


Before Alan had left for the film set on Akrotiri in October, they were tourists in a two-car caravan west on Crete to Ano Vouves where the oldest olive tree in the world still lived and produced olives. Two local masked driver-guides had been glad to take them from Heraklion to Chania along the stony northern coast road. For the twins, it was too long a drive for one day, so they broke it into three days-two nights, staying at *taverna*/inns glad to welcome them after the summer people had departed and wouldn't return until March for spring skiing.

The tree was a national treasure, protected by a low stone fence. All it meant to Arno and Dylan was that they couldn't climb it, but they liked a big emoji-happy-face cactus plant in a terracotta urn; they argued whether its two green protrusions were open arms or huge ears. Alan, David, and Mercedes were glad to see the cactus's spines appeared clipped. Occasions for sin and injury. Tutor Alice internationally-shared images and video on her phone. She and David, Alan observed, "were umbilically connected to the outside world."

As were Drew and Vera, all November, working on promotion for ***Blue Monkeys***. A Zoom interview was orchestrated into a mini-documentary trailer featuring the Columbia scholars on Whidbey Island intercut with the three stars' movie-making at Akroteri. "The film depicts the 1960's dig on modern Santorini Island north of Crete – that unearthed Atlantis! – where bulljumper Pasikennae's voyages began!" This circus aired, and "media attention erupted" for both ***Blue Monkeys*** and THE FIRST END OF THE WORLD.

A few days after, Alan phoned Pidge privately.

"They had to hype *erupted*," Alan said.

"*Caldera* is a new 'word of the day,' I'm told. Also that the special effects volcano footage overlaps of Santorini's layered cliffs," Pidge commiserated, "are on Tik Tok and Instagram."

"David ferried up from Heraklion with the boys and entourage for a visit," Alan said.

"We took the ferry to Seattle once already. We have to do book signings on the West Coast. Drew Burgos has also got me writing a children's book series like the ones I wrote for Dylan and Arno and Micheline. Pearl's already involved writing a Shoshone grammar text with a group at U. Idaho. No luck in our attempts to hide out. We're still wearing masks. You'd think an island in the middle of nowhere would be an escape."

"Nowhere is everywhere now. LARA CROFT TOMB RAIDER was filmed here. We *are* the escape."

"Clever. How are you, dear?"

The actor reacted with a catch in his voice, "Wanted to see and hear you." Then he shifted back to chat, "Dylan and Arno saw the real blue monkeys fresco in the site's Beta House. They'd seen the copies in Athens when we first landed. We do interior shots in an Athens studio. Might as well be on a soundstage in Queens. Short version: boys do not like museums, guides, or guards. You know the 'boxing boys' wall next to the antelopes?"

"Oh, yes."

"When our guide said the boxers were six-to-ten years old, they took it as a cue. Pow-pow. We were not highly popular on that tour. Kids want to run through crumbled stone streets and into building ruins, not stay on roped-off museum paths."

"Pasikennae's home town," Pidge said. "She walked there."

Alan heard the homesickness in Pidge's voice.

He said, "Marwa and her detective did well, I heard. A signed confession *and* a baby."

"How's your weather?" Pidge asked.

"The water is still warm."

At a park on Whidbey Island, Pidge reported the conversation to Pearl.

"The rest of it went on like that."

Pearl was distracted, managing Honey and the new retractable leash. Fort Casey State Park looked west at a watery expanse that dwarfed the Hudson River. She looked to their right, north, toward a border to Canada. Pidge followed Pearl's view. Honey bounded back to them.

"The Strait of Juan de Fuca," Pidge spanned her arms, "opens to the giant Pacific. Puget Sound is a fjord." She pointed to a snowy peak and pronounced as a weather report, "Mount Rainier? Mount Rain-Year? It certainly is."

The trio returned to walking.

"No rain clouds now. You miss skyscraper canyons and crowds of people instead of those pines?" Pearl asked.

Pidge looked at the back of an ungloved hand. It was a topography of knuckles, veins, and ligaments visible under freckled skin.

"I miss a map. Juan de Fuca was Ioannis Phokas, a sixteenth century Greek sailing for Spain. What a journey, like Pasikennae. I miss the sound of the City. Here, it's so quiet at night. Stark still like the days of empty sky after 9/11. I hear my heartbeat in my left ear."

"It's the same sky. We've been silent places before."

A jet from the nearby Naval Air Station roared overhead. Honey barked at it.

"Thank you," Pearl laughed.

Cheered, Pidge said, "I always expected to return *home*."

"A word that translates as it moves."

Pidge nodded. "Even Teddy Roosevelt's statue is moving to North Dakota."

"About time. I can picture Pasikennae on a beach like this."

"In the Orkneys? Homesick?"

"No, she was already busy creating chapter stones for us to decipher. Firing 'em in kilns. Cladding them in copper."

"You think she could imagine us?"

"The future is all blue monkeys."

"What?"

Suddenly, the sun spread massed white clouds easily mistaken for the Cascade Mountains. Pearl looked up and squinted into the brightness. "*Blue monkeys danced with Sky,*" she recited.

Then, neither spoke for a while. In the gift of sunshine, they walked along the sandy beach past driftwood and scattered stones. Honey nosed as much as she could.

"We've gone far enough." Pidge stopped, looked at their path back.

"Pasikennae must have felt more at home on water. She could navigate mountains and valleys at sea. Who can trust land? People steal it and get stolen from it."

"Enough to make a dervish dizzy," Pearl agreed. Then she hummed a tune and sang, "But it wouldn't be make-believe, if you believed…"

Pidge smiled. "What now?"

"That grad student of yours who saw us on the Zoom interview, we went to see STREETCAR how many years ago with him in New York? It had that dizzy revolving set! 2016? He texted you that he married on a Whidbey beach. Maybe this one."

Pidge said his name. "He takes the ferry here with his wife several times a year. With their two kids. Parleyed linguistics into whatever arcane voodoo they do in Seattle."

"Then we'll be seeing them," Pearl said, "at home."


The cries woke John who turned and lifted his namesake out of the co-sleeper and into Marwa's sleepy arms. Back from the bathroom, he stood in the near dawn and watched mother and child together. Her nipple overflowed the baby's mouth.

"Hail Marwa," he said. "full of milk."

Her eyes were on the infant, then up at John. Sated, the baby slept. She lifted him into John's arms and smiled invitingly. He replaced Donnelly in the co-sleeper.

Marwa said, "I hope his voice will be as low as yours one day. A baritone arouses an erotic reflex."

In his rush to return to bed, John jarred his night table. The professors' book-marked best seller fell to the floor.

After, he quickly showered, dressed, and found Beckett and her grandfather breakfasting at the kitchen counter. He left for the precinct as the sun rose. In this November in his soul, John Donnelly felt no need to board Melville's *Pequod*. Whale oil had been superseded. *Sapiens* needed to speed up energy evolution before annihilating too many more species – and itself. After this morning's encounter with Her, John's faith in Gaia was another kind of booster shot. Not a bad mood to begin a new day in. Behind his mask, no one could see he was grinning.

The City busied like a morning hive. Jets and helicopters flew overhead. He could almost believe he felt the subway below the cement. The crowds and masks meant more than – he never could remember the terms from poetry – Schenectady was always the path to one – *synecdoche*. And the other one, *metonymy*? A teacher's voice, 'The White House stands for the President.' Whatever, the masks and returning crowds meant something. The image on the cover of ***Blue Monkeys*** came to mind.

*CODA*

Finally, on Christmas morning, 2021, the new Webb Telescope successfully launched atop an Ariane 5 rocket from Europe's Spaceport in French Guiana. Past midnight on a night in January, 2022, a crane descended in the wintry dark on the bronze statue of Theodore Roosevelt, lifting his upper body from the pedestal where it had presided at New York's American Museum of Natural History since 1940. The remainder of the sculpture, surrounded by scaffolding, was scheduled to leave for North Dakota in pieces through the week. Detective Donnelly quoted Shelley, *My name is Ozymandias, King of Kings; Look on my Works, ye Mighty, and despair!*

On the Whidbey Island kitchen wall, catty-corner to a built-in upper cabinet wine rack, Pidge had put up the framed photo of the Linear A tablet whose second line's first symbol meant *wine*.

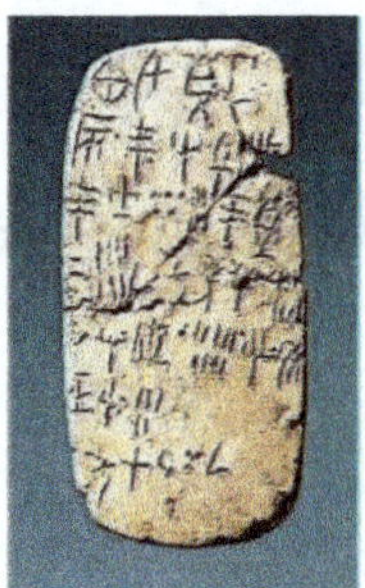

In New York, there had been no space for it in the kitchen -- nor a wine rack. "It lived in the steamy bathroom," Pearl told guests. Pidge added, "We had it reframed here. Like us."     X-rated scenes in the film THE FIRST END OF THE WORLD went "viral" -- repeatedly seen and heard, soundtracked to Aretha Franklin's 1967 *Chain of Fools*; the one chord song climbed to the top of Billboard again. Eager for a follow-up sequel, the film's producers were competing to option **Blue Monkeys** with intentions to TITANIC-frame the story of the elderly professors telling Pasikennae's epic saga. A-list actresses already vied to play her at the different stages of her life.

David Rochester's article, *The Long Etcetera*, appeared in an issue of *The New York Times Magazine*. It began with a quotation of Newton's Third Law of Motion: *For every action, there is an equal and opposite reaction.* "New waves repeat old ones: plague, book-banning, axis/alliances, culture, Cold, and now, another horrible hot war. But under the Sun, novelties as Newton and Darwin (*etcetera*) described also occur."

With apologies to "the Capek brothers' THE INSECT PLAY," David included in his essay a detail that six-year-old Arno had brought to his attention: *"Scientists in South Africa discovered that at night, dung beetles rolled balls of dung in straight lines, guided by the Milky Way."* Dylan painted the beetles blue on a large canvas Alan taught him how to stretch. Dylan named it *Dung Bugs*, and Alan had it framed in a shop in Heraklion. When they finally returned to New York City (without Mercedes), the painting was hung in the living room above the baby grand piano.

Another work of art -- Pidge called it "savant-level" -- was a framed pen and ink enlarged portrait Alan created (at Pearl's texted request) before they left Crete, of the real Phaistos Disk in the nearby Heraklion Archeological Museum.

"He got every glyph exactly correct!" Pidge hung Alan's picture above a small table featuring their museum replicas of the disk and a Minoan-like vase she filled with dried eucalyptus leaves. They gave off a pleasant, musty fragrance.

As Dylan had asked, Alan sent a framed print of *Dung Bugs* (with *The Long Etcetera* as caption-provenance, its first page taped to the back) to Micheline in Inwood. Then, on his own, Alan sent one to everyone who'd attended that first December dinner party, the one David had co-opted from Susanna and James. In each home, it became a reminder, a story, and connection. It kept them friends.

It snowed in Seattle for Christmas and in Athens in January. As Omicron numbers rose, Pidge and Pearl had little intention of budging from their island condo, let alone ferry to see Alan's costar. She was the sleep-walking Lady in THE TRAGEDY OF MACBETH, a new film playing

on the mainland through the anniversary of the January 6ᵗʰ attack on the U.S. Capitol. Alan had

messaged Pidge the actress's praise for his Scottish accent in THE FIRST END OF THE

WORLD. "*Pom* said, 'Glad Mac and I didn't need to try the burr!'"

*Blue Monkeys* began months on the best seller lists, in America and worldwide across print,

e-book, and audio formats. A-list actors were lining up for parts as Drew participated in the

competition for movie rights.

Over speakerphone, the agent told Pidge, "Your old Vassar Girl classmate wants in."

"I'm older. She was a freshman when I was a senior. Our paths never crossed."

"Maybe now they will. She wants to play Pasikennae white-haired in the Orkneys."

Pearl said, "It's a luxury for a life to have a coda."

When Pidge took Honey for walks around their Whidbey neighborhood, she thought of the

monkey glyph that meant 'welcome.' She hoped that Pasikennae had walked with a puppy on

Orkney's paved streets or along its beaches of sand and banded, rounded stones. That she

remembered Lake Superior where her pet had delighted baby Sueaysua. That Pasikennae

imagined blue monkeys dancing on the wall in her Orkney home.

When he eventually travelled with the family to the Long Island house, Alan learned that

Brian and Abby had left the North Fork, whereabouts unknown. Brian's brother, who had taken

over the art store and was raising their two abandoned children, described his sibling not as the

"rolling stone he thought he was, but a tumbleweed." Both of Abby's parents had died of the

plague.

Death and taxes, weather and war – only historians would remember that this time,

Switzerland and Sweden took a side. Sunflowers were planted and refugees fled to unfamiliar terrain. Lost names and places sent echoes far *upwhen* where archeology might find them difficult to decipher.

### *from Blue Monkeys by Paloma Shapiro & Pearl Feria*

*...Since the Orkneys had been the cultural center of the British Isles four millennia ago, Pasikennae was likely not the only one of the stranded citizens of the Minoan empire who lived out their lives so far north among its paved streets and painted houses. Among these few, Pasikennae appeared not only welcomed but also recognized and revered, identified as a bull vaulter, sea captain, teacher, and healer. Of all the priceless items found in her tomb, among bracelets and rings, were tablets chosen by the people who buried her. Clearly, the most valued were the four copper-clad boxes.*

*Many of these appeared to be primers Pasikennae created. The tablets were stories, maps, songs, and what looked like mathematical and/or geometric knowledge that remains to be explained – if possible. Of all these, though, one stood out. It was a black stone she had kept all her life. Unlike the smooth-surfaced others, the copper sheath of this fourth had hammered circles all around, the largest one centered on top. Its raised ridges identified it as the three concentric circles of Mnkallis before the volcanic catastrophe.*

*Inside its copper container, this unique tablet was obsidian, unlike the others of etched common stone or inscribed, fired clay with remnants of paint color. The tablet evidences that Pasikennae wasn't an artisan, but she was an experienced scribe. We understood this shiny black relic to be Pasikennae's last words. So let them be ours.*

*Approach and hold mighty horns.*
*The great bull lifts and tosses*
*like ocean waves our fragile barque,*
*buoys the sailor through blue sky.*
*Vault through the Crown to land*

https://en.wikipedia.org/wiki/Minoan_Bull-leaper

It feels like a long time ago that I first became curious about the first end of the world. Cosmic, geologic, and biological timelines catalog eons. Fin de siècle feeling about the end of the 20th century has morphed into focus on developments and cataclysms already occurring in the first quarter of our 21$^{st}$. Atlantis, Vesuvius and Krakatoa were words I grew up with. To Pompeii I added Akroteri – and even Gobekli Tepe. If those names (and Linear A) are new, there are bookshelves – and Google – sources awaiting you.

A short summary: Early on, I was captivated by Rodney Castleden's **MINOAN LIFE IN BRONZE AGE CRETE** (Routledge 1993)/. Special thanks go to Mr. Castleden, who replied to an email question with influential insights into Minoan beliefs & behaviors, and to Margalit Fox's **THE RIDDLE OF THE LABYRINTH THE QUEST TO CRACK AN ANCIENT CODE** (Ecco Press, 2013) that introduced me to the brilliant Cretan language scholar-investigator, Alice Kober, the inspiration for Pidge & Pearl. Essential to my story of archaic Crete-meeting-Lake Superior was research into the proto-Ojibway people, which included Johann Georg Kohl's epic **KITCHI-GAMI** (Chapman & Hall, 1860; Minnesota Historical Society Press, 1985).

More thanks to the authors of **AN INTRODUCTION TO THE SHOSHONI LANGUAGE** (The University of Utah Press, 2002) Drusilla Gould and Christopher Loether at Idaho State University's Shoshoni Language Project. Ms. Gould, whose mother "was of the Salmon-Eater Shoshoni located in Lemhi, Idaho, and father of the Yellow-Forelock of the Eastern Shoshoni people of Fort Washakie, Wyoming, on the Wind River Reservation," generously emailed back and forth with me, sharing so much about Indigenous culture.

Back East, Manhattan's Upper West Side is the home of dear friend Stephanie Cowell https://www.stephaniecowell.com/, author of historical fiction and patient source of answers to too many questions. Teacher-restauranteur Marla Chait Cornejo generously advised on all Spanish language queries. Michael C. Nelson (CUNY, Queens College) pointed in helpful directions. Real-life NYPD Detective Karen Dougherty Mattiolo [retired] answered Detective John Donnelly's questions [any errors are mine, not hers!]

My grandmother was a telegrapher on Wall Street a century ago. She taught me to read and tapped out messages in Morse Code on the arm of a chair. I'm a native New Yorker, grateful to be living in Roger Williams's Rhode Island. The intersection of cyberspace with spacetime keeps me on daily alert. I wear progressive lenses and try to traverse C.P. Snow's bridge between the 'two cultures' of art/science.

www.ingramcontent.com/pod-product-compliance
Lightning Source LLC
Chambersburg PA
CBHW070405120726
47909CB00008B/3000